Classic
HORROR STORIES

Classic
HORROR STORIES

SIXTEEN LEGENDARY STORIES
OF THE SUPERNATURAL

EDITED *by*

CHARLES A. COULOMBE

THE LYONS PRESS
GUILFORD, CONNECTICUT

The Lyons Press is an imprint of The Globe Pequot Press.

10   9   8   7   6   5   4   3   2   1

Printed in the United States of America

Designed by Claire Zoghb

ISBN 1-59228-200-8

Library of Congress Cataloging-in-Publication data is avail-
able on file

Contents

CONTENTS

Introduction

F ear is a basic human instinct. We all feel it from time to time—fear of losing our jobs, our friends, and our loved ones. Behind these lingers the greatest of all: the fear of death. One major way with which we cope is maintenance of routine. Not only in terms of doing things which of themselves may stave off the objects of our fear, such as working hard at our jobs and following our doctor's medical advice strictly; no, there is also the atavistic belief that if we blot out our terror with the minutiae of unchanging schedule, that which we dread will somehow pass us by. In cities under siege, with no help of relief from enemy assault, people will continue to go to work and then to their accustomed restaurants and cabarets; all the while doing their best to ignore the impending doom which threatens. This is true of all of us in some degree, since all must, in the end, die.

True as this is of the natural fears which surround us, for so long as we have records we know that human beings have revelled in tales of supernatural horrors, of beings against which neither routine nor locked doors can protect us. Given the doom which awaits all, we might well wonder why this should be. With the specters of disease, war, poverty, and so forth, why should humanity look for demons under the bed?

Perhaps it is because, paradoxically, they give relief both from the boredom of that routine we protect ourselves with, and from the tedium of the everyday fears we seek to escape. Although we live in an ever more secular and unbelieving society, that which frightened our ancestors can still reach out to us, for all our electric lights and computers. And on some level, we are happy that it is so.

But there have, of course, been some changes over time. For one thing, prior to the Reformation, there was no distinction between horrific or fantastic literature, and the "mainstream." As we know, Shakespeare confronted his historical figures in *Hamlet, Macbeth,* and *Julius Caesar*, with ghosts and witches; in this he followed all the great writers who preceded him, from Homer to Chaucer. Interestingly, this has remained somewhat the practice in lands less affected by the Reformation and the Enlightenment than the English-speaking world has been. Asked at a literary conference by a fan for advice on writing horror or fantasy, Peter S. Beagle, author of *The Last Unicorn*, replied, "write in Spanish. That way, instead of being pigeon-holed as a genre writer, you'll be hailed as a 'magic realist' and win the Nobel Prize!"

However that may be, such distinctions did not exist in early Western literature. As a salute to that fact, in this collection we include not only an early vampire story from the *Metamorphoses* of Apuleius, but what must be the earliest account of a séance, the story of the Witch of Endor from the Old Testament. In the early days of Christianity, such things were accepted as a matter of course, and much time and energy went into driving off the forces of darkness from the faithful.

Most of our selections, however, come from the 19th century, when the literary distinction just referred to had become a reality. This was truly the Golden Age of horror writing. Much of the impetus for this came from the Romantic Revival, which arose in Europe and America as a protest against the materialism and rationalism of the Enlightenment, a movement blamed by many both for the bloodshed of the French and succeeding revolutions, and the ugliness of industrialism. It is no surprise that from much the same milieu arose the Occult Revival of the 19th century, with its self-proclaimed mission of re-enchanting daily life. New forces were in the air, and in the face of them, dreamers, poets, and writers of all sorts sought refuge in ancient fears and modern wonders.

Among the folk whose work we will enjoy in the following pages are those legitimizers of American literature, Nathaniel Hawthorne and Washington Irving; the European Romantic Nikolay Gogol; and the Scots giant, Sir Walter Scott. Rudyard Kipling will show what haunted the weird landscape of India. Charles Dickens, Robert W. Chambers, and Ambrose Bierce will put in their appearances, of course, and a number of lesser known (but equally disturbing) contemporaries shall also join us. We shall shiver at a werewolf with Saki, and tremble at ghosts with R. S. Hawker.

We halt our survey at the commencement of the 20th century, and dedicated horror fans will note some differences between our authors and more recent ones. A great chasm between older material and post-Lovecraft work is the eventual breaking free from the traditional folklore embraced by the Romantics, and its gradual replacement with pure literary constructs. So too, the moral stance of horror novels altered, as the horrific came to be less and less depicted as the work of creatures under the control of the devil, and more as simply part of a cosmic (if malevolent) unknown. As scientific opinion was getting ever more precise, so the spiritual was becoming foggier.

For another thing, the sexual element is much lighter. This is important simply because many contemporary commentators (particularly of a so-called "Conservative" bent) maintain—and cite a good deal of more modern horrific fiction to support said contention—that supernatural literature finds its root in perverse sexuality. It might be replied that all fiction today is far more sexual in content than that of the past. A true cynic might observe that this phenomenon has been accompanied by a rise in advertising for Viagra and similar products; leading one to wonder if all the talk masks increasing inability.

But if that fear is unique to our time, supernatural fear is not. Moreover, it is as visceral as belief in religion, of which it is the flip side, so to speak. But need practitioners of the craft be believers in the supernatural themselves, to write effectively? Answers on this question are decidedly mixed, such authorities as H. P. Lovecraft and Montague Summers disagreeing violently thereon. This disagreement mirrors the changes in the genre just referred to. What is certain is that writers of horror need to suspend disbelief, for at least a time, in their readers—that is, in you and me. However one tries to interpret the work of such writers in the abstract, I

believe the ones represented here accomplish that
task. For which, in an age of terrorism and mystery
diseases, we may all be grateful.

Charles A. Coulombe
Arcadia, California
30 April 2003
Walpurgis Night
May Eve

Ancient Horrors

We begin our journey with the "Ancient World"—Judea and Greece.

Our first tale is that of Saul and the Witch of Endor, from the Old Testament (I Kings 28.1-25). Here we see King Saul consulting what we would call today a trance medium to call up the Prophet Samuel; as with many desperate folk down through the ages, Saul sought wisdom from beyond for very practical matters—with little good result.

From Greece comes an account of the Vampire-like Empusa. Here we see the horrid thing dealt with by Apollonius of Tyana, a wonder-worker of pre-Christian days, whose miracles were often cited after the birth of the Church, in order to show that pagans could also perform supernatural marvels.

CHAPTER 28

The Philistines go out to war against Israel. Saul being forsaken by God, hath recourse to a witch. Samuel appeareth to him.

And it came to pass in those days, that the Philistines gathered together their armies to be prepared for war against Israel: and Achis said to David: Know thou now assuredly, that thou shalt go out with me to the war, thou, and thy men.

2 And David said to Achis: Now thou shalt know what thy servant will do.

And Achis said to David: And I will appoint thee to guard my life for ever.

3 Now Samuel was dead, and all Israel mourned for him, and buried him in Ramatha his city. And Saul had put away all the magicians and soothsayers out of the land.

4 And the Philistines were gathered together, and came and camped in Sunam: and Saul also gathered together all Israel, and came to Gelboe.

5 And Saul saw the army of the Philistines, and was afraid, and his heart was very much dismayed.

6 And he consulted the Lord, and he answered him not, neither by dreams, nor by priests, nor by prophets.

7 And Saul said to his servants: Seek me a woman that hath a divining spirit, and I will go to her, and inquire by her. And his servants said to him: There is a woman that hath a divining spirit at Endor.

8 Then he disguised himself: and put on other clothes, and he went, and two men with him, and they came to the woman by night, and he said to her: Divine to me by thy divining spirit, and bring me up him whom I shall tell thee.

9 And the woman said to him: Behold thou knowest all that Saul hath done, and how he hath rooted out the magicians and soothsayers from the land: why then dost thou lay a snare for my life, to cause me to be put to death?

10 And Saul swore unto her by the Lord, saying: As the Lord liveth there shall no evil happen to thee for this thing.

11 And the woman said to him: Whom shall I bring up to thee? And he said, Bring me up Samuel.

12 And when the woman saw Samuel, she cried out with a loud voice, and said to Saul: Why hast thou deceived me? for thou art Saul.

13 And the king said to her: Fear not: what hast thou seen? And the woman said to Saul: I saw gods ascending out of the earth.

14 And he said to her: What form is he of? And she said: An old man cometh up, and he is covered

with a mantle. And Saul understood that it was Samuel, and he bowed himself with his face to the ground, and adored.

15 And Samuel said to Saul: Why hast thou disturbed my rest, that I should be brought up? And Saul said, I am in great distress: For the Philistines fight against me, and God is departed from me, and would not hear me, neither by the hand of prophets, nor by dreams: therefore I have called thee, that thou mayest shew me what I shall do.

16 And Samuel said: Why askest thou me, seeing the Lord has departed from thee, and is gone over to thy rival:

17 For the Lord will do to thee as he spoke by me, and he will rend thy kingdom out of thy hand, and will give it to thy neighbour David:

18 Because thou didst not obey the voice of the Lord, neither didst thou execute the wrath of his indignation upon Amalec. Therefore hath the Lord done to thee what thou sufferest this day.

19 And the Lord also will deliver Israel with thee into the hands of the Philistines: and to morrow thou and thy sons shall be with me: and the Lord will also deliver the army of Israel into the hands of the Philistines.

20 And forthwith Saul fell all along on the ground, for he was frightened with the words of

Samuel, and there was no strength in him, for he had eaten no bread all that day.

21 And the woman came to Saul (for he was very much troubled) and said to him: Behold thy hand-maid hath obeyed thy voice, and I have put my life in my hand and I hearkened unto the words which thou spokest to me.

22 Now therefore hear thou also the voice of thy handmaid, and let me set before thee a morsel of bread, that thou mayest eat and recover strength, and be able to go on thy journey.

23 But he refused, and said: I will not eat. But his servants and the woman forced him, and at length hearkening to their voice, he arose from the ground and sat upon the bed.

24 Now the woman had a fatted calf in the house, and she made haste and killed it: and taking meal kneaded it, and baked some unleavened bread,

25 And set it before Saul, and before his servants. And when they had eaten they rose up, and walked all that night.

Life of Apollonius of Tyana by Philostratus, book IV, xxv. In discussing the pupils of the great philosopher his biographer tells us: "Among the latter was Menippus, a Lycian of twenty-five years of age, well endowed with good judgement, and of a physique so beautifully proportioned that in mien he resembled a fine and gentlemanly athlete. Now this Menippus was supposed by most people to be loved by a foreign woman, who was good-looking and extremely dainty, and said that she was rich; although she was really, as it turned out, none of these things, but was only so in semblance. For as he was walking all alone along the road towards Cenchreæ, he met with an apparition, and it was a woman who clasped his hand and declared that she had been long in love with him, and that she was a Phoenician woman and lived in a suburb of Corinth, and she mentioned the name of the particular suburb, and said: 'When you reach the place this evening, you will hear my voice as I sing to you, and you shall have wine such as you never before drank, and there will be no rival to disturb you; and we two beautiful beings will live together.' The youth consented to this, for although he was in general a strenuous philosopher, he was nevertheless susceptible to the tender passion; and he visited her in the evening, and for the future constantly sought her company as his darling, for he did not yet realize that she was a mere apparition.

"Then Apollonius looked over Menippus as a sculptor might do and he sketched an outline of the youth and examined him, and having observed his foibles, he said: 'You are a fine youth and are hunted by fine women, but in this case you are cherishing a serpent, and a serpent cherishes you.' And when Menippus expressed his surprise he added: 'For this lady is of a kind you cannot marry. Why should you? Do you think that she loves you?' 'Indeed I do,' said the youth, 'since she behaves to me as if she loves me.' 'And would you then marry her?' said Apollonius. 'Why, yes, for it would be delightful to marry a woman who loves you.' Thereupon Apollonius asked when the wedding was to be. 'Perhaps to-morrow,' said the other, 'for it brooks no delay.' Apollonius therefore waited for the occasion of the wedding breakfast, and then, presenting himself before the guests who had just arrived, he said: 'Where is the dainty lady at whose instance ye are come?' 'Here she is,' replied Menippus, and at the same moment he rose slightly from his seat, blushing. 'And to which of you belong the silver and gold and all the rest of the decorations of the banqueting hall?' 'To the lady,' replied the youth, 'for this is all I have of my own,' pointing to the philosopher's cloak which he wore.

"And Apollonius said: 'Have you heard of the gardens of Tantalus, how they exist and yet do not exist?' 'Yes,' they answered, 'in the poems of Homer, for we certainly never went down to Hades.' 'As such,' replied Apollonius, 'you must regard this adornment, for it is not reality but the semblance of reality. And that you may realize the truth of what I say, this fine bride is one of the vampires, that is to say of those beings whom the many regard as lamias and hobgoblins. These beings fall in love, and they are devoted to the delights of Aphrodite, but especially to the flesh of human beings, and they decoy with such delights those whom they mean to devour in their feasts.' And the lady said: 'Cease your ill-omened talk and begone'; and she pretended to be disgusted at what she heard, and no doubt she was inclined to rail at philosophers and say that they always talked nonsense. When, however, the goblets of gold and the show of silver were proved as light as air and all fluttered away out of their sight, while the wine-bearers and the cooks and all the retinue of servants vanished before the rebukes of Apollonius, the phantom pretended to weep, prayed him not to torture her nor to compel her to confess what she really was. But Apollonius insisted and would not let her off, and then she admitted that she was a vampire, and was fattening up Menippus with pleasures before devouring his body, for it was her habit to feed upon young and beautiful bodies, because their blood is pure and strong. I have related at length, because it was necessary to do so, this the best-known story of Apollonius; for many people are aware of it and know that the incident occurred in the centre of Hellas; but they have only heard in a general and vague manner that he once caught and overcame a lamia in Corinth but they have never learned what she was about, nor that he did it to save Menippus, but I owe my own account to Damis and to the work which he wrote."

The Feast of Redgauntlet

[SIR WALTER SCOTT]

The Romantic Movement crossed the Channel; no better or more famous exponent of it could be found in all the Three Kingdoms of the British Isles than Sir Walter Scott. In keeping with the practice of his Continental colleagues, he reached into the past of his own country, Scotland, to produce such masterpieces as Ivanhoe *and* Waverly. *But he also followed those contemporaries in looking to the folk beliefs of the local peasantry with respect and mining them as a source for stories. In the following, Sir Walter melds history and superstition with a master's touch—and adds some wry comments on human nature as well.*

Ye maun have heard of Sir Robert Redgauntlet of that Ilk, who lived in these parts before the dear years. The country will lang mind him; and our fathers used to draw breath thick if ever they heard him named. He was out wi' the Hielandmen in Montrose's time; and again he was in the hills wi' Glencairn in the saxteen hundred and fifty-twa; and sae when King Charles the Second came in, wha was in sic favor as the Laird of Redgauntlet? He was knighted at Lonon court, wi' the King's ain sword; and being a red-hot prelatist, he came down here, rampauging like a lion, with commissions of lieutenancy (and of lunacy, for what I ken), to put down a' the Whigs and Covenanters in the country. Wild wark they made of it; for the Whigs were as dour as the Cavaliers were fierce, and it was which should first tire the other. Redgauntlet was aye for the strong hand; and his name is kenn'd as wide in the country as Claverhouse's or Tam Dalyell's. Glen, nor dargle, nor mountain, nor cave could hide the puir Hill-folk when Redgauntlet was out with bugle and bloodhound after them, as if they had been sae mony deer. And troth when they fand them, they didna mak muckle mair ceremony than a Hielandman wi' a roebuck. It was just, "Will ye tak the test?" If not, "Make ready—present—fire!" and there lay the recusant.

Far and wide was Sir Robert hated and feared. Men thought he had a direct compact with Satan; that he was proof against steel, and that bullets happed aff his buff-coat like hailstanes from a hearth; that he had a mear that would turn a hare on the side of Carrifra Gauns—and muckle to the same purpose, of whilk mair anon. The best blessing they wared on him was, "Deil scowp wi' Redgauntlet!" He wasna a bad maister to his ain folk though, and was weel aneugh liked by his tenants; and as for the lackies and troopers that raid out wi' him to the persecutions, as the Whigs ca'd those killing times, they wad hae drunken themsells blind to his health at ony time.

Now you are to ken that my gudesire lived on Redgauntlet's grund; they ca' the place Primrose Knowe. We had lived on the grund, and under the Redgauntlets, since the riding days, and lang before. It was a pleasant bit; and I think the air is callerer and fresher there than onywhere else in the country. It's a' deserted now; and I sat on the broken door-cheek three days since, and was glad I couldna see the plight the place was in; but that's a' wide o' the mark. There dwelt my gudesire, Steenie Steenson, a rambling, rattling chiel he had been in his young days, and could play weel on the pipes; he was famous at "Hoopers and Girders," a' Cumberland couldna touch him at "Jockie Lattin," and he had the finest finger for the backlilt between Berwick and Carlisle. The like o' Steenie wasna the sort that they made Whigs o'. And so he became a Tory, as they ca' it, which we now ca' Jacobites, just out of a kind of needcessity, that he might belang to some side or other. He had nae ill-will to the Whig bodies, and liked little to see the blude rin, though being obliged to follow Sir Robert in hunting and hosting, watching and warding, he saw muckle mischief, and maybe did some, that he couldna avoid.

Now Steenie was a kind of favorite with his master, and kenn'd a' the folks about the castle, and was often sent for to play the pipes when they were at their merriment. Auld Dougal MacCallum, the butler, that had followed Sir Robert through gude and ill, thick and thin, pool and stream, was specially fond of the pipes, and aye gae my gudesire his gude word wi' the laird; for Dougal could turn his master round his finger.

Weel, round came the Revolution, and it had like to have broken the hearts baith of Dougal and his master. But the change was not a'thegither sae great as they feared, and other folk thought for. The Whigs made an unco crawing what they wad do with their auld enemies, and in special wi' Sir Robert Redgauntlet. But there were ower mony great folks dipped in the same doings to mak a spick and span new warld. So Parliament passed it a' ower easy; and Sir Robert, bating that he was held to hunting foxes instead of Covenanters, remained just the man he was. His revel was as loud, and his hall as weel lighted, as ever it had been, though maybe he lacked the fines of the Nonconformists, that used to come to stock his larder and cellar; for it is certain he began to be keener about the rents than his tenants used to find him before, and they behoved to be prompt to the rent-day, or else the laird wasna pleased. And he was sic an awsome body that naebody cared to anger him; for the oaths he swore, and the rage that he used to get into, and the looks that he put on, made men sometimes think him a devil incarnate.

Weel, my gudesire was nae manager—no that he was a very great misguider—but he hadna the saving gift, and he got twa terms' rent in arrear. He got the first brash at Whitsunday put ower wi' fair word nd piping; but when Martinmas came, there was a summons from the grund-officer to come wi' the rent on a day preceese, or else Steenie behoved to flit. Sair wark he had to get the siller; but he was weel-freended, and at last he got the haill scraped thegither—a thousand merks; the maist of it was from a neighbor they ca'd Laurie Lapraik a sly tod. Laurie had walth o' gear—could hunt wi' the hound and rin wi' the hare—and be Whig or Tory, saunt or sinner, as the wind stood. He was a professor in this Revolution warld; but he liked an orra sough of this warld, and a tune on the pipes weel aneugh at a bytime; and abune a' he thought he had gude security for the siller he lent my gudesire ower the stocking at Primrose Knowe.

Away trots my gudesire to Redgauntlet Castle, wi' a heavy purse and a light heart, glad to be out of the laird's danger. Weel, the first thing he learned at the castle was that Sir Robert had fretted himself into a fit of the gout, because he did not appear before twelve o'clock. It wasna a'thegither for sake of the money, Dougal thought; but because he didna like to part wi' my gudesire aff the grund. Dougal was glad to see Steenie, and brought him into the great oak parlor, and there sat the laird his leesome lane, excepting that he had beside him a great ill-favored jackanape, that was a special pet of his—a cankered beast it was, and mony an ill-natured trick it played; ill to please it was, and easily angered—ran about the haill castle, chattering and yowling, and pinching and biting folk, especially before ill weather, or distur-bances in the state. Sir Robert ca'd it Major Weir after the warlock that was burnt;[1] and few folk liked either the name or the conditions of the creature— they thought there was something in it by ordinar— and my gudesire was not just easy in mind when the door shut on him, and he saw himself in the room wi' naebody but the laird, Dougal MacCallum, and the major, a thing that hadna chanced to him before.

---

[1] A celebrated wizard, executed (1670) at Edinburgh for sorcery and other crimes.

Sir Robert sat, or, I should say, lay, in a great armed chair, wi' his grand velvet gown, and his feet on a cradle; for he had baith gout and gravel, and his face looked as gash and ghastly as Satan's. Major Weir sat opposite to him, in a red laced coat, and the laird's wig on his head; and aye as Sir Robert girned wi' pain, the jackanape girned too, like a sheep's-head between a pair of tangs—an ill-faured, fearsome couple they were. The laird's buff-coat was hung on a pin behind him, and his broadsword and his pistols within reach; for he keepit up the auld fashion of having the weapons ready, and a horse saddled day and night, just as he used to do when he was able to loup on horseback, and away after ony of the Hill-folk he could get speerings of. Some said it was for fear of the Whigs taking vengeance, but I judge it was just his auld custom—he wasna gien to fear onything. The rental-book, wi' its black cover and brass clasps, was lying beside him; and a book of sculduggery sangs was put betwixt the leaves, to keep it open at the place where it bore evidence against the goodman of Primrose Knowe, as behind the hand with his mails and duties. Sir Robert gave my gudesire a look as if he would have withered his heart in his bosom. Ye maun ken he had a way of bending his brows that men saw the visible mark of a horseshoe in his forehead, deep-dinted, as if it had been stamped there.

"Are ye come light-handed, ye son of a toom whistle?" said Sir Robert. "Zounds! if you are———"

My gudesire, with as gude a countenance as he could put on, made a leg, and placed the bag of money on the table wi' a dash, like a man that does something clever. The laird drew it to him hastily. "Is it all here, Steenie, man?"

"Your honor will find it right," said my gudesire.

"Here, Dougal," said the laird, "gie Steenie a tass of brandy downstairs, till I count the siller and write the receipt."

But they werena weel out of the room when Sir Robert gied a yelloch that garr'd the castle rock. Back ran Dougal—in flew the livery-men—yell on yell gied the laird, ilk ane mair awfu' than the ither. My gudesire knew not whether to stand or flee, but he ventured back into the parlor, where a' was gaun hirdie-girdie—naebody to say "come in" or "gae out." Terribly the laird roared for cauld water to his feet, and wine to cool his throat; and "Hell, hell, hell, and its flames," was aye the word in his mouth. They brought him water, and when they plunged his swoln feet into the tub, he cried out it was burning; and folk say that it did bubble and sparkle like a seething caldron. He flung the cup at Dougal's head, and said he had given him blood instead of burgundy; and, sure aneugh, the lass washed clotted blood aff the carpet the neist day. The jackanape they ca'd Major Weir, it jibbered and cried as if it was mocking its master. My gudesire's head was like to turn: he forgot baith siller and receipt, and downstairs he banged; but as he ran, the shrieks came faint and fainter; there was a deep-drawn shivering groan, and word gaed through the castle that the laird was dead.

Weel, away came my gudesire wi' his finger in his mouth, and his best hope was that Dougal had seen the money-bag, and heard the laird speak of writing the receipt. The young laird, now Sir John, came from Edinburgh to see things put to rights. Sir John and his father never gree'd weel. Sir John had been bred an advocate, and afterward sat in the last Scots Parliament and voted for the Union, having gotten, it was thought, a rug of the compensations; if his father could have come out of his grave he would have brained him for it on his ain hearthstane. Some thought it was easier counting with the auld rough knight than the fair-spoken young ane—but mair of that anon.

Dougal MacCallum, poor body, neither grat nor graned, but gaed about the house looking like a corpse, but directing, as was his duty, a' the order of the grand funeral. Now, Dougal looked aye waur and waur when night was coming, and was aye the last to gang to his bed, whilk was in a little round just opposite the chamber of dais, whilk his master occu-

pied while he was living, and where he now lay in
state, as they ca'd it, weel-a-day! The night before the
funeral, Dougal could keep his awn counsel nae
langer: he came doun with his proud spirit, and fairly
asked auld Hutcheon to sit in his room with him for
an hour. When they were in the round, Dougal took
ae tass of brandy to himself and gave another to
Hutcheon, and wished him all health and lang life,
and said that, for himself, he wasna lang for this
world; for that, every night since Sir Robert's death,
his silver call had sounded from the state chamber,
just as it used to do at nights in his lifetime, to call
Dougal to help to turn him in his bed. Dougal said
that, being alone with the dead on that floor of the
tower (for naebody cared to wake Sir Robert
Redgauntlet like another corpse), he had never dau-
red to answer the call, but that now his conscience
checked him for neglecting his duty; for, "though
death breaks service," said MacCallum, "it shall
never break my service to Sir Robert; and I will
answer his next whistle, so be you will stand by me,
Hutcheon."

Hutcheon had nae will to work, but he had stood
by Dougal in battle and broil, and he wad not fail
him at this pinch; so down the carles sat ower a stoup
of brandy, and Hutcheon, who was something of a
clerk, would have read a chapter of the Bible; but

Dougal would hear neathing but a blaud of Davie
Lindsay, whilk was the waur preparation.

When midnight came, and the house was quiet as
the grave, sure aneugh the silver whistle sounded as
sharp and shrill as if Sir Robert was blowing it, and
up gat the twa auld serving-men and tottered into
the room where the dead man lay. Hutcheon saw
aneugh at the first glance; for there were torches in
the room, which showed him the foul fiend in his
ain shape, sitting on the laird's coffin! Ower he
couped as if he had been dead. He could not tell
how lang he lay in a trance at the door, but when he
gathered himself he cried on his neighbor, and getting nae answer, raised the house, when Dougal was
found lying dead within twa steps of the bed where
his master's coffin was placed. As for the whistle, it
was gaen anes and aye; but mony a time was it heard
at the top of the house on the bartizan, and amang
the auld chimneys and turrets, where the howlets
have their nests. Sir John hushed the matter up, and
the funeral passed over without mair bogle-wark.

But when a' was ower, and the laird was beginning
to settle his affairs, every tenant was called up for his
arrears, and my gudesire for the full sum that stood
him in the rental-book. Weel, away he trots to the
castle, to tell his story, and there he is introduced to
Sir John, sitting in his father's chair, in deep mourn-

ing, with weepers and hanging cravat, and a small walking rapier by his side, instead of the auld broadsword that had a hundredweight of steel about it, what with blade, chape, and basket-hilt. I have heard their communing so often tauld ower, that I almost think I was there myself, though I couldna be born at the time. (In fact, Alan, my companion mimicked, with a good deal of humor, the flattering, conciliating tone of the tenant's address, and the hypocritical melancholy of the laird's reply. His grandfather, he said, had, while he spoke, his eye fixed on the rental-book, as if it were a mastiff-dog that he was afraid would spring up and bite him.)

"I wuss ye joy, sir, of the head seat, and the white loaf, and the braid lairdship. Your father was a kind man to friends and followers; muckle grace to you, Sir John, to fill his shoon—his boots, I suld say, for he seldom wore shoon, unless it were muils when he had the gout."

"Ay, Steenie," quoth the laird, sighing deeply, and putting his napkin to his een, "his was a sudden call, and he will be missed in the country; no time to set his house in order: weel prepared Godward, no doubt, which is the root of the matter, but left us behind a tangled hesp to wind, Steenie. Hem! hem! We maun go to business, Steenie; much to do, and little time to do it in."

Here he opened the fatal volume. I have heard of

a thing they call Doomsday Book—I am clear it has been a rental of back-ganging tenants.

"Stephen," said Sir John, still in the same soft, sleekit tone of voice—"Stephen Stevenson, or Steenson, ye are down here for a year's rent behind the hand, due at last term."

Stephen. "Please your honor, Sir John, I paid it to your father."

Sir John. "Ye took a receipt then, doubtless, Stephen, and can produce it?"

Stephen. "Indeed I hadna time, an it like your honor; for nae sooner had I set doun the siller, and just as his honor Sir Robert, that's gaen, drew it till him to count it, and write out the receipt, he was ta'en wi' the pains that removed him."

"That was unlucky," said Sir John, after a pause. "But ye maybe paid it in the presence of somebody. I want but a talis qualis evidence, Stephen. I would go ower strictly to work with no poor man."

Stephen. "Troth, Sir John, there was naebody in the room but Dougal MacCallum, the butler. But, as your honor kens, he has e'en followed his auld master."

"Very unlucky again, Stephen," said Sir John, without altering his voice a single note. "The man to whom ye paid the money is dead; and the man who witnessed the payment is dead too; and the siller, which should have been to the fore, is neither seen nor heard tell of in the repositories. How am I to believe a' this?"

Stephen. "I dinna ken, your honor; but there is a bit memorandum note of the very coins—for, God help me! I had to borrow out of twenty purses—and I am sure that ilka man there set down will take his grit oath for what purpose I borrowed the money."

Sir John. "I have little doubt ye *borrowed* the money, Steenie. It is the *payment* to my father that I want to have some proof of."

Stephen. "The siller maun be about the house, Sir John. And since your honor never got it, and his honor that was canna have ta'en it wi' him, maybe some of the family may have seen it."

Sir John. "We will examine the servants, Stephen; that is but reasonable."

But lackey and lass, and page and groom, all denied stoutly that they had ever seen such a bag of money as my gudesire described. What was waur, he had unluckily not mentioned to any living soul of them his purpose of paying his rent. Ae quean had noticed something under his arm, but she took it for the pipes.

Sir John Redgauntlet ordered the servants out of the room, and then said to my gudesire: "Now, Steenie, ye see you have fair play; and, as I have little doubt ye ken better where to find the siller than any other body, I beg, in fair terms, and for your own sake, that you will end this fashcrie; for, Stephen, ye maun pay or flit."

"The Lord forgie your opinion," said Stephen, driven almost to his wit's-end—"I am an honest man."

"So am I, Stephen," said his honor; "and so are all the folks in the house, I hope. But if there be a knave among us, it must be he that tells the story he can not prove." He paused, and then added, mair sternly: "If I understand your trick, sir; you want to take advantage of some malicious reports concerning things in this family, and particularly respecting my father's sudden death, thereby to cheat me out of the money, and perhaps take away my character, by insinuating that I have received the rent I am demanding. Where do you suppose this money to be? I insist upon knowing."

My gudesire saw everything look sae muckle against him that he grew nearly desperate; however, he shifted from one foot to another, looked to every corner of the room, and made no answer.

"Speak out, sirrah," said the laird, assuming a look of his father's—a very particular one, which he had when he was angry: it seemed as if the wrinkles of his frown made that selfsame fearful shape of a horse's shoe in the middle of his brow—"speak out, sir! I *will* know your thought. Do you suppose that I have this money?"

"Far be it frae me to say so," said Stephen.

"Do you charge any of my people with having taken it?"

"I wad be laith to charge them that may be inno-cent," said my gudesire; "and if there be any one that is guilty, I have nae proof."

"Somewhere the money must be, if there is a word of truth in your story," said Sir John; "I ask where you think it is, and demand a correct answer?"

"In hell, if you *will* have my thoughts of it," said my gudesire, driven to extremity—"in hell! with your father, his jackanape, and his silver whistle."

Down the stairs he ran, for the parlor was nae place for him after such a word, and he heard the laird swearing blood and wounds behind him, as fast as ever did Sir Robert, and roaring for the bailie and the baron-officer.

Away rode my gudesire to his chief creditor, him they ca'd Laurie Lapraik, to try if he could make onything out of him; but when he tauld his story, he got but the warst word in his wame—thief, beggar, and dyvour were the safest terms; and to the boot of these hard terms, Laurie brought up the auld story of his dipping his hand in the blood of God's saunts, just as if a tenant could have helped riding with the laird, and that a laird like Sir Robert Redgauntlet. My gudesire was by this time far beyond the bounds of patience, and while he and Laurie were at deil speed the liars, he was wanchancie aneugh to abuse Lapraik's doctrine as weel as the man, and said things that garr'd folks' flesh grue that heard them; he wasna just himsell, and he had lived wi' a wild set in his day.

At last they parted, and my gudesire was to ride hame through the wood of Pitmurkie, that is a' fou of black firs, as they say. I ken the wood, but the firs may be black or white for what I can tell. At the entry of the wood there is a wild common, and on the edge of the common a little lonely change-house, that was keepit then by a hostler-wife—they suld hae ca'd her Tibbie Faw—and there puir Stee-nie cried for a mutchkin of brandy, for he had had no refreshment the haill day. Tibbie was earnest wi' him to take a bite o' meat, but he couldna think o't, nor would he take his foot out of the stirrup, and took off the brandy wholly at twa drafts, and named a toast to each—the first was, the memory of Sir Robert Redgauntlet, and might he never lie quiet in his grave till he had righted his poor bond-tenant; and the second was, a health to Man's Enemy, if he would but get him back the pock of siller, or tell him what came o't, for he saw the haill world was like to regard him as a thief and a cheat, and he took that waur than even the ruin of his house and hauld.

On he rode, little caring where. It was a dark night turned, and the trees made it yet darker, and he let the beast take its ain road through the wood; when, all of a sudden, from tired and wearied that it was before, the nag began to spring, and flee, and stend, that my gudesire could hardly keep the saddle; upon the whilk, a horseman, suddenly riding up beside him, said, "That's a mettle beast of yours, freend; will you sell him?" So saying, he touched the horse's neck with his riding-wand, and it fell into its auld heigh-ho of a stumbling trot. "But his spunk's soon out of him, I think," continued the stranger, "and that is like money a man's courage, that thinks he wad do great things till he come to the proof."

My gudesire scarce listened to this, but spurred his horse, with "Gude e'en to you, freend."

But it's like the stranger was ane that doesna lightly yield his point; for, ride as Steenie liked, he was aye beside him at the salfsame pace. At last my gudesire, Steenie Steenson, grew half angry and, to say the truth, half feared.

"What is it that ye want with me, freend?" he said. "If ye be a robber, I have nae money; if ye be a leal man, wanting company, I have nae heart to mirth or speaking; and if ye want to ken the road, I scarce ken it mysell."

"If you will tell me your grief," said the stranger, "I am one that, though I have been sair misca'd in the world, am the only hand for helping my freends."

So my gudesire, to ease his ain heart, mair than from any hope of help, told him the story from beginning to end.

"It's a hard pinch," said the stranger; "but I think I can help you."

"If you could lend the money, sir, and take a lang day—I ken nae other help on earth," said my gudesire.

"But there may be some under the earth," said the stranger. "Come, I'll be frank wi' you; I could lend you the money on bond, but you would maybe scruple my terms. Now, I can tell you that your auld laird is disturbed in his grave by your curses, and the wailing of your family, and if ye daur venture to go to see him, he will give you the receipt."

My gudesire's hair stood on end at this proposal, but he thought his companion might be some humorsome chield that was trying to frighten him, and might end with lending him the money. Besides, he was bauld wi' brandy, and desperate wi' distress; and he said he had courage to go to the gate of hell, and a step farther, for that receipt.

The stranger laughed.

Weel, they rode on through the thickest of the wood, when, all of a sudden, the horse stopped at the door of a great house; and, but that he knew the place was ten miles off, my gudesire would have thought he was at Redgauntlet Castle. They rode into the outer courtyard, through the muckle fauld-ing yetts, and aneath the auld portcullis; and the whole front of the house was lighted, and there were pipes and fiddles, and as much dancing and deray within as used to be in Sir Robert's house at Pace and Yule, and such high seasons. They lap off, and my gudesire, as seemed to him, fastened his horse to the very ring he had tied him to that morning, when he gaed to wait on the young Sir John.

"God!" said my gudesire, "if Sir Robert's death be but a dream!"

He knocked at the ha' door just as he was wont, and his auld acquaintance, Dougal MacCallum, just after his wont, too, came to open the door, and said, "Piper Steenie, are ye there, lad? Sir Robert has been crying for you."

My gudesire was like a man in a dream; he looked for the stranger, but he was gane for the time. At last he just tried to say, "Ha! Dougal Driveower, are ye living? I thought ye had been dead."

"Never fash yoursell wi' me," said Dougal, "but look to yourself; and see ya tak naething frae ony-body here, neither meat, drink, or siller, except just the receipt that is your ain."

So saying, he led the way out through halls and trances that were weel kenn'd to my gudesire, and into the auld oak parlor; and there was as much singing of profane sangs, and birling of red wine,

and speaking blasphemy and sculduddry, as had ever
been in Redgauntlet Castle when it was at the
blythest.

But, Lord take us in keeping! what a set of ghastly
revelers they were that sat round that table! My
gudesire kenn'd mony that had long before gane to
their place, for often had he piped to the most part in
the hall of Redgauntlet. There was the fierce Mid-
dleton, and the dissolute Rothes, and the crafty
Lauderdale; and Dalyell, with his bald head and a
beard to his girdle; and Earlshell, with Cameron's
blue on his hand; and wild Bonshaw, that tied blessed
Mr. Cargill's limbs till the blude sprung; and Dumb-
arton Douglas, the twice-turned traitor baith to
country and king. There was the Bluidy Advocate
MacKenyie, who, for his worldly wit and wisdom,
had been to the rest as a god. And there was Claverhouse, as beautiful as when he lived, with his long
dark, curled locks, streaming down over his laced
buff-coat, and his left hand always on his right spule-
blade, to hide the wound that the silver bullet had
made. He sat apart from them all, and looked at
them with a melancholy, haughty countenance;
while the rest hallooed, and sung, and laughed, that
the room rang. But their smiles were fearfully con-
torted from time to time; and their laughter passed
into such wild sounds as made my gudesire's very
nails grow blue, and chilled the marrow in his banes.

They that waited at the table were just the wicked servingmen and troopers that had done their work and cruel bidding on earth. There was the Lang Lad of the Nethertown, that helped to take Argyle; and the bishop's summoner, that they called the Deil's Rattle-bag; and the wicked guardsmen, in their laced coats; and the savage Highland Amorites, that shed blood like water; and mony a proud serving-man, haughty of heart and bloody of hand, cringing to the rich, and making them wickeder than they would be; grinding the poor to powder, when the rich had broken them to fragments. And mony, mony mair were coming and ganging, a' as busy in their vocation as if they had been alive.

Sir Robert Redgauntlet, in the midst of a' this fearful riot, cried, wi' a voice like thunder, on Steenie Piper to come to the board-head where he was sitting, his legs stretched out before him, and swathed up with flannel, with his holster pistols aside him, while the great broad-sword rested against his chair, just as my gudesire had seen him the last time upon earth—the very cushion for the jackanape was close to him, but the creature itsell was not there; it wasna its hour, it's likely; for he heard them say as he came forward, "Is not the major come yet?" And another answered, "The jackanape will be here betimes the morn." And when my gudesire came forward, Sir Robert, or his ghaist, or the deevil in his likeness, said, "Weel, piper, hae ye settled wi' my son for the year's rent?"

With much ado my father gat breath to say that Sir John would not settle without his honor's receipt.

"Ye shall hae that for a tune of the pipes, Steenie," said the appearance of Sir Robert. "Play us up, 'Weel hoddled, Luckie.'"

Now this was a tune my gudesire learned frae a warlock, that heard it when they were worshiping Satan at their meetings, and my gudesire had sometimes played it at the ranting suppers in Redgauntlet Castle, but never very willingly; and now he grew cauld at the very name of it, and said, for excuse, he hadna his pipes wi' him.

"MacCallum, ye limb of Beelzebub," said the fearfu' Sir Robert, "bring Steenie the pipes that I am keeping for him!"

MacCallum brought a pair of pipes might have served the piper of Donald of the Isles. But he gave my gudesire a nudge as he offered them; and looking secretly and closely, Steenie saw that the chanter was of steel, and heated to a white heat; so he had fair warning not to trust his fingers with it. So he excused himself again, and said he was faint and frightened, and had not wind enough to fill the bag.

"Then ye maun eat and drink, Steenie," said the figure; "for we do little else here; and it's ill speaking between a fou man and a fasting."

Now these were the very words that the bloody Earl of Douglas said to keep the king's messenger in hand, while he cut the head off MacLellan of Bombie, at the Threave Castle, and that put Steenie mair and mair on his guard. So he spoke up like a man, and said he came neither to eat, or drink, or make minstrelsy, but simply for his ain—to ken what was come o' the money he had paid, and to get a discharge for it; and he was so stout-hearted by this time, that he charged Sir Robert for conscience' sake (he had no power to say the holy name), and as he hoped for peace and rest, to spread no snares for him, but just to give him his ain.

The appearance gnashed its teeth and laughed, but it took from a large pocket-book the receipt, and handed it to Steenie. "There is your receipt, ye pitiful cur; and for the money, my dog-whelp of a son may go look for it in the Cat's Cradle."

My gudesire uttered mony thanks, and was about to retire when Sir Robert roared aloud: "Stop though, thou sackdoudling son of a whore! I am not done with thee. *Here* we do nothing for nothing; and you must return on this very day twelvemonth to pay your master the homage that you owe me for my protection."

My father's tongue was loosed of a suddenty, and he said aloud: "I refer myself to God's pleasure, and not to yours."

He had no sooner uttered the word than all was dark around him, and he sunk on the earth with such a sudden shock that he lost both breath and sense.

How lang Steenie lay there, he could not tell; but when he came to himself, he was lying in the auld kirkyard of Redgauntlet parochine, just at the door of the family aisle, and the scutcheon of the auld knight, Sir Robert, hanging over his head. There was a deep morning fog on grass and gravestane around him, and his horse was feeding quietly beside the minister's twa cows. Steenie would have thought the whole was a dream, but he had the receipt in his hand, fairly written and signed by the auld laird; only the last letters of his name were a little disorderly, written like one seized with sudden pain.

Sorely troubled in his mind, he left that dreary place, rode through the mist to Redgauntlet Castle, and with much ado he got speech of the laird.

"Well, you dyvour bankrupt," was the first word, "have you brought me my rent?"

"No," answered my gudesire, "I have not; but I have brought your honor Sir Robert's receipt for it."

"How, sirrah? Sir Robert's receipt! You told me he had not given you one."

"Will your honor please to see if that bit line is right?"

Sir John looked at every line, and at every letter,

with much attention, and at last at the date, which my gudesire had not observed—" 'From my appointed place,' " he read, " 'this twenty-fifth of November.' What! That is yesterday! Villain, thou must have gone to Hell for this!"

"I got it from your honor's father; whether he be in Heaven or Hell, I know not," said Steenie.

"I will delate you for a warlock to the privy council!" said Sir John. "I will send you to your master, the devil, with the help of a tar-barrel and a torch!"

"I intend to delate myself to the presbytery," said Steenie, "and tell them all I have seen last night, whilk are things fitter for them to judge of than a borrell man like me."

Sir John paused, composed himself, and desired to hear the full history; and my gudesire told it him from point to point, as I have told it you—word for word, neither more nor less.

Sir John was silent again for a long time, and at last he said, very composedly: "Steenie, this story of yours concerns the honor of many a noble family besides mine; and if it be a leasing-making, to keep yourself out of my danger, the least you can expect is to have a red-hot iron driven through your tongue, and that will be as bad as scauding your fingers with a red-hot chanter. But yet it may be true, Steenie; and if the money cast up, I shall not know what to think of it. But where shall we find the Cat's Cradle?

There are cats enough about the old house, but I think they kitten without the ceremony of bed or cradle."

"We were best ask Hutcheon," said my gudesire; "he kens a' the odd corners about as weel as— another serving-man that is now gane, and that I wad not like to name."

Aweel, Hutcheon, when he was asked, told them that a ruinous turret, lang disused, next to the clock-house, only accessible by a ladder, for the opening was on the outside, and far above the battlements, was called of old the Cat's Cradle.

"There will I go immediately," said Sir John; and he took (with what purpose, Heaven kens) one of his father's pistols from the hall-table, where they had lain since the night he died, and hastened to the battlements.

It was a dangerous place to climb, for the ladder was auld and frail, and wanted ane or twa rounds. However, up got Sir John, and entered at the turret door, where his body stopped the only little light that was in the bit turret. Something flees at him wi' a vengeance, maist dang him back ower; bang gaed the knight's pistol, and Hutcheon, that held the ladder, and my gudesire that stood beside him, hears a loud skelloch. A minute after, Sir John flings the body of the jackanape down to them, and cries that the siller is fund, and that they should come up and help him. And there was the bag of siller sure aneugh, and mony orra things besides that had been missing for mony a day. And Sir John, when he had riped the turret weel, led my gudesire into the dining-parlor, and took him by the hand, and spoke kindly to him, and said he was sorry he should have doubted his word, and that he would hereafter be a good master to him, to make amends.

"And now, Steenie," said Sir John, "although this vision of yours tends, on the whole, to my father's credit, as an honest man, that he should, even after his death, desire to see justice done to a poor man like you, yet you are sensible that ill-dispositioned men might make bad constructions upon it, concerning his soul's health. So, I think, we had better lay the haill dirdum on that ill-deedie creature, Major Weir, and say naething about your dream in the wood of Pitmurkie. You had taken ower muckle brandy to be very certain about onything; and, Steenie, this receipt (his hand shook while he held it out), it's but a queer kind of document, and we will do best, I think, to put it quietly in the fire."

"Od, but for as queer as it is, it's a' the voucher I have for my rent," said my gudesire, who was afraid, it may be, of losing the benefit of Sir Robert's discharge.

"I will bear the contents to your credit in the rental-book, and give you a discharge under my own hand," said Sir John, "and that on the spot. And, Steenie, if you can hold your tongue about this matter, you shall sit, from this term downward, at an easier rent."

"Mony thanks to your honor," said Steenie, who saw easily in what corner the wind was; "doubtless I will be conformable to all your honor's commands; only I would willingly speak wi' some powerful minister on the subject, for I do not like the sort of summons of appointment whilk your honor's father——"

"Do not call the phantom my father!" said Sir John, interrupting him.

"Weel, then, the thing that was so like him," said my gudesire; "he spoke of my coming back to him this time twelvemonth, and it's a weight on my conscience."

"Aweel, then," said Sir John, "if you be so much distressed in mind, you speak to our minister of the parish; he is a douce man, regards the honor of our family, and the mair that he may look for some patronage from me."

Wi' that my gudesire readily agreed that the receipt should be burned, and the laird threw it into the chimney with his ain hand. Burn it would not for them, though; but away it flew up the lum, wi' a lang train of sparks at its tail, and a hissing noise like a squib.

My gudesire gaed down to the manse, and the minister, when he had heard the story, said it was his real opinion that, though my gudesire had gaen very far in tampering with dangerous matters, yet, as he had refused the devil's arles (for such was the offer of meat and drink), and had refused to do homage by piping at his bidding, he hoped, that if he held a circumspect walk hereafter, Satan could take little advantage by what was come and gane. And, indeed, my gudesire, of his ain accord, lang foreswore baith the pipes and the brandy; it was not even till the year was out, and the fatal day passed, that he would so much as take the fiddle, or drink usquebaugh or tippenny.

Sir John made up his story about the jackanape as he liked himself; and some believe till this day there was no more in the matter than the filching nature of the brute. Indeed, ye'll no hinder some to threap that it was name o' the Auld Enemy that Dougal and Hutcheon saw in the laird's room, but only that wanchancie creature, the major, capering on the coffin; and that, as to the blawing on the laird's whistle that was heard after he was dead, the filthy brute could do that as weel as the laird himself, if no better. But Heaven kens the truth, whilk first came out by the minister's wife, after Sir John and her ain gudeman were baith in the molds. And then, my gudesire, wha was failed in his limbs, but not in his

judgment or memory—at least nothing to speak
of—was obliged to tell the real narrative to his
freends for the credit of his good name. He might
else have been charged for a warlock.

The shades of evening were growing thicker around
us as my conductor finished his long narrative with
this moral: "Ye see, birkie, it is nae chancy thing to
tak a stranger traveler for a guide when ye are in an
uncouth land."

"I should not have made that inference," said I.
"Your grandfather's adventure was fortunate for
himself, whom it saved from ruin and distress; and
fortunate for his landlord also, whom it prevented
from committing a gross act of injustice."

"Ay, but they had baith to sup the sauce o't sooner
or later," said Wandering Willie. "What was fristed
wasna forgiven. Sir John died before he was much
over three-score; and it was just like of a moment's
illness. And for my gudesire, though he departed in
fullness of years, yet there was my father, a yauld man
of forty-five, fell down betwixt the stilts of his
pleugh, and raise never again, and left nae bairn, but
me, a puir sightless, fatherless, motherless creature,
could neither work nor want. Things gaed weel
aneugh at first; for Sir Redwald Redgauntlet, the
only son of Sir John, and the oye of auld Sir Robert,
and, wae's me! the last of the honorable house, took

the farm off our hands, and brought me into his household to have care of me. He liked music, and I had the best teachers baith England and Scotland could gie me. Mony a merry year was I wi' him; but wae's me! he gaed out with other pretty men in the Forty-five—I'll say nae mair about it. My head never settled weel since I lost him; and if I say another word about it, deil a bar will I have the heart to play the night. Look out, my gentle chap," he resumed, in a different tone, "ye should see the lights in Brokenburn Glen by this time."

The Adventure of the German Student

[WASHINGTON IRVING]

Romanticism, once established in Great Britain, leapt another, greater, body of water—the Atlantic. But where Europe had a treasury of folklore in its immemorial past from which to draw, the United States had only four sources: the Indians, the earliest settlements, the revolution, and the ongoing romance of the frontier (which latter had been used—albeit less than accurately—by the great French Romantic, Chateaubriand). Not too surprisingly, all four of these themes were used by the first American writer to gain great fame abroad, Washington Irving.

A native of New York, he became famous for using the strange lore of the early Dutch settlers of his native state to great effect in such works as A Knickerbocker's History of New-York, Rip Van Winkle, *and* The Legend of Sleepy Hollow. *But he returned Chateaubriand's compliment by also looking to old Europe for settings and material, as in the following tale, which also abandons his trademark geniality for a subdued, but nonetheless effective, fear-smithing.*

On a stormy night, in the tempestuous times of the French Revolution, a young German was returning to his lodgings, at a late hour, across the old part of Paris. The lightning gleamed, and the loud claps of thunder rattled through the lofty narrow streets—but I should first tell you something about this young German.

Gottfried Wolfgang was a young man of good family. He had studied for some time at Gottingen, but being of a visionary and enthusiastic character, he had wandered into those wild and speculative doctrines which have so often bewildered German students. His secluded life, his intense application, and the singular nature of his studies, had an effect on both mind and body. His health was impaired; his imagination diseased. He had been indulging in fanciful speculations on spiritual essences, until, like Swedenborg, he had an ideal world of his own around him. He took up a notion, I do not know from what cause, that there was an evil influence hanging over him; an evil genius or spirit seeking to ensnare him and ensure his perdition. Such an idea working on his melancholy temperament produced the most gloomy effects. He became haggard and desponding. His friends discovered the mental malady preying upon him, and determined that the best cure was a change of scene; he was sent, therefore, to finish his studies amidst the splendors and gayeties of Paris.

Wolfgang arrived at Paris at the breaking out of the revolution. The popular delirium at first caught his enthusiastic mind, and he was captivated by the political and philosophical theories of the day: but the scenes of blood which followed shocked his sensitive nature, disgusted him with society and the world, and made him more than ever a recluse. He shut himself up in a solitary apartment in the *Pays Latin,* the quarter of students. There, in a gloomy street not far from the monastic walls of the Sorbonne, he pursued his favorite speculations. Sometimes he spent hours together in the great libraries of Paris, those catacombs of departed authors, rummaging among their hoards of dusty and obsolete works in quest of food for his unhealthy appetite. He was, in a manner, a literary ghoul, feeding in the charnel-house of decayed literature.

Wolfgang, thought solitary and recluse, was of an ardent temperament, but for a time it operated merely upon his imagination. He was too shy and ignorant of the world to make any advances to the fair, but he was a passionate admirer of female beauty, and in his lonely chamber would often lose himself in reveries on forms and faces which he had seen, and his fancy would deck out images of loveliness far surpassing the reality.

While his mind was in this excited and sublimated state, a dream produced an extraordinary effect upon him. It was of a female face of transcendent beauty. So strong was the impression made, that he dreamt of it again and again. It haunted his thoughts by day, his slumbers by night; in fine, he became passionately enamored of this shadow of a dream. This lasted so long that it became one of those fixed ideas which haunt the minds of melancholy men, and are at times mistaken for madness.

Such was Gottfried Wolfgang, and such his situation at the time I mentioned. He was returning home late one stormy night, through some of the old and gloomy streets of the *Marais,* the ancient part of Paris. The loud claps of thunder rattled among the high houses of the narrow streets. He came to the *Place de Greve,* the square, where public executions are performed. The lightning quivered about the pinnacles of the ancient *Hotel de Ville,* and shed flickering gleams over the open space in front. As Wolfgang was crossing the square, he shrank back with horror at finding himself close by the guillotine. It was the height of the reign of terror, when this dreadful instrument of death stood ever ready, and its scaffold was continually running with the blood of the virtuous and the brave. It had that very day been actively employed in the work of carnage, and there it stood in grim array, amidst a silent and sleeping city, waiting for fresh victims.

Wolfgang's heart sickened within him, and he was turning shuddering from the horrible engine when he beheld a shadowy form, cowering as it were at the foot of the steps which led up to the scaffold. A succession of vivid flashes of lightning revealed it more distinctly. It was a female figure, dressed in black. She was seated on one of the lower steps of the scaffold, leaning forward, her face hid in her lap; and her long dishevelled tresses hanging to the ground, streaming with the rain which fell in torrents. Wolfgang paused. There was something awful in this solitary monument of woe. The female had the appearance of being above the common order. He knew the times to be full of vicissitude, and that many a fair head, which had once been pillowed on down, now wandered houseless. Perhaps this was some poor mourner whom the dreadful axe had rendered desolate, and who sat here heart-broken on the strand of existence, from which all that was dear to her had been launched into eternity.

He approached, and addressed her in the accents of sympathy. She raised her head and gazed wildly at him. What was his astonishment at beholding, by the bright glare of the lighting, the very face which had haunted him in his dreams. It was pale and disconsolate, but ravishingly beautiful.

Trembling with violent and conflicting emotions, Wolfgang again accosted her. He spoke something of her being exposed at such an hour of the night, and to the fury of such a storm, and offered to conduct her to her friends. She pointed to the guillotine with a gesture of dreadful signification.

"I have no friend on earth!" said she.

"But you have a home," said Wolfgang.

"Yes—in the grave!"

The heart of the student melted at the words.

"If a stranger dare make an offer," said he, "without danger of being misunderstood, I would offer my humble dwelling as a shelter; myself as a devoted friend. I am friendless myself in Paris, and a stranger in the land; but if my life could be of service, it is at your disposal, and should be sacrificed before harm or indignity should come to you."

There was an honest earnestness in the young man's manner that had its effect. His foreign accent, too, was in his favor; it showed him not to be a hackneyed inhabitant of Paris. Indeed, there is an eloquence in true enthusiasm that is not to be doubted. The homeless stranger confided herself implicitly to the protection of the student.

He supported her faltering steps across the *Pont Neuf,* and by the place where the statue of Henry the Fourth had been overthrown by the populace.

The storm had abated, and the thunder rumbled at a distance. All Paris was quiet; that great volcano of human passion slumbered for a while, to gather fresh strength for the next day's eruption. The student conducted his charge through the ancient streets of the *Pays Latin,* and by the dusky walls of the Sorbonne, to the great dingy hotel which he inhabited. The old portress who admitted them stared with surprise at the unusual sight of the melancholy Wolfgang, with a female companion.

On entering his apartment, the student, for the first time, blushed at the scantiness and indifference of his dwelling. He had but one chamber—an old-fashioned saloon—heavily carved, and fantastically furnished with the remains of former magnificence, for it was one of those hotels in the quarter of the Luxembourg palace, which had once belonged to nobility. It was lumbered with books and papers, and all the usual apparatus of a student, and his bed stood in a recess at one end.

When lights were brought, and Wolfgang had a better opportunity of contemplating the stranger, he was more than ever intoxicated by her beauty. Her face was pale, but of a dazzling fairness, set off by a profusion of raven hair that hung clustering about it. Her eyes were large and brilliant, with a singular expression approaching almost to wildness. As far as her black dress permitted her shape to be seen, it was of perfect symmetry. Her whole appearance was highly striking, though she was dressed in the simplest style. The only thing approaching to an ornament which she wore, was a broad black band round her neck, clasped by diamonds.

The perplexity now commenced with the student how to dispose of the helpless being thus thrown upon his protection. He thought of abandoning his chamber to her, and seeking shelter for himself elsewhere. Still he was so fascinated by her charms, there seemed to be such a spell upon his thoughts and senses, that he could not tear himself from her presence. Her manner, too, was singular and unaccountable. She spoke no more of the guillotine. Her grief had abated. The attentions of the student had first won her confidence, and then, apparently, her heart. She was evidently an enthusiast like himself, and enthusiasts soon understood each other.

In the infatuation of the moment, Wolfgang avowed his passion for her. He told her the story of his mysterious dream, and how she had possessed his heart before he had even seen her. She was strangely affected by his recital, and acknowledged to have felt an impulse towards him equally unaccountable. It was the time for wild theory and wild actions. Old prejudices and superstitions were done away; everything was under the sway of the "Goddess of Rea-son." Among other rubbish of the old times, the forms and ceremonies of marriage began to be con-sidered superfluous bonds for honorable minds. Social compacts were the vogue. Wolfgang was too much of a theorist not to be tainted by the liberal doctrines of the day.

"Why should we separate?" said he: "our hearts are united; in the eye of reason and honor we are as one. What need is there of sordid forms to bind high souls together?"

The stranger listened with emotion: she had evi-dently received illumination at the same school.

"You have no home nor family," continued he: "Let me be everything to you, or rather let us be everything to one another. If form is necessary, form shall be observed—there is my hand. I pledge myself to you forever."

"Forever?" said the stranger, solemnly.

"Forever!" repeated Wolfgang.

The stranger clasped the hand extended to her: "then I am yours," murmured she, and sank upon his bosom.

The next morning the student left his bride sleep-ing, and sallied forth at an early hour to seek more spacious apartments suitable to the change in his sit-uation. When he returned, he found the stranger lying with her head hanging over the bed, and one arm thrown over it. He spoke to her, but received no reply. He advanced to awaken her from her uneasy posture. On taking her hand, it was cold—there was no pulsation—her face was pallid and ghastly. In a word, she was a corpse.

Horrified and frantic, he alarmed the house. A scene of confusion ensued. The police was summoned. As the officer of police entered the room, he started back on beholding the corpse.

"Great heaven!" cried he, "how did this woman come here?"

"Do you know anything about her?" said Wolfgang eagerly.

"Do I?" exclaimed the officer: "she was guillotined yesterday."

He stepped forward; undid the black collar round the neck of the corpse, and the head rolled on the floor!

The student burst into a frenzy. "The fiend! the fiend has gained possession of me!" shrieked he: "I am lost forever."

They tried to soothe him, but in vain. He was possessed with the frightful belief that an evil spirit had reanimated the dead body to ensnare him. He went distracted, and died in a mad-house.

Here the old gentleman with the haunted head finished his narrative.

"And is this really a fact?" said the inquisitive gentleman.

"A fact not to be doubted," replied the other. "I had it from the best authority. The student told it me himself. I saw him in a mad-house in Paris."

Feathertop

❧

[NATHANIEL HAWTHORNE]

*A sterner bunch than Irving's jolly Dutchmen in New York were
the Puritans of old New England—famous for the Salem Witch
Trials. Not surprisingly their weird lore was much darker.
Hawthorne, a descendant of one of the trial judges, reflected this
in such stories as the oft-anthologized "Young Goodman
Brown." Here, however, he uses the witch legends of his native
region with an almost Irvingesque lightness—almost. Being
Hawthorne, however, his conclusions about humanity are as
frightening as anything in* The House of the Seven Gables.

"Dickon," cried Mother Rigby, "a coal for
my pipe!"

The pipe was in the old dame's mouth
when she said these words. She had thrust it there
after filling it with tobacco, but without stooping to
light it at the hearth, where indeed there was no

appearance of a fire having been kindled that morning. Forthwith, however, as soon as the order was
given, there was an intense red glow out of the bowl
of the pipe, and a whiff of smoke from Mother
Rigby's lips. Whence the coal came, and how
brought thither by an invisible hand, I have never
been able to discover.

"Good!" quoth Mother Rigby, with a nod of her
head. "Thank ye, Dickon! And now for making this
scarecrow. Be within call, Dickon, in case I need you
again."

The good woman had risen thus early (for as yet it
was scarcely sunrise) in order to set about making a
scarecrow, which she intended to put in the middle
of her corn-patch. It was now the latter week of
May, and the crows and blackbirds had already discovered the little, green, rolled-up leaf of the Indian
corn just peeping out of the soil. She was determined, therefore, to contrive as lifelike a scarecrow as
ever was seen, and to finish it immediately, from top
to toe, so that it should begin its sentinel's duty that
very morning. Now Mother Rigby (as everybody
must have heard) was one of the most cunning and
potent witches in New England, and might, with
very little trouble, have made a scarecrow ugly
enough to frighten the minister himself. But on this
occasion, as she had awakened in an uncommonly
pleasant humor, and was further dulcified by her

pipe of tobacco, she resolved to produce something fine, beautiful, and splendid, rather than hideous and horrible.

"I don't want to set up a hobgoblin in my own corn-patch, and almost at my own doorstep," said Mother Rigby to herself, puffing out a whiff of smoke; "I could do it if I pleased, but I'm tired of doing marvellous things, and so I'll keep within the bounds of every-day business just for variety's sake. Besides, there is no use in scaring the little children for a mile roundabout, though 't is true I'm a witch."

It was settled, therefore, in her own mind, that the scarecrow should represent a fine gentleman of the period, so far as the materials at hand would allow. Perhaps it may be as well to enumerate the chief of the articles that went to the composition of this figure.

The most important item of all, probably, although it made so little show, was a certain broom stick, on which Mother Rigby had taken many an airy gallop at midnight, and which now served the scarecrow by way of a spinal column, or, as the unlearned phrase it, a backbone. One of its arms was a disabled flail which used to be wielded by Good-man Rigby, before his spouse worried him out of this troublesome world; the other, if I mistake not, was composed of the pudding stick and a broken rung of a chair, tied loosely together at the elbow. As for its legs, the right was a hoe handle, and the left an undistinguished and miscellaneous stick from the woodpile. Its lungs, stomach, and other affairs of that kind were nothing better than a meal bag stuffed with straw. Thus we have made out the skeleton and entire corporosity of the scarecrow, with the exception of its head; and this was admirably supplied by a somewhat withered and shrivelled pumpkin, in which Mother Rigby cut two holes for the eyes, and a slit for the mouth, leaving a bluish-colored knob in the middle to pass for a nose. It was really quite a respectable face.

"I've seen worse ones on human shoulders, at any rate," said Mother Rigby. "And many a fine gentleman has a pumpkin head, as well as my scarecrow."

But the clothes, in this case, were to be the making of the man. So the good old woman took down from a peg an ancient plum-colored coat of London make, and with relics of embroidery on its seams, cuffs, pocket-flaps, and button-holes, but lamentably worn and faded, patched at the elbows, tattered at the skirts, and threadbare all over. On the left breast was a round hole, whence either a star of nobility had been rent away, or else the hot heart of some former wearer had scorched it through and through. The neighbors said that this rich garment belonged to the Black Man's wardrobe, and that he kept it at Mother Rigby's cottage for the convenience of slipping it on whenever he wished to make a grand appearance at the governor's table. To match the coat there was a velvet waistcoat of very ample size, and formerly embroidered with foliage that had been as brightly golden as the maple leaves in October, but which had now quite vanished out of the substance of the velvet. Next came a pair of scarlet breeches, once worn by the French governor of Louisbourg, and the knees of which had touched the lower step of the throne of Louis le Grand. The Frenchman had given these smallclothes to an Indian powwow, who parted with them to the old witch for a gill of strong waters, at one of their dances in the forest. Furthermore, Mother Rigby produced a pair of silk stockings and put them on the figure's legs, where they showed as unsubstantial as a dream, with the wooden reality of the two sticks making itself miserably apparent through the holes. Lastly, she put her dead husband's wig on the bare scalp of the pumpkin, and surmounted the whole with a dusty three-cornered hat, in which was stuck the longest tail feather of a rooster.

Then the old dame stood the figure up in a corner of her cottage and chuckled to behold its yellow semblance of a visage, with its nobby little nose thrust into the air. It had a strangely self-satisfied aspect, and seemed to say, "Come look at me!"

Then the old dame stood the figure up in a corner

of her cottage and chuckled to behold its yellow semblance of a visage, with its nobby little nose thrust into the air. It had a strangely self-satisfied aspect, and seemed to say, "Come look at me!"

"And you are well worth looking at, that's a fact!" quoth Mother Rigby, in admiration at her own handiwork. "I've made many a puppet since I've been a witch, but methinks this is the finest of them all. 'T is almost too good for a scarecrow. And, by the by, I'll just fill a fresh pipe of tobacco and then take him out to the corn-patch."

While filling her pipe the old woman continued to gaze with almost motherly affection at the figure in the corner. To say the truth, whether it were chance, or skill, or downright witchcraft, there was something wonderfully human in this ridiculous shape, bedizened with its tattered finery; and as for the countenance, it appeared to shrivel its yellow surface into a grin—a funny kind of expression betwixt scorn and merriment, as if it understood itself to be a jest at mankind. The more Mother Rigby looked the better she she was pleased.

"Dickon," cried she sharply, "another coal for my pipe!"

Hardly had she spoken, than, just as before, there was a red-glowing coal on the top of the tobacco. She drew in a long whiff and puffed it forth again into the bar of morning sunshine which struggled through the one dusty pane of her cottage window. Mother Rigby always liked to flavor her pipe with a coal of fire from the particular chimney corner whence this had been brought. But where that chimney corner might be, or who brought the coal from it—further than that the invisible messenger seemed to respond to the name of Dickon—I cannot tell.

"That puppet yonder," thought Mother Rigby, still with her eyes fixed on the scarecrow, "is too good a piece of work to stand all summer in a corn-patch, frightening away the crows and blackbirds. He's capable of better things. Why, I've danced with a worse one, when partners happened to be scarce, at our witch meetings in the forest! What if I should let him take his chance among the other men of straw and empty fellows who go bustling about the world?"

The old witch took three or four more whiffs of her pipe and smiled.

"He'll meet plenty of his brethren at every street corner!" continued she. "Well; I didn't mean to dabble in witchcraft to-day, further than the lighting of my pipe, but a witch I am, and a witch I'm likely to be, and there's no use trying to shirk it. I'll make a man of my scarecrow, were it only for the joke's sake!"

While muttering these words, Mother Rigby took

the pipe from her own mouth and thrust it into the crevice which represented the same feature in the pumpkin visage of the scarecrow.

"Puff, darling, puff!" said she. "Puff away, my fine fellow! your life depends on it!"

This was a strange exhortation, undoubtedly, to be addressed to a mere thing of sticks, straw, and old clothes, with nothing better than a shrivelled pumpkin for a head—as we know to have been the scarecrow's case. Nevertheless, as we must carefully hold in remembrance, Mother Rigby was a witch of singular power and dexterity; and, keeping this fact duly before our minds, we shall see nothing beyond credibility in the remarkable incidents of our story. Indeed, the great difficulty will be at once got over, if we can only bring ourselves to believe that, as soon as the old dame bade him puff, there came a whiff of smoke from the scarecrow's mouth. It was the very feeblest of whiffs, to be sure; but it was followed by another and another, each more decided than the preceding one.

"Puff away, my pet! puff away, my pretty one!" Mother Rigby kept repeating, with her pleasantest smile. "It is the breath of life to ye; and that you may take my word for."

Beyond all question the pipe was bewitched. There must have been a spell either in the tobacco or in the fiercely-glowing coal that so mysteriously

burned on top of it, or in the pungently-aromatic
smoke which exhaled from the kindled weed. The
figure, after a few doubtful attempts, at length blew
forth a volley of smoke extending all the way from
the obscure corner into the bar of sunshine. There it
eddied and melted away among the motes of dust. It
seemed a convulsive effort; for the two or three next
whiffs were fainter, although the coal still glowed
and threw a gleam over the scarecrow's visage. The
old witch clapped her skinny hands together, and
smiled encouragingly upon her handiwork. She saw
that the charm worked well. The shrivelled, yellow
face, which heretofore had been no face at all, had
already a thin, fantastic haze, as it were of human
likeness, shifting to and fro across it; sometimes vanishing entirely, but growing more perceptible than
ever with the next whiff from the pipe. The whole
figure, in like manner, assumed a show of life, such as
we impart to ill-defined shapes among the clouds,
and half deceive ourselves with the pastime of our
own fancy.

If we must needs pry closely into the matter, it
may be doubted whether there was any real change,
after all, in the sordid, worn-out, worthless, and ill-
jointed substance of the scarecrow; but merely a
spectral illusion, and a cunning effect of light and
shade so colored and contrived as to delude the eyes
of most men. The miracles of witchcraft seem

always to have had a very shallow subtlety; and, at least, if the above explanation does not hit the truth of the process, I can suggest no better.

"Well puffed, my pretty lad!" still cried old Mother Rigby. "Come, another good stout whiff, and let it be with might and main. Puff for thy life, I tell thee! Puff out of the very bottom of thy heart, if any heart thou hast, or any bottom to it! Well done, again! Thou didst suck in that mouthful as if for the pure love of it."

And then the witch beckoned to the scarecrow, throwing so much magnetic potency into her gesture that it seemed as if it must inevitably be obeyed, like the mystic call of the loadstone when it summons the iron.

"Why lurkest thou in the corner, lazy one?" said she. "Step forth! Thou hast the world before thee!"

Upon my word, if the legend were not one which I heard on my grandmother's knee, and which had established its place among things credible before my childish judgment could analyze its probability, I question whether I should have the face to tell it now.

In obedience to Mother Rigby's word, and extending its arm as if to reach her outstretched hand, the figure made a step forward—a kind of hitch and jerk, however, rather than a step—then tottered and almost lost its balance. What could the witch expect? It was nothing, after all, but a scarecrow stuck upon two sticks. But the strong-willed old beldam scowled, and beckoned, and flung the energy of her purpose so forcibly at this poor combination of rotten wood, and musty straw, and ragged garments, that it was compelled to show itself a man, in spite of the reality of things. So it stepped into the bar of sunshine. There it stood—poor devil of a contrivance that it was!—with only the thinnest vesture of human similitude about it, through which was evident the stiff, rickety, incongruous, faded, tattered, good-for-nothing patchwork of its substance, ready to sink in a heap upon the floor, as conscious of its own unworthiness to be erect. Shall I confess the truth? At its present point of vivification, the scarecrow reminds me of some of the lukewarm and abortive characters, composed of heterogeneous materials, used for the thousandth time, and never worth using, with which romance writers (and myself, no doubt, among the rest) have so over peopled the world of fiction.

But the fierce old hag began to get angry and show a glimpse of her diabolic nature (like a snake's head, peeping with a hiss out of her bosom), at this pusillanimous behavior of the thing which she had taken the trouble to put together.

"Puff away, wretch!" cried she, wrathfully. "Puff, puff, puff, thou thing of straw and emptiness! thou rag or two! thou meal bag! thou pumpkin head!

thou nothing! Where shall I find a name vile enough to call thee by? Puff, I say, and suck in thy fantastic life along with the smoke! else I snatch the pipe from thy mouth and hurl thee where that red coal came from."

Thus threatened, the unhappy scarecrow had nothing for it but to puff away for dear life. As need was, therefore, it applied itself lustily to the pipe, and sent forth such abundant volleys of tobacco smoke that the small cottage kitchen became all vaporous. The one sunbeam struggled mistily through, and could but imperfectly define the image of the cracked and dusty window pane on the opposite wall. Mother Rigby, meanwhile, with one brown arm akimbo and the other stretched towards the figure, loomed grimly amid the obscurity with such port and expression as when she was wont to heave a ponderous nightmare on her victims and stand at the bedside to enjoy their agony. In fear and trembling did this poor scarecrow puff. But its efforts it must be acknowledged, served an excellent purpose for, with each successive whiff, the figure lost more and more of its dizzy and perplexing tenuity and seemed to take denser substance. Its very garments, moreover, partook of the magical change, and shone with the gloss of novelty and glistened with the skilfully embroidered gold that had long ago been rent away.

And, half revealed among the smoke, a yellow visage bent its lustreless eyes on Mother Rigby.

At last the old witch clinched her fist and shook it at the figure. Not that she was positively angry, but merely acting on the principle—perhaps untrue, or not the only truth, though as high a one as Mother Rigby could be expected to attain—that feeble and torpid natures, being incapable of better inspiration, must be stirred up by fear. But here was the crisis. Should she fail in what she now sought to effect, it was her ruthless purpose to scatter the miserable simulacre into its original elements.

"Thou hast a man's aspect," said she, sternly. "Have also the echo and mockery of a voice! I bid thee speak!"

The scarecrow gasped, struggled, and at length emitted a murmur, which was so incorporated with its smoky breath that you could scarcely tell whether it were indeed a voice or only a whiff of tobacco. Some narrators of this legend hold the opinion that Mother Rigby's conjurations and the fierceness of her will had compelled a familiar spirit into the figure, and that the voice was his.

"Mother," mumbled the poor stifled voice, "be not so awful with me! I would fain speak; but being without wits, what can I say?"

"Thou canst speak, darling, canst thou?" cried

Mother Rigby, relaxing her grim countenance into a smile. "And what shalt thou say, quotha! Say, indeed! Art thou of the brotherhood of the empty skull, and demandest of me what thou shalt say? Thou shalt say a thousand things, and saying them a thousand times over, thou shalt still have said nothing! Be not afraid, I tell thee! When thou comest into the world (whither I purpose sending thee forthwith) thou shalt not lack the wherewithal to talk. Talk! Why, thou shalt babble like a millstream, if thou wilt. Thou hast brains enough for that, I trow!"

"At your service, mother," responded the figure.

"And that was well said, my pretty one," answered Mother Rigby. "Then thou speakest like thyself, and meant nothing. Thou shalt have a hundred such set phrases, and five hundred to the boot of them. And now, darling, I have taken so much pains with thee and thou art so beautiful, that, by my troth, I love thee better than any witch's puppet in the world; and I've made them of all sorts—clay, wax, straw, sticks, night fog, morning mist, sea foam, and chimney smoke. But thou art the very best. So give heed to what I say."

"Yes, kind mother," said the figure, "with all my heart!"

"With all thy heart!" cried the old witch, setting her hands to her sides and laughing loudly. "Thou hast such a pretty way of speaking. With all thy heart! And thou didst put thy hand to the left side of thy waistcoat as if thou really hadst one!"

So now, in high good humor with this fantastic contrivance of hers, Mother Rigby told the scarecrow that it must go and play its part in the great world, where not one man in a hundred, she affirmed, was gifted with more real substance than itself. And, that he might hold up his head with the best of them, she endowed him, on the spot, with an unreckonable amount of wealth. It consisted partly of a gold mine in Eldorado, and of ten thousand shares in a broken bubble, and of half a million acres of vineyard at the North Pole, and of a castle in the air, and a chateau in Spain, together with all the rents and income therefrom accruing. She further made over to him the cargo of a certain ship, laden with salt of Cadiz, which she herself, by her necromantic arts, had caused to founder, ten years before, in the deepest part of midocean. If the salt were not dissolved, and could be brought to market, it would fetch a pretty penny among the fishermen. That he might not lack ready money, she gave him a copper farthing of Birmingham manufacture, being all the coin she had about her, and likewise a great deal of brass, which she applied to his forehead, thus making it yellower than ever.

"With that brass alone," quoth Mother Rigby, "thou canst pay thy way all over the earth. Kiss me, pretty darling! I have done my best for thee."

Furthermore, that the adventurer might lack no possible advantage towards a fair start in life, this excellent old dame gave him a token by which he was to introduce himself to a certain magistrate, member of the council, merchant, and elder of the church (the four capacities constituting but one man), who stood at the head of society in the neighboring metropolis. The token was neither more nor less than a single word, which Mother Rigby whispered to the scarecrow, and which the scarecrow was to whisper to the merchant.

"Gouty as the old fellow is, he'll run thy errands for thee, when once thou hast given him that word in his ear," said the old witch. "Mother Rigby knows the worshipful Justice Gookin, and the worshipful Justice knows Mother Rigby!"

Here the witch thrust her wrinkled face close to the puppet's, chuckling irrepressibly, and fidgeting all through her system, with delight at the idea which she meant to communicate.

"The worshipful Master Gookin," whispered she, "hath a comely maiden to his daughter. And hark ye, my pet! Thou hast a fair outside, and a pretty wit enough of thine own. Yea, a pretty wit enough! Thou wilt think better of it when thou hast seen more of other people's wits. Now, with thy outside and thy inside, thou art the very man to win a young girl's heart. Never doubt it! I tell thee it shall be so. Put but a bold face on the matter, sigh, smile, flourish thy hat, thrust forth thy leg like a dancing-master, put thy right hand to the left side of thy waistcoat, and pretty Polly Gookin is thine own!"

All this while the new creature had been sucking in and exhaling the vapory fragrance of his pipe, and seemed now to continue this occupation as much for the enjoyment it afforded as because it was an essential condition of his existence. It was wonderful to see how exceedingly like a human being it behaved. Its eyes (for it appeared to possess a pair) were bent on Mother Rigby, and at suitable junctures it nodded or shook its head. Neither did it lack words proper for the occasion: "Really! Indeed! Pray tell me! Is it possible! Upon my word! By no means! Oh! Ah! Hem!" and other such weighty utterances as imply attention, inquiry, acquiescence, or dissent on the part of the auditor. Even had you stood by and seen the scarecrow made, you could scarcely have resisted the conviction that it perfectly understood the cunning counsels which the old witch poured into its counterfeit of an ear. The more earnestly it applied its lips to the pipe, the more distinctly was its human likeness stamped among visible realities, the more sagacious grew its expression, the more lifelike its gestures and movements, and the more intelligibly audible its voice. Its garments, too, glistened so much the brighter with an illusory magnificence. The very pipe, in which burned the spell of all this wonder-work, ceased to appear as a smoke-blackened earthen stump, and became a meerschaum, with painted bowl and amber mouthpiece.

It might be apprehended, however, that as the life of the illusion seemed identical with the vapor of the pipe, it would terminate simultaneously with the reduction of the tobacco to ashes. But the beldam foresaw the difficulty.

"Hold thou the pipe, my precious one," said she, "while I fill it for thee again."

It was sorrowful to behold how the fine gentle-man began to fade back into a scarecrow while Mother Rigby shook the ashes out of the pipe and proceeded to replenish it from her tobacco-box.

"Dickon," cried she, in her high, sharp tone, "another coal for this pipe!"

No sooner said than the intensely red speck of fire was glowing within the pipe-bowl; and the scare-crow, without waiting for the witch's bidding, applied the tube to his lips and drew in a few short, convulsive whiffs, which soon, however, became reg-ular and equable.

"Now, mine own heart's darling," quoth Mother Rigby, "whatever may happen to thee, thou must stick to thy pipe. Thy life is in it; and that, at least, thou knowest well, if thou knowest nought besides. Stick to thy pipe, I say! Smoke, puff, blow thy cloud; and tell the people, if any question be made, that it is for thy health, and that so the physician orders thee to do. And, sweet one, when thou shalt find thy pipe getting low, go apart into some corner, and (first filling thyself with smoke) cry sharply, 'Dickon, a fresh pipe of tobacco!' and, 'Dickon, another coal for my pipe!' and have it into thy pretty mouth as speedily as may be. Else, instead of a gallant gentleman in a gold-laced coat, thou wilt be but a jumble of sticks and tattered clothes, and a bag of straw, and a withered pumpkin! Now depart, my treasure, and good luck go with thee!"

"Never fear, mother!" said the figure, in a stout voice, and sending forth a courageous whiff of smoke, "I will thrive, if an honest man and a gentleman may!"

"Oh, thou wilt be the death of me!" cried the old witch, convulsed with laughter. "That was well said. If an honest man and a gentleman may! Thou playest thy part to perfection. Get along with thee for a smart fellow; and I will wager on thy head, as a man of pith and substance, with a brain and what they call a heart, and all else that a man should have, against any other thing on two legs. I hold myself a better witch than yesterday, for thy sake. Did not I make thee? And I defy any witch in New England to make such another! Here; take my staff along with thee!"

The staff, though it was but a plain oaken stick, immediately took the aspect of a gold-headed cane.

"That gold head has as much sense in it as thine own," said Mother Rigby, "and it will guide thee straight to worshipful Master Gookin's door. Get thee gone, my pretty pet, my darling, my precious one, my treasure; and if any ask thy name, it is Feathertop. For thou hast a feather in thy hat, and I have thrust a handful of feathers into the hollow of thy head, and thy wig, too, is of the fashion they call Feathertop—so be Feathertop thy name!"

And, issuing from the cottage, Feathertop strode manfully towards town. Mother Rigby stood at the threshold, well pleased to see how the sunbeams glistened on him, as if all his magnificence were real, and how diligently and lovingly he smoked his pipe, and how handsomely he walked, in spite of a little stiffness of his legs. She watched him until out of sight, and threw a witch benediction after her darling, when a turn of the road snatched him from her view.

Betimes in the forenoon, when the principal street of the neighboring town was just at its acme of life and bustle, a stranger of very distinguished figure was seen on the sidewalk. His port as well as his garments betokened nothing short of nobility. He wore a richly-embroidered plum-colored coat, a waistcoat of costly velvet, magnificently adorned with golden foliage, a pair of splendid scarlet breeches, and the finest and glossiest of white silk stockings. His head was covered with a peruke, so daintily powdered and adjusted that it would have been sacrilege to disorder it with a hat; which, therefore (and it was a gold-laced hat, set off with a snowy feather), he carried beneath his arm. On the breast of his coat glistened a star. He managed his gold-headed cane with an airy grace, peculiar to the fine gentlemen of the period; and, to give the highest possible finish to his equipment, he had lace ruffles at his wrist, of a most ethereal delicacy, sufficiently avouching how idle and aristocratic must be the hands which they half concealed.

It was a remarkable point in the accoutrement of this brilliant personage that he held in his left hand a fantastic kind of a pipe, with an exquisitely painted bowl and an amber mouthpiece. This he applied to his lips as often as every five or six paces, and inhaled a deep whiff of smoke, which, after being retained a moment in his lungs, might be seen to eddy gracefully from his mouth and nostrils.

As may well be supposed, the street was all astir to find out the stranger's name.

"It is some great nobleman, beyond question," said

one of the townspeople. "Do you see the star at his breast?"

"Nay; it is too bright to be seen," said another. "Yes; he must needs be a nobleman, as you say. But by what conveyance, think you, can his lordship have voyaged or travelled hither? There has been no vessel from the old country for a month past; and if he have arrived overland from the southward, pray where are his attendants and equipage?"

"He needs no equipage to set off his rank," remarked a third. "If he came among us in rags, nobility would shine through a hole in his elbow. I never saw such dignity of aspect. He has the old Norman blood in his veins, I warrant him."

"I rather take him to be a Dutchman, or one of your high Germans," said another citizen. "The men of those countries have always the pipe at their mouths."

"And so has a Turk," answered his companion. "But, in my judgment, this stranger hath been bred at the French court, and hath there learned polite-ness and grace of manner, which none understand so well as the nobility of France. That gait, now! A vul-gar spectator might deem it stiff—he might call it a hitch and jerk—but, to my eye, it hath an unspeak-able majesty, and must have been acquired by con-stant observation of the deportment of the Grand Monarque. The stranger's character and office are evident enough. He is a French ambassador, come to treat with our rulers about the cession of Canada."

"More probably a Spaniard," said another, "and hence his yellow complexion; or, most likely, he is from the Havana, or from some port on the Spanish main, and comes to make investigation about the piracies which our government is thought to connive at. Those settlers in Peru and Mexico have skins as yellow as the gold which they dig out of their mines."

"Yellow or not," cried a lady, "he is a beautiful man!—so tall, so slender! such a fine, noble face, with so well-shaped a nose, and all that delicacy of expression about the mouth! And, bless me, how bright his star is! It positively shoots out flames!"

"So do your eyes, fair lady," said the stranger, with a bow and a flourish of his pipe; for he was just passing at the instant. "Upon my honor, they have quite dazzled me."

"Was ever so original and exquisite a compliment?" murmured the lady, in an ecstasy of delight.

Amid the general admiration excited by the stranger's appearance, there were only two dissenting voices. One was that of an impertinent cur, which, after snuffing at the heels of the glistening figure, put its tail between its legs and skulked into its master's back yard, vociferating an execrable howl. The other dissentient was a young child, who squalled at the

fullest stretch of his lungs, and babbled some unintelligible nonsense about a pumpkin.

Feathertop meanwhile pursued his way along the
street. Except for the few complimentary words to
the lady, and now and then a slight inclination of the
head in requital of the profound reverences of the
bystanders, he seemed wholly absorbed in his pipe.
There needed no other proof of his rank and conse-
quence than the perfect equanimity with which he
comported himself, while the curiosity and admiration of the town swelled almost into clamor around
him. With a crowd gathering behind his footsteps,
he finally reached the mansion-house of the worshipful Justice Gookin, entered the gate, ascended the
steps of the front door, and knocked. In the interim,
before his summons was answered, the stranger was
observed to shake the ashes out of his pipe.

"What did he say in that sharp voice?" inquired
one of the spectators.

"Nay, I know not," answered his friend. "But the
sun dazzles my eyes strangely. How dim and faded
his lordship looks all of a sudden! Bless my wits,
what is the matter with me?"

"The wonder is," said the other, "that his pipe,
which was out only an instant ago, should be all
alight again, and with the reddest coal I ever saw.
There is something mysterious about this stranger.
What a whiff of smoke was that! Dim and faded did

you call him? Why, as he turns about the star on his breast is all ablaze."

"It is, indeed," said his companion; "and it will go near to dazzle pretty Polly Gookin, whom I see peeping at it out of the chamber window."

The door being now opened, Feathertop turned to the crowd, made a stately bend of his body like a great man acknowledging the reverence of the meaner sort, and vanished into the house. There was a mysterious kind of a smile, if it might not better be called a grin or grimace, upon his visage; but, of all the throng that beheld him, not an individual appears to have possessed insight enough to detect the illusive character of the stranger except a little child and a cur dog.

Our legend here loses somewhat of its continuity, and, passing over the preliminary explanation between Feathertop and the merchant, goes in quest of the pretty Polly Gookin. She was a damsel of a soft, round figure, with light hair and blue eyes, and a fair, rosy face, which seemed neither very shrewd nor very simple. This young lady had caught a glimpse of the glistening stranger while standing at the threshold, and had forthwith put on a laced cap, a string of beads, her finest kerchief, and her stiffest damask petticoat in preparation for the interview. Hurrying from her chamber to the parlor, she had ever since been viewing herself in the large looking-glass and practising pretty airs—now a smile, now a ceremonious dignity of aspect, and now a softer smile than the former, kissing her hand likewise, tossing her head, and managing her fan; while within the mirror an unsubstantial little maid repeated every gesture and did all the foolish things that Polly did, but without making her ashamed of them. In short, it was the fault of pretty Polly's ability rather than her will if she failed to be as complete an artifice as the illustrious Feathertop himself; and, when she thus tampered with her own simplicity, the witch's phantom might well hope to win her.

No sooner did Polly hear her father's gouty footsteps approaching the parlor door, accompanied with the stiff clatter of Feathertop's high-heeled shoes, than she seated herself bolt upright and innocently began warbling a song.

"Polly! daughter Polly!" cried the old merchant. "Come hither, child."

Master Gookin's aspect, as he opened the door, was doubtful and troubled.

"This gentleman," continued he, presenting the stranger, "is the Chevalier Feathertop—nay, I beg his pardon, my Lord Feathertop—who hath brought me a token of remembrance from an ancient friend of mine. Pay your duty to his lordship, child, and honor him as his quality deserves."

After these few words of introduction, the worshipful magistrate immediately quitted the room. But, even in that brief moment, had the fair Polly glanced aside at her father instead of devoting herself wholly to the brilliant guest, she might have taken warning of some mischief nigh at hand. The old man was nervous, fidgety, and very pale. Purposing a smile of courtesy, he had deformed his face with a sort of galvanic grin, which, when Feathertop's back was turned, he exchanged for a scowl, at the same time shaking his fist and stamping his gouty foot—an incivility which brought its retribution along with it. The truth appears to have been that Mother Rigby's word of introduction, whatever it might be, had operated far more on the rich merchant's fears than on his good will. Moreover, being a man of wonderfully acute observation, he had noticed that these painted figures on the bowl of Feathertop's pipe were in motion. Looking more closely, he became convinced that these figures were a party of little demons, each duly provided with horns and a tail, and dancing hand in hand, with gestures of diabolical merriment, round the circumference of the pipe bowl. As if to confirm his suspicions, while Master Gookin ushered his guest along a dusky passage from his private room to the parlor, the star on Feathertop's breast had scintillated actual flames, and threw a flickering gleam upon the wall, the ceiling, and the floor.

With such sinister prognostics manifesting themselves on all hands, it is not to be marvelled at that the merchant should have felt that he was committing his daughter to a very questionable acquaintance. He cursed, in his secret soul, the insinuating elegance of Feathertop's manners, as this brilliant personage bowed, smiled, put his hand on his heart, inhaled a long whiff from his pipe, and enriched the atmosphere with the smoky vapor of a fragrant and visible sigh. Gladly would poor Master Gookin have thrust his dangerous guest into the street, but there was a constraint and terror within him. This respectable old gentleman, we fear, at an earlier period of life, had given some pledge or other to the evil principle, and perhaps was now to redeem it by the sacrifice of his daughter.

It so happened that the parlor door was partly of glass, shaded by a silken curtain, the folds of which hung a little awry. So strong was the merchant's interest in witnessing what was to ensue between the fair Polly and the gallant Feathertop that, after quitting the room, he could by no means refrain from peeping through the crevice of the curtain.

But there was nothing very miraculous to be seen; nothing—except the trifles previously noticed—to confirm the idea of a supernatural peril environing the pretty Polly. The stranger it is true was evidently a thorough and practised man of the world, system-

atic and self-possessed, and therefore the sort of a
person to whom a parent ought not to confide a
simple, young girl without due watchfulness for the
result. The worthy magistrate, who had been con-
versant with all degrees and qualities of mankind,
could not but perceive every motion and gesture of
the distinguished Feathertop came in its proper
place; nothing had been left rude or native in him; a
well-digested conventionalism had incorporated
itself thoroughly with his substance and transformed
him into a work of art. Perhaps it was this peculiar-
ity that invested him with a species of ghastliness and
awe. It is the effect of anything completely and con-
summately artificial, in human shape, that the person
impresses us as an unreality and as having hardly pith
enough to cast a shadow upon the floor. As regarded
Feathertop, all this resulted in a wild, extravagant,
and fantastical impression, as if his life and being
were akin to the smoke that curled upward from his
pipe.

But pretty Polly Gookin felt not thus. The pair
were now promenading the room: Feathertop with
his dainty stride and no less dainty grimace; the girl
with a native maidenly grace, just touched, not
spoiled, by a slightly affected manner, which seemed
caught from the perfect artifice of her companion.
The longer the interview continued, the more
charmed was pretty Polly, until, within the first quar-

ter of an hour (as the old magistrate noted by his watch), she was evidently beginning to be in love. Nor need it have been witchcraft that subdued her in such a hurry; the poor child's heart, it may be, was so very fervent that it melted her with its own warmth as reflected from the hollow semblance of a lover. No matter what Feathertop said, his words found depth and reverberation in her ear; no matter what he did, his action was heroic to her eye. And by this time it is to be supposed there was a blush on Polly's cheek, a tender smile about her mouth, and a liquid softness in her glance; while the star kept coruscating on Feathertop's breast, and the little demons careered with more frantic merriment than ever about the circumference of his pipe bowl. O pretty Polly Gookin, why should these imps rejoice so madly that a silly maiden's heart was about to be given to a shadow! Is it so unusual a misfortune, so rare a triumph?

By and by Feathertop paused, and throwing himself into an imposing attitude, seemed to summon the fair girl to survey his figure and resist him longer if she could. His star, his embroidery, his buckles glowed at that instant with unutterable splendor; the picturesque hues of his attire took a richer depth of coloring; there was a gleam and polish over his whole presence betokening the perfect witchery of well-ordered manners. The maiden raised her eyes and suffered them to linger upon her companion with a bashful and admiring gaze. Then, as if desirous of judging what value her own simple comeliness might have side by side with so much brilliancy, she cast a glance towards the full-length looking-glass in front of which they happened to be standing. It was one of the truest plates in the world and incapable of flattery. No sooner did the images therein reflected meet Polly's eye than she shrieked, shrank from the stranger's side, gazed at him for a moment in the wildest dismay, and sank insensible upon the floor. Feathertop likewise had looked towards the mirror, and there beheld, not the glittering mockery of his outside show, but a picture of the sordid patchwork of his real composition, stripped of all witchcraft.

The wretched simulacrum! We almost pity him. He threw up his arms with an expression of despair that went further than any of his previous manifestations towards vindicating his claims to be reckoned human; for, perchance the only time since this so often empty and deceptive life of mortals began its course, an illusion had seen and fully recognized itself.

Mother Rigby was seated by her kitchen hearth in the twilight of this eventful day, and had just shaken the ashes out of a new pipe, when she heard a hurried tramp along the road. Yet it did not seem so much the tramp of human footsteps as the clatter of sticks or the rattling of dry bones.

"Ha!" thought the old witch, "what step is that? Whose skeleton is out of its grave now, I wonder?"

A figure burst headlong into the cottage door. It was Feathertop! His pipe was still alight; the star still flamed upon his breast; the embroidery still glowed upon his garments; nor had he lost, in any degree or manner that could be estimated, the aspect that assimilated him with our mortal brotherhood. But yet, in some indescribable way (as is the case with all that has deluded us when once found out), the poor reality was felt beneath the cunning artifice.

"What has gone wrong?" demanded the witch. "Did yonder sniffling hypocrite thrust my darling from his door? The villain! I'll set twenty fiends to torment him till he offer thee his daughter on his bended knees!"

"No, mother," said Feathertop despondingly; "it was not that."

"Did the girl scorn my precious one?" asked Mother Rigby, her fierce eyes glowing like two coals of Tophet. "I'll cover her face with pimples! Her nose shall be as red as the coal in thy pipe! Her front teeth shall drop out! In a week hence she shall not be worth thy having!"

"Let her alone, mother," answered poor Feathertop; "the girl was half won; and methinks a kiss from her sweet lips might have made me altogether human. But," he added, after a brief pause and then a howl of self-contempt, "I've seen myself, mother! I've seen myself for the wretched, ragged, empty thing I am! I'll exist no longer!"

Snatching the pipe from his mouth, he flung it with all his might against the chimney, and at the same instant sank upon the floor, a medley of straw and tattered garments, with some sticks protruding from the heap, and a shrivelled pumpkin in the midst. The eyeholes were now lustreless; but the rudely-carved gap, that just before had been a mouth, still seemed to twist itself into a despairing grin, and was so far human.

"Poor fellow!" quoth Mother Rigby, with a rueful glance at the relics of her ill-fated contrivance. "My poor, dear, pretty Feathertop! There are thousands upon thousands of coxcombs and charlatans in the world, made up of just such a jumble of worn-out, forgotten, and good-for-nothing trash as he was! Yet they live in fair repute, and never see themselves for what they are. And why should my poor puppet be the only one to know himself and perish for it?"

While thus muttering, the witch had filled a fresh pipe of tobacco, and held the stem between her fingers, as doubtful whether to thrust it into her mouth or Feathertop's.

"Poor Feathertop!" she continued. "I could easily

give him another chance and send him forth again to-morrow. But no; his feelings are too tender, his sensibilities too deep. He seems to have too much heart to bustle for his own advantage in such an empty and heartless world. Well! well! I'll make a scarecrow of him after all. 'T is an innocent and useful vocation, and will suit my darling well; and, if each of his human brethren had as fit a one, 't would be the better for mankind; and as for this pipe of tobacco, I need it more than he."

So saying, Mother Rigby put the stem between her lips. "Dickon!" cried she, in her high, sharp tone, "another coal for my pipe!"

The Werewolf

[H. B. MARRYAT]

*The lore of the werewolf is ancient indeed, and so of course was
seized on by the Romantics. Here, Marryat makes full use of the
folklore of the Hartz Mountains, and follows it fairly closely—
with some literary flourishes.*

My father was not born, or originally a resident, in the Hartz Mountains; he was
the serf of a Hungarian nobleman of
great possessions in Transylvania; but although a serf,
he was not by any means a poor or illiterate man. In
fact, he was rich, and his intelligence and respectability were such that he had been raised by his lord to
the stewardship; but whoever may happen to be
born a serf, a serf must he remain, even though he
become a wealthy man; such was the condition of
my father. My father had been married for about

five years and by his marriage had three children—
my elder brother, Caesar, myself (Hermann), and a
sister named Marcella. Latin is still the language spoken in that country, and that will account for our
high-sounding names. My mother was a very beautiful woman, unfortunately more beautiful than virtuous: She was seen and admired by the lord of the
soil; my father was sent away upon some mission; and
during his absence, my mother, flattered by the
attentions and won by the assiduities of this nobleman, yielded to his wishes. It so happened that my
father returned very unexpectedly and discovered
the intrigue. The evidence of my mother's shame
was positive; he surprised her in the company of her
seducer! Carried away by the impetuosity of his
feelings, he watched the opportunity of a meeting
taking place between them and murdered both his
wife and her seducer. Conscious that, as a serf, not
even the provocation which he had received would
be allowed as a justification of his conduct, he hastily
collected together what money he could lay his
hands on, and as we were then in the depth of winter, he put his horses to the sleigh, and taking his
children with him, he set off in the middle of the
night and was far away before the tragical circumstance had become known. Aware that he would be
pursued and that he had no chance of escape if he

remained in any portion of his native country (in which the authorities could lay hold of him), he continued his flight without intermission until he had buried himself in the intricacies and seclusion of the Hartz Mountains. Of course, all that I have now told you I learned afterward. My oldest recollections are knit to a rude, yet comfortable, cottage in which I lived with my father, brother, and sister. It was on the confines of one of those vast forests which cover the northern part of Germany; around it were a few acres of ground, which, during the summer months, my father cultivated, and which, though they yielded a doubtful harvest, were sufficient for our support. In the winter we remained much indoors, for as my father followed the chase, we were left alone, and the wolves, during that season, incessantly prowled about. My father had purchased the cottage and land about it from one of the rude foresters, who gain their livelihood partly by hunting and partly by burning charcoal for the purpose of smelting the ore from the neighboring mines. It was distant about two miles from any other habitation. I can call to mind the whole landscape now: the tall pines which rose up on the mountain above us and the wide expanse of forest beneath, on the topmost boughs and heads of whose trees we looked down from our cottage, as the mountain below us rapidly descended into the distant valley. In summertime the prospect was beautiful, but during the severe winter, a more desolate scene could not well be imagined.

I said that in the winter my father occupied himself with the chase; every day he left us, and often would he lock the door, that we might not leave the cottage. He had no one to assist him or to take care of us—indeed, it was not easy to find a female servant who would live in such a solitude; but could he have found one, my father would not have received her, for he had imbibed a horror of the sex, as a difference of his conduct toward us, his two boys, and my poor little sister, Marcella, evidently proved. You may suppose we were sadly neglected; indeed, we suffered much, for my father, fearful that we might come to some harm, would not allow us fuel when he left the cottage; and we were obliged, therefore, to creep under the heaps of bearskins and there to keep ourselves as warm as we could until he returned in the evening, when a blazing fire was our delight. That my father chose this restless sort of life may appear strange, but the fact was that he could not remain quiet; whether from remorse for having committed murder or from the misery consequent on his change of situation or from both combined, he was never happy unless he was in a state of activity. Children, however, when left much to themselves, acquire a thoughtfulness not common to their age. So it was with us; and during the short cold days of winter we would sit silent, longing for the happy hours when the snow would melt and the leaves burst out and the birds begin their songs and when we should again be set at liberty.

Such was our peculiar and savage sort of life until my brother Caesar was nine, myself seven, and my sister five years old, when the circumstances occurred on which is based the extraordinary narrative which I am about to relate.

One evening my father returned home rather later than usual; he had been unsuccessful, and as the weather was very severe and many feet of snow were upon the ground, he was not only very cold, but in a very bad humor. He had brought in wood, and we were all three of us gladly assisting each other in blowing on the embers to create the blaze, when he caught poor little Marcella by the arm and threw her aside; the child fell, struck her mouth, and bled very much. My brother ran to raise her up. Accustomed to ill usage and afraid of my father, she did not dare to cry, but looked up in his face very piteously. My father drew his stool nearer to the hearth, muttered something in abuse of women, and busied himself with the fire, which both my brother and I had deserted when our sister was so unkindly treated. A cheerful blaze was soon the result of his exertions; but we did not, as usual, crowd around it. Marcella, still bleeding, retired to a corner, and my brother and I took our seats beside her, while my father hung over the fire gloomily and alone. Such had been our position for about half an hour, when the howl of a wolf, close under the window of the cottage, fell on our ears. My father started up and seized his gun; the howl was repeated, he examined the priming and then hastily left the cottage, shutting the door after him. We all waited (anxiously listening), for we thought that if he succeeded in shooting the wolf, he would return in a better humor; and although he was harsh to all of us, and particularly so to our little sister, still we loved our father and loved to see him cheerful and happy, for what else had we to look up to? And I may here observe that perhaps there never were three children who were fonder of each other; we did not, like other children, fight and dispute together; and if, by chance, any disagreement did arise between my brother and me, little Marcella would run to us, and kissing us both, seal, through her entreaties, the peace between us. Marcella was a lovely, amiable child; I can recall her beautiful features even now—Alas! poor little Marcella.

We waited for some time, but the report of the gun did not reach us, and my elder brother then said, "Our father has followed the wolf and will not be back for some time. Marcella, let us wash the blood from your mouth, and then we will leave this corner and go to the fire and warm ourselves."

We did so and remained there until near midnight, every minute wondering, as it grew later, why our father did not return. We had no idea that he was in any danger, but we thought that he must have chased the wolf for a very long time. "I will look out and see if father is coming," said my brother Caesar, going to the door. "Take care," said Marcella, "the wolves must be about now, and we cannot kill them, Brother." My brother opened the door very cautiously and but a few inches; he peeped out. "I see nothing," said he after a time, and once more he joined us at the fire. "We have had no supper," said I, for my father usually cooked the meat as soon as he came home, and during his absence we had nothing but the fragments of the preceding day.

"And if our father comes home after his hunt, Caesar," said Marcella, "he will be pleased to have some supper; let us cook it for him and for ourselves." Caesar climbed upon the stool and reached down some meat—I forget now whether it was venison or bear's meat; but we cut off the usual quantity and proceeded to dress it, as we used to do under our father's superintendence. We were all busied putting it into the platters before the fire to await his coming, when we heard the sound of a horn. We listened—there was a noise outside, and a minute afterward my father entered, ushering in a young female and a large dark man in a hunter's dress.

Perhaps I had better now relate what was only known to me many years afterward. When my father had left the cottage, he perceived a large white wolf about thirty yards from him; as soon as the animal saw my father, it retreated slowly, growling and snarling. My father followed; the animal did not run but always kept at some distance, and my father did not like to fire until he was pretty certain that his ball would take effect: Thus they went on for some time, the wolf now leaving my father far behind, and then stopping and snarling defiance at him, and then again, on his approach, setting off at speed.

Anxious to shoot the animal (for the white wolf is very rare), my father continued the pursuit for several hours, during which he continually ascended the mountain.

You must know that there are peculiar spots on those mountains which are supposed, and as my story will prove, truly supposed, to be inhabited by the evil influences; they are well known to the huntsmen, who invariably avoid them. Now one of these spots, an open space in the pine forests above us, had been pointed out to my father as dangerous on that account. But whether he disbelieved these wild stories or whether, in his eager pursuit of the chase, he disregarded them, I know not; certain, however, it is that he was decoyed by the white wolf to this open space, where the animal appeared to slacken her speed. My father approached, came close up to her, raised his gun to his shoulder, and was about to fire, when the wolf suddenly disappeared. He thought that the snow on the ground must have dazzled his sight, and he let down his gun to look for the beast—but she was gone; how she could have escaped over the clearance, without his seeing her, was beyond his comprehension. Mortified at the ill success of his chase, he was about to retrace his steps, when he heard the distant sound of a horn. Astonishment at such a sound—at such an hour—in such a wilderness, made him forget for the moment his disappointment, and he remained riveted to the spot. In a minute the horn was blown a second time and at no great distance; my father stood still and listened: A third time it was blown. I forget the term used to express it, but it was the signal which, my father well knew, implied that the party was lost in the woods. In a few minutes more my father beheld a man on horseback, with a female seated on the crupper, enter the cleared space and ride up to him. At first, my father called to mind the strange stories which he had heard of the supernatural beings who were said to frequent these mountains; but the nearer approach of the parties satisfied him that they were mortals like himself. As soon as they came up to him, the man who guided the horse accosted him. "Friend hunter, you are out late, the better fortune for us: We have ridden far and are in fear of our lives, which are eagerly sought after. These mountains have enabled us to elude our pursuers, but if we find not shelter and refreshment, that will avail us little, as we must perish from hunger and the inclemency of the night. My daughter, who rides behind me, is now more dead than alive—say, can you assist us in our difficulty?"

"My cottage is some few miles distant," replied my father, "but I have little to offer you besides a shelter from the weather; to the little I have you are welcome. May I ask whence you come?"

"Yes, friend, it is no secret now; we have escaped from Transylvania, where my daughter's honor and my life were equally in jeopardy!"

This information was quite enough to raise an interest in my father's heart. He remembered his own escape: He remembered the loss of his wife's honor and the tragedy by which it was wound up. He immediately, and warmly, offered all the assistance which he could afford them.

"There is no time to be lost, then, good sir," observed the horseman; "my daughter is chilled with the frost and cannot hold out much longer against the severity of the weather."

"Follow me," replied my father, leading the way toward home.

"I was lured away in pursuit of a large white wolf," observed my father; "it came to the very window of my hut, or I should not have been out at this time of night."

"The creature passed by us just as we came out of the wood," said the female in a silvery tone.

"I was nearly discharging my piece at it," observed the hunter; "but since it did us such good service, I am glad that I allowed it to escape."

In about an hour and a half, during which my father walked at a rapid pace, the party arrived at the cottage and, as I said before, came in.

"We are in good time, apparently," observed the dark hunter, catching the smell of the roasted meat, as he walked to the fire and surveyed my brother and sister and myself. "You have young cooks here, Mynheer." "I am glad that we shall not have to wait," replied my father. "Come, mistress, seat yourself by the fire; you require warmth after your cold ride." "And where can I put up my horse, Mynheer?" observed the huntsman. "I will take care of him," replied my father, going out of the cottage door.

The female must, however, be particularly described. She was young and apparently twenty years of age. She was dressed in a traveling dress, deeply bordered with white fur, and wore a cap of white ermine on her head. Her features were very beautiful, at least I thought so, and so my father has since declared. Her hair was flaxen, glossy, and shining, and bright as a mirror; and her mouth, although somewhat large when it was open, showed the most brilliant teeth I have ever beheld. But there was something about her eyes, bright as they were, which made us children afraid; they were so restless, so furtive; I could not at that time tell why, but I felt as if there were cruelty in her eye; and when she beckoned us to come to her, we approached her with fear and trembling. Still she was beautiful, very beautiful. She spoke kindly to my brother and myself, patted our heads, and caressed us; but Marcella would not come near her; on the contrary, she slunk away and hid herself in the bed and would not wait for supper, which half an hour before she had been so anxious for.

My father, having put the horse into a close shed, soon returned, and supper was placed upon the table. When it was over, my father requested that the young lady take possession of his bed, and he would remain at the fire and sit up with her father. After some hesitation on her part, this arrangement was agreed to, and I and my brother crept into the other bed with Marcella, for we had as yet always slept together.

But we could not sleep; there was something so
unusual, not only in seeing strange people, but in
having those people sleep at the cottage, that we
were bewildered. As for poor little Marcella, she was
quiet, but I perceived that she trembled during the
whole night, and sometimes I thought that she was
checking a sob. My father had brought out some
spirits, which he rarely used, and he and the strange
hunter remained drinking and talking before the
fire. Our ears were ready to catch the slightest whisper—so much was our curiosity excited.

"You said you came from Transylvania?" observed
my father.

"Even so, Mynheer," replied the hunter. "I was a
serf to the noble house of—; my master would insist
upon my surrendering up my fair girl to his wishes;
it ended in my giving him a few inches of my hunting knife."

"We are countrymen and brothers in misfortune,"
replied my father, taking the huntsman's hand and
pressing it warmly.

"Indeed! Are you, then, from that country?"

"Yes; and I too have fled for my life. But mine is a
melancholy tale."

"Your name?" inquired the hunter.

"Krantz."

"What! Krantz of—I have heard your tale; you
need not renew your grief by repeating it now. Wel-

come, most welcome, Mynheer, and, I may say, my worthy kinsman. I am your second cousin, Wilfred of Barnsdorf," cried the hunter, rising up and embracing my father.

They filled their horn mugs to the brim and drank to one another, after the German fashion. The conversation was then carried on in a low tone; all that we could collect from it was that our new relative and his daughter were to take up their abode in our cottage, at least for the present. In about an hour they both fell back in their chairs and appeared to sleep.

"Marcella, dear, did you hear?" said my brother in a low tone.

"Yes," replied Marcella in a whisper, "I heard all. Oh! Brother, I cannot bear to look upon that woman—I feel so frightened."

My brother made no reply, and shortly afterward we were all three fast asleep.

When we awoke the next morning, we found that the hunter's daughter had risen before us. I thought she looked more beautiful than ever. She came up to Marcella and caressed her; the child burst into tears and sobbed as if her heart would break.

But not to detain you with too long a story, the huntsman and his daughter were accommodated in the cottage. My father and he went out hunting daily, leaving Christina with us. She performed all the household duties, was very kind to us children, and gradually the dislike even of little Marcella wore away. But a great change took place in my father; he appeared to have conquered his aversion to the sex and was most attentive to Christina. Often, after her father and we were in bed, would he sit up with her, conversing in a low tone by the fire. I ought to have mentioned that my father and the huntsman Wilfred slept in another portion of the cottage and the bed which he formerly occupied and which was in the same room as ours, had been given up to the use of Christina. These visitors had been about three weeks at the cottage, when one night, after we children had been sent to bed, a consultation was held. My father had asked Christina in marriage and had obtained both her own consent and that of Wilfred; after this a conversation took place, which was, as nearly as I can recollect, as follows:

"You may take my child, Mynheer Krantz, and my blessing with her, and I shall then leave you and seek some other habitation—it matters little where."

"Why not remain here, Wilfred?"

"No, no, I am called elsewhere; let that suffice, and ask no more questions. You have my child."

"I thank you for her and will duly value her; but there is one difficulty."

"I know what you would say; there is no priest here in this wild country: True, neither is there any law to bind; still must some ceremony pass between you, to satisfy a father. Will you consent to marry her after my fashion? If so, I will marry you directly."

"I will," replied my father.

"Then take her by the hand. Now, Mynheer, swear."

"I swear," repeated my father.

"By all the spirits of the Hartz Mountains—"

"Nay, why not by Heaven?" interrupted my father.

"Because it is not my humor," rejoined Wilfred; "if I prefer that oath, less binding perhaps, than another, surely you will not thwart me."

"Well, be it so then; have your humor. Will you make me swear by that in which I do not believe?"

"Yet many do so, who in outward appearance are Christians," rejoined Wilfred. "Say, will you be married, or shall I take my daughter away with me?"

"Proceed," replied my father impatiently.

"I swear by all the spirits of the Hartz Mountains, by all their power for good or for evil, that I take Christina for my wedded wife; that I will ever protect her, cherish her, and love her; that my hand shall never be raised against her to harm her."

My father repeated the words after Wilfred.

"And if I fail in this, my vow, may all the vengeance of the spirits fall upon me and upon my children; may they perish by the vulture, by the wolf or other beasts of the forest; may their flesh be torn from their limbs and their bones blanch in the wilderness; all this I swear."

My father hesitated as he repeated the last words; little Marcella could not restrain herself, and as my father repeated the last sentence, she burst into tears. This sudden interruption appeared to discompose the party, particularly my father; he spoke harshly to the child, who controlled her sobs, burying her face under the bedclothes.

Such was the second marriage of my father. The next morning the hunter Wilfred mounted his horse and rode away.

My father resumed his bed, which was in the same room as ours; and things went on much as before the marriage, except that our new stepmother did not show any kindness toward us; indeed, during my father's absence, she would often beat us, particularly little Marcella, and her eyes would flash fire as she looked eagerly upon the fair and lovely child.

One night, my sister awoke me and my brother.

"What is the matter?" said Caesar.

"She has gone out," whispered Marcella.

"Gone out!"

"Yes, gone out the door, in her night clothes," replied the child; "I saw her get out of bed, look at my father to see if he slept, and then she went out the door."

What could induce her to leave her bed, and all undressed to go out, in such bitter wintry weather, with the snow deep on the ground, was to us incomprehensible; we lay awake, and in about an hour we heard the growl of a wolf, close under the window.

"There is a wolf," said Caesar; "she will be torn to pieces."

"Oh no!" cried Marcella.

A few minutes afterward our stepmother appeared; she was in her nightdress, as Marcella had stated. She let down the latch of the door, so as to make no noise, went to a pail of water and washed her face and hands, and then slipped into the bed where my father lay.

We all three trembled, we hardly knew why, but we resolved to watch the next night: We did so—and not only on the ensuing night, but on many others, and always at about the same hour, would our stepmother rise from her bed and leave the cottage—and after she was gone, we invariably heard the growl of a wolf under our window and always saw her, on her return, wash herself before she retired to bed. We observed, also, that she seldom sat down to meals and that when she did, she appeared to eat with dislike; but when the meat was taken down, to be prepared for dinner, she would often furtively put a raw piece into her mouth.

My brother Caesar was a courageous boy; he did

not like to speak to my father until he knew more. He resolved that he would follow her out and ascertain what she did. Marcella and I endeavored to dissuade him from this project, but he would not be controlled, and the very next night he lay down in his clothes, and as soon as our stepmother had left the cottage, he jumped up, took down my father's gun, and followed her.

You may imagine in what a state of suspense Marcella and I remained during his absence. After a few minutes, we heard the report of a gun. It did not awaken my father, and we lay trembling with anxiety. A minute afterward we saw our stepmother enter the cottage—her dress was bloody. I put my hand to Marcella's mouth to prevent her crying out, although I was myself in great alarm. Our stepmother approached my father's bed, looked to see if he was asleep, and then went to the chimney and blew the embers into a blaze.

"Who is there?" said my father, waking up.

"Lie still, dearest," replied my stepmother, "it is only me; I have lighted the fire to warm some water; I am not quite well."

My father turned around and was soon asleep, but we watched our stepmother. She changed her linen and threw the garments she had worn into the fire; and we then perceived that her right leg was bleeding profusely, as if from a gunshot wound. She bandaged it up, and then dressing herself, remained before the fire until the break of day.

Poor little Marcella, her heart beat quickly as she pressed me to her side—so indeed did mine. Where was our bother Caesar? At last my father rose, and then for the first time I spoke, saying, "Father, where is my brother Caesar?"

"Your brother!" exclaimed he. "Why, where can he be?"

"Merciful Heaven! I thought as I lay very restless last night," observed our stepmother, "that I heard somebody open the latch of the door; and, dear me, Husband, what has become of your gun?"

My father cast his eyes up above the chimney and perceived that his gun was missing. For a moment he looked perplexed, then seizing a broad ax, he went out of the cottage without saying another word.

He did not remain away from us long: In a few minutes he returned, bearing in his arms the mangled body of my poor brother; he laid it down and covered up his face.

My stepmother rose up and looked at the body, while Marcella and I threw ourselves by its side, wailing and sobbing bitterly.

"Go to bed again, children," said she sharply. "Husband," continued she, "your boy must have taken the gun down to shoot a wolf, and the animal has been too powerful for him. Poor boy! He has paid dearly for his rashness."

My father made no reply; I wished to speak—to tell all—but Marcella, who perceived my intention, held me by the arm and looked at me so imploringly that I desisted.

My father, therefore, was left in his error; but Marcella and I, although we could not comprehend it, were conscious that our stepmother was in some way connected with my brother's death.

That day my father went out and dug a grave, and when he laid the body in the earth, he piled up stones over it, so that the wolves should not be able to dig it up. The shock of this catastrophe was to my poor father very severe; for several days he never went to the chase, although at times he would utter bitter anathemas and vengeance against the wolves.

But during this time of mourning on his part, my stepmother's nocturnal wanderings continued with the same regularity as before.

At last, my father took down his gun to repair to the forest; but he soon returned and appeared much annoyed.

"Would you believe it, Christina, that the wolves—perdition to the whole race—have actually contrived to dig up the body of my poor boy, and now there is nothing left of him but his bones?"

"Indeed!" replied my stepmother. Marcella looked at me, and I saw in her intelligent eyes all she would have uttered.

"A wolf growls under our window every night, Father," said I.

"Aye, indeed?—why did you not tell me, boy?—wake me the next time you hear it."

I saw my stepmother turn away; her eyes flashed fire, and she gnashed her teeth.

My father went out again and covered up with a larger pile of stones the little remnants of my poor brother which the wolves had spared. Such was the first act of the tragedy.

The spring now came on: The snow disappeared, and we were permitted to leave the cottage; but never would I quit, for one moment, my dear little sister, to whom, since the death of my brother, I was more ardently attached than ever; indeed, I was afraid to leave her alone with my stepmother, who appeared to have a particular pleasure in ill-treating the child. My father was now employed upon his little farm, and I was able to render him some assistance.

Marcella used to sit by us while we were at work, leaving my stepmother alone in the cottage. I ought to observe that, as the spring advanced, so did my stepmother decrease her nocturnal rambles, and that we never heard the growl of the wolf under the window after I had spoken of it to my father.

One day, when my father and I were in the field, Marcella being with us, my stepmother came out, saying that she was going into the forest to collect some herbs my father wanted and that Marcella must go to the cottage and watch the dinner. Marcella went, and my stepmother soon disappeared in the forest, taking a direction quite contrary to that in which the cottage stood, and leaving my father and me, as it were, between her and Marcella.

About an hour afterward we were startled by shrieks from the cottage, evidently the shrieks of little Marcella. "Marcella has burned herself, Father," said I, throwing down my spade. My father threw down his, and we both hastened to the cottage. Before we could gain the door, out darted a large white wolf, which fled with the utmost celerity. My father had no weapon; he rushed into the cottage and there saw poor little Marcella expiring; her body was dreadfully mangled, and the blood pouring from it had formed a large pool on the cottage floor. My father's first intention had been to seize his gun and pursue, but he was checked by this horrid spectacle; he knelt down by his dying child and burst into tears: Marcella could just look kindly on us for a few seconds, and then her eyes were closed in death.

My father and I were still hanging over my poor sister's body, when my stepmother came in. At the dreadful sight she expressed much concern, but she did not appear to recoil from the sight of blood, as most women do.

"Poor child!" said she. "It must have been that great white wolf which passed me just now and frightened me so—she's quite dead, Krantz."

"I know it—I know it!" cried my father in agony. I thought my father would never recover from the effects of this second tragedy: He mourned bitterly over the body of his sweet child and for several days would not consign it to its grave, although frequently requested by my stepmother to do so. At last he yielded and dug a grave for her close by that of my poor brother and took every precaution that the wolves should not violate her remains.

I was now really miserable as I lay alone in the bed which I had formerly shared with my brother and sister. I could not help thinking that my stepmother was implicated in both their deaths, although I could not account for the manner; but I no longer felt afraid of her: My little heart was full of hatred and revenge.

The night after my sister had been buried, as I lay awake, I perceived my stepmother get up and go out of the cottage. I waited for some time, then dressed myself and looked out through the door, which I

half opened. The moon shone bright, and I could
see the spot where my brother and my sister had
been buried; and what was my horror, when I perceived my stepmother busily removing the stones
from Marcella's grave.

She was in her white nightdress, and the moon
shone full upon her. She was digging with her hands
and throwing away the stones behind her with all the
ferocity of a wild beast. It was some time before I
could collect my senses and decide what to do. At
last, I perceived that she had arrived at the body and
raised it up to the side of the grave. I could bear it
no longer; I ran to my father and awoke him.

"Father! Father!" cried I. "Dress yourself, and get
your gun."

"What!" cried my father. "The wolves are there,
are they?"

He jumped out of bed, threw on his clothes, and
in his anxiety did not appear to perceive the absence
of his wife. As soon as he was ready, I opened the
door, he went out, and I followed him.

Imagine his horror, when (unprepared as he was
for such a sight) he beheld as he advanced toward the
grave, not a wolf, but his wife, in her nightdress on
her hands and knees, crouching by the body of my
sister and tearing off large pieces of the flesh and
devouring them with all the avidity of a wolf. She
was too busy to be aware of our approach. My father

dropped his gun, his hair stood on end; so did mine; he breathed heavily, and then his breath for a time stopped. I picked up the gun and put it into his hand. Suddenly he appeared as if concentrated rage had restored him to double vigor; he leveled his piece, fired, and with a loud shriek, down fell the wretch whom he had fostered in his bosom.

"God of Heaven!" cried my father, sinking down upon the earth in a swoon as soon as he had discharged his gun.

I remained some time by his side before he recovered. "Where am I?" said he. "What has happened?—Oh!—yes, yes! I recollect now. Heaven forgive me!"

He rose, and we walked up to the grave; what again was our astonishment and horror to find that instead of the dead body of my stepmother, as we expected, there was lying over the remains of my poor sister, a large white she-wolf.

"The white wolf!" exclaimed my father. "The white wolf which decoyed me into the forest—I see it all now—I have dealt with the spirits of the Hartz Mountains."

For some time my father remained in silence and deep thought. He then carefully lifted up the body of my sister, replaced it in the grave, and covered it over as before, having struck the head of the dead animal with the heel of his boot, and raving like a madman. He walked back to the cottage, shut the door, and threw himself on the bed; I did the same, for I was in a stupor of amazement.

Early in the morning we were both roused by a loud knocking at the door, and in rushed the hunter Wilfred.

"My daughter!—man—my daughter!—where is my daughter!" cried he in a rage.

"Where the wretch, the fiend, should be, I trust," replied my father, starting up and displaying equal choler, "where she should be—in hell!—Leave this cottage or you may fare worse."

"Ha-ha!" replied the hunter. "Would you harm a potent spirit of the Hartz Mountains? Poor mortal, who must needs wed a werewolf."

"Out, demon! I defy thee and thy power."

"Yet shall you feel it; remember your oath—your solemn oath—never to raise your hand against her to harm her."

"I made no compact with evil spirits."

"You did; and if you failed in your vow, you were to meet the vengeance of the spirits. Your children were to perish by the vulture, the wolf—"

"Out, out, demon!"

"And their bones blanch in the wilderness. Ha!—Ha!"

My father, frantic with rage, seized his ax and raised it over Wilfred's head to strike.

"All this I swear," continued the huntsman, mockingly.

The ax descended; but it passed through the form of the hunter, and my father lost his balance and fell heavily on the floor.

"Mortal!" said the hunter, striding over my father's body. "We have power over only those who have committed murder. You have been guilty of double murder—you shall pay the penalty attached to your marriage vow. Two of your children are gone; the third is yet to follow—and follow them he will, for your oath is registered. Go—it were kindness to kill you—your punishment is—that you live!"

St. John's Eve

[NIKOLAY GOGOL]

Romanticism went East as well as West, and in the first half of the 19th century was as prominent in Russia as anywhere else. Gogol, in true Romantic fashion, used the beliefs of the Russian peasantry in framing this unsettling piece set during the holiday of the title, a magic night (also called Midsummer's Eve). In practically all European folklore, anything might happen, and the forces of supernature were out en masse—a sort of Hallowe'en in Summer, so to speak. But be warned: this is no light romp, as in Shakespeare's A Midsummer Night's Dream. *Darker forces are at work, to be sure.*

No one could have recognized this village of ours a little over a hundred years ago: a hamlet it was, the poorest kind of a hamlet. Half a score of miserable *izbás,* unplastered, badly thatched, were scattered here and there about the fields. There was not an enclosure or a decent shed to shelter animals or wagons. That was the way the wealthy lived: and if you had looked for our brothers, the poor,—why, a hole in the ground,—that was a cabin for you! Only by the smoke could you tell that a God-created man lived there. You ask why they lived so? It was not entirely through poverty: almost every one led a wandering, Cossack life, and gathered not a little plunder in foreign lands; it was rather because there was no reason for setting up a well-ordered *khata* (wooden house). How many people were wandering all over the country,—Crimeans, Poles, Lithuanians! It was quite possible that their own countrymen might make a descent, and plunder every thing. Any thing was possible.

In this hamlet a man, or rather a devil in human form, often made his appearance. Why he came, and whence, no one knew. He prowled about, got drunk, and suddenly disappeared as if into the air, and there was not a hint of his existence. Then, again, behold, and he seemed to have dropped from the sky, and went flying about the street of the village, of which no trace now remains, and which was not more than a hundred paces from Dikanka. He would collect together all the Cossacks he met; then there were songs, laughter, money in abundance, and vodka flowed like water. . . . He would address the pretty girls, and give them ribbons, earrings, strings of beads—more than they knew what to do with. It is true that the pretty girls rather hesitated about accepting his presents: God knows, perhaps they had passed through unclean hands. My grandfather's aunt, who kept a tavern at that time, in which Basavriuk (as they called that devil-man) often had his carouses, said that no consideration on the face of the earth would have induced her to accept a gift from him. And then, again, how avoid accepting? Fear seized on every one when he knit his bristly brows, and gave a sidelong glance which might send your feet, God knows whither: but if you accept, then the next night some fiend from the swamp, with horns on his head, comes to call, and begins to squeeze your neck, when there is a string of beads upon it; or bite your finger, if there is a ring upon it; or drag you by the hair, if ribbons are braided in it. God have mercy, then, on those who owned such gifts! But here was the difficulty: it was impossible to get rid of them; if you threw them into the water, the diabolical ring or necklace would skim along the surface, and into your hand.

There was a church in the village—St. Pantelei, if I remember rightly. There lived there a priest, Father Athanasii of blessed memory. Observing that Basavriuk did not come to church, even on Easter, he determined to reprove him, and impose penance upon him. Well, he hardly escaped with his life. "Hark ye, *pannótche!*"[1] he thundered in reply, "learn to mind your own business instead of meddling in other people's, if you don't want that goat's throat of yours stuck together with boiling *kutya*."[2] What was to be done with this unrepentant man? Father Athanasii contented himself with announcing that any one who should make the acquaintance of Basavriuk would be counted a Catholic, an enemy of Christ's church, not a member of the human race.

In this village there was a Cossack named Korzh, who had a laborer whom people called Peter the Orphan—perhaps because no one remembered either his father or mother. The church starost, it is true, said that they had died of the pest in his second year; but my grandfather's aunt would not hear to that, and tried with all her might to furnish him with parents, although poor Peter needed them about as much as we need last year's snow. She said that his father had been in Zaporozhe, taken prisoner by the Turks, underwent God only knows what tortures, and having, by some miracle, disguised himself as a eunuch, had made his escape. Little cared the

---

[1] Sir.

[2] A dish of rice or wheat flour, with honey and raisins, which is brought to the church on the celebration of memorial masses.

black-browed youths and maidens about his parents. They merely remarked, that if he only had a new coat, a red sash, a black lambskin cap, with dandified blue crown, on his head, a Turkish sabre hanging by his side, a whip in one hand and a pipe with handsome mountings in the other, he would surpass all the young men. But the pity was, that the only thing poor Peter had was a gray *svitka* with more holes in it than there are gold pieces in a Jew's pocket. And that was not the worst of it, but this: that Korzh had a daughter, such a beauty as I think you can hardly have chanced to see. My deceased grandfather's aunt used to say—and you know that it is easier for a woman to kiss the Evil One than to call anybody a beauty, without malice be it said—that this Cossack maiden's cheeks were as plump and fresh as the pinkest poppy when just bathed in God's dew, and, glowing, it unfolds its petals, and coquets with the rising sun; that her brows were like black cords, such as our maidens buy nowadays, for their crosses and ducats, of the Moscow peddlers who visit the villages with their baskets, and evenly arched as though peeping into her clear eyes; that her little mouth, at sight of which the youths smacked their lips, seemed made to emit the songs of nightingales; that her hair, black as the raven's wing, and soft as young flax (our maidens did not then plait their hair in clubs interwoven with pretty, bright-hued ribbons), fell in curls over her *kuntush*.[1] Eh! may I never intone another alleluia in the choir, if I would not have kissed her, in spite of the gray which is making its way all through the old wool which covers my pate, and my old woman beside me, like a thorn in my side! Well, you know what happens when young men and maids live side by side. In the twilight the heels of red boots were always visible in the place where Pidórka chatted with her Petrus. But Korzh would never have suspected any thing out of the way, only one day—it is evident that none but the Evil One could have inspired him—Petrus took it into his head to kiss the Cossack maiden's rosy lips with all his heart in the passage, without first looking well about him; and that same Evil One—may the son of a dog dream of the holy cross!—caused the old graybeard, like a fool, to open the cottage-door at that same moment. Korzh was petrified, dropped his jaw, and clutched at the door for support. Those unlucky kisses had completely stunned him. It surprised him more than the blow of a pestle on the wall, with which, in our days, the muzhik generally drives out his intoxication for lack of fusees and powder.

Recovering himself, he took his grandfather's hunting-whip from the wall, and was about to bela-

[1]Upper garment in Little Russia.

bor Peter's back with it, when Pidórka's little six-year-old brother Ivas rushed up from somewhere or other, and, grasping his father's legs with his little hands, screamed out, "Daddy, daddy! don't beat Petrus!" What was to be done? A father's heart is not made of stone. Hanging the whip again upon the wall, he led him quietly from the house. "If you ever show yourself in my cottage again, or even under the windows, look out, Petró! by Heaven, your black mustache will disappear; and your black locks, though wound twice about your ears, will take leave of your pate, or my name is not Terentiy Korzh." So saying, he gave him a little taste of his fist in the nape of his neck, so that all grew dark before Petrus, and he flew headlong. So there was an end of their kissing. Sorrow seized upon our doves; and a rumor was rife in the village, that a certain Pole, all embroidered with gold, with mustaches, sabre, spurs, and pockets jingling like the bells of the bag with which our sacristan Taras goes through the church every day, had begun to frequent Korzh's house. Now, it is well known why the father is visited when there is a black-browed daughter about. So, one day, Pidórka burst into tears, and clutched the hand of her Ivas. "Ivas, my dear! Ivas, my love! fly to Petrus, my child of gold, like an arrow from a bow. Tell him all: I would have loved his brown eyes, I would have kissed his white face, but my fate decrees not so.

More than one towel have I wet with burning tears.
I am sad, I am heavy at heart. And my own father is
my enemy. I will not marry that Pole, whom I do
not love. Tell him they are preparing a wedding, but
there will be no music at our wedding: ecclesiastics
will sing instead of pipes and *kobzas*.[1] I shall not
dance with my bridegroom: they will carry me out.
Dark, dark will be my dwelling—of maple wood;
and, instead of chimneys, a cross will stand upon the
roof."

Petró stood petrified, without moving from the
spot, when the innocent child lisped out Pidórka's
words to him. "And I, unhappy man, thought to go
to the Crimea and Turkey, win gold and return to
thee, my beauty! But it may not be. The evil eye has
seen us. I will have a wedding, too, dear little fish, I
too; but no ecclesiastics will be at that wedding. The
black crow will caw, instead of the pope, over me;
the smooth field will be my dwelling; the dark blue
clouds my roof-tree. The eagle will claw out my
brown eyes: the rain will wash the Cossack's bones,
and the whirlwinds will dry them. But what am I?
Of whom, to whom, am I complaining? 'Tis plain,
God willed it so. If I am to be lost, then so be it!"
and he went straight to the tavern.

My late grandfather's aunt was somewhat sur-

---

[1] Eight-stringed musical instrument.

prised on seeing Petrus in the tavern, and at an hour when good men go to morning mass; and she stared at him as though in a dream, when he demanded a jug of brandy, about half a pailful. But the poor fellow tried in vain to drown his woe. The vodka stung his tongue like nettles, and tasted more bitter than worm-wood. He flung the jug from him upon the ground. "You have sorrowed enough, Cossack," growled a bass voice behind him. He looked round—Basavriuk! Ugh, what a face! His hair was like a brush, his eyes like those of a bull. "I know what you lack: here it is." Then he jingled a leather purse which hung from his girdle, and smiled diabolically. Petró shuddered. "He, he, he! yes, how it shines!" he roared, shaking out ducats into his hand: "he, he, he! and how it jingles! And I only ask one thing for a whole pile of such shiners."—"It is the Evil One!" exclaimed Petró:—"Give them here! I'm ready for any thing!" They struck hands upon it. "See here, Petró, you are ripe just in time: to-morrow is St. John the Baptist's day. Only on this one night in the year does the fern blossom. Delay not. I will await thee at midnight in the Bear's ravine."

I do not believe that chickens await the hour when the woman brings their corn, with as much anxiety as Petrus awaited the evening. And, in fact, he looked to see whether the shadows of the trees were not lengthening, if the sun were not turning red towards setting; and, the longer he watched, the more impatient he grew. How long it was! Evidently, God's day had lost its end somewhere. And now the sun is gone. The sky is red only on one side, and it is already growing dark. It grows colder in the fields. It gets dusky, and more dusky, and at last quite dark. At last! With heart almost bursting from his bosom, he set out on his way, and cautiously descended through the dense woods into the deep hollow called the Bear's ravine. Basavriuk was already waiting there. It was so dark, that you could not see a yard before you. Hand in hand they penetrated the thin marsh, clinging to the luxuriant thorn-bushes, and stumbling at almost every step. At last they reached an open spot. Petró looked about him: he had never chanced to come there before. Here Basavriuk halted.

"Do you see, before you stand three hillocks? There are a great many sorts of flowers upon them. But may some power keep you from plucking even one of them. But as soon as the fern blossoms, seize it, and look not round, no matter what may seem to be going on behind thee."

Petró wanted to ask—and behold, he was no longer there. He approached the three hillocks— where were the flowers? He saw nothing. The wild steppe-grass darkled around, and stifled every thing

in its luxuriance. But the lightning flashed; and
before him stood a whole bed of flowers, all wonderful, all strange: and there were also the simple
fronds of fern. Petró doubted his senses, and stood
thoughtfully before them, with both hands upon his
sides.

"What prodigy is this? One can see these weeds
ten times in a day: what marvel is there about them?
Was not devil's-face laughing at me?"

Behold! the tiny flower-bud crimsons, and moves
as though alive. It is a marvel, in truth. It moves, and
grows larger and larger, and flushes like a burning
coal. The tiny star flashes up, something bursts softly,
and the flower opens before his eyes like a flame,
lighting the others about it. "Now is the time,"
thought Petró, and extended his hand. He sees hundreds of shaggy hands reach from behind him, also
for the flower; and there is a running about from
place to place, in the rear. He half shut his eyes,
plucked sharply at the stalk, and the flower remained
in his hand. All became still. Upon a stump sat
Basavriuk, all blue like a corpse. He moved not so
much as a finger. His eyes were immovably fixed on
something visible to him alone: his mouth was half
open and speechless. All about, nothing stirred. Ugh!
it was horrible!—But then a whistle was heard,
which made Petró's heart grow cold within him; and
it seemed to him that the grass whispered, and the

flowers began to talk among themselves in delicate voices, like little silver bells; the trees rustled in waving contention;—Basavriuk's face suddenly became full of life, and his eyes sparkled. "The witch has just returned," he muttered between his teeth. "See here, Petró: a beauty will stand before you in a moment; do whatever she commands; if not—you are lost forever." Then he parted the thorn-bush with a knotty stick, and before him stood a tiny *izbá,* on chicken's legs, as they say. Basavriuk smote it with his fist, and the wall trembled. A large black dog ran out to meet them, and with a whine, transforming itself into a cat, flew straight at his eyes. "Don't be angry, don't be angry, you old Satan!" said Basavriuk, employing such words as would have made a good man stop his ears. Behold, instead of a cat, an old woman with a face wrinkled like a baked apple, and all bent into a bow: her nose and chin were like a pair of nutcrackers. "A stunning beauty!" thought Petró; and cold chills ran down his back. The witch tore the flower from his hand, bent over, and muttered over it for a long time, sprinkling it with some kind of water. Sparks flew from her mouth, froth appeared on her lips.

"Throw it away," she said, giving it back to Petró.

Petró threw it, and what wonder was this? the flower did not fall straight to the earth, but for a long while twinkled like a fiery ball through the darkness, and swam through the air like a boat: at last it began to sink lower and lower, and fell so far away, that the little star, hardly larger than a poppy-seed, was barely visible. "Here!" croaked the old woman, in a dull voice: and Basavriuk, giving him a spade, said, "Dig here, Petró: here you will see more gold than you or Korzh ever dreamed of."

Petró spat on his hands, seized the spade, applied his foot, and turned up the earth, a second, a third, a fourth time. . . . There was something hard: the spade clinked, and would go no farther. Then his eyes began to distinguish a small, iron-bound coffer. He tried to seize it; but the chest began to sink into the earth, deeper, farther, and deeper still: and behind him he heard a laugh, more like a serpent's hiss. "No, you shall not see the gold until you procure human blood," said the witch, and led up to him a child of six, covered with a white sheet, indicating by a sign that he was to cut off his head. Petró was stunned. A trifle, indeed, to cut off a man's, or even an innocent child's, head for no reason whatever! In wrath he tore off the sheet enveloping his head, and behold! before him stood Ivas. And the poor child crossed his little hands, and hung his head. . . . Petró flew upon the witch with the knife like a madman, and was on the point of laying hands on her. . . .

"What did you promise for the girl?" . . . thundered Basavriuk; and like a shot he was on his back.

The witch stamped her foot: a blue flame flashed from the earth; it illumined it all inside, and it was as if moulded of crystal; and all that was within the earth became visible, as if in the palm of the hand. Ducats, precious stones in chests and kettles, were piled in heaps beneath the very spot they stood on. His eyes burned, . . . his mind grew troubled. . . . He grasped the knife like a madman, and the inno-cent blood spurted into his eyes. Diabolical laughter resounded on all sides. Misshaped monsters flew past him in herds. The witch, fastening her hands in the headless trunk, like a wolf, drank its blood. . . . All went round in his head. Collecting all his strength, he set out to run. Every thing turned red before him. The trees seemed steeped in blood, and burned and groaned. The sky glowed and glowered. . . . Burning points, like lightning, flickered before his eyes. Utterly exhausted, he rushed into his miserable hovel, and fell to the ground like a log. A death-like sleep overpowered him.

Two days and two nights did Petró sleep, without once awakening. When he came to himself, on the third day, he looked long at all the corners of his hut; but in vain did he endeavor to recollect; his memory was like a miser's pocket, from which you cannot entice a quarter of a kopek. Stretching himself, he heard something clash at his feet. He looked,—two bags of gold. Then only, as if in a dream, he recollected that he had been seeking some treasure, that something had frightened him in the woods. . . . But at what price he had obtained it, and how, he could by no means understand.

Korzh saw the sacks—and was mollified. "Such a Petrus, quite unheard of! yes, and did I not love him? Was he not to me as my own son?" And the old fellow carried on his fiction until it reduced him to tears. Pidórka began to tell him how some passing gypsies had stolen Ivas; but Petró could not even recall him—to such a degree had the Devil's influence darkened his mind! There was no reason for delay. The Pole was dismissed, and the wedding-feast prepared; rolls were baked, towels and handkerchiefs embroidered; the young people were seated at table; the wedding-loaf was cut; *banduras,* cymbals, pipes, k*obzi,* sounded, and pleasure was rife. . . .

A wedding in the olden times was not like one of the present day. My grandfather's aunt used to tell—what doings!—how the maidens—in festive head-dresses of yellow, blue, and pink ribbons, above which they bound gold braid; in thin chemisettes embroidered on all the seams with red silk, and strewn with tiny silver flowers; in morocco shoes, with high iron heels—danced the gorlitza as swimmingly as peacocks, and as wildly as the whirlwind; how the youths—with their ship-shaped caps upon their heads, the crowns of gold brocade, with a little slit at the nape where the hair-net peeped through, and two horns projecting, one in front and another behind, of the very finest black lambskin; in *kuntushas* of the finest blue silk with red borders— stepped forward one by one, their arms akimbo in stately form, and executed the *gopak;* how the lads— in tall Cossack caps, and light cloth *svitkas,* girt with silver embroidered belts, their short pipes in their teeth—skipped before them, and talked nonsense. Even Korzh could not contain himself, as he gazed at the young people, from getting gay in his old age. Bandura in hand, alternately puffing at his pipe and singing, a brandy-glass upon his head, the gray-beard began the national dance amid loud shouts from the merry-makers. What will not people devise in merry mood! They even began to disguise their faces. They did not look like human beings. They are not to be compared with the disguises which we have at our weddings nowadays. What do they do now? Why, imitate gypsies and Moscow peddlers. No! then one used to dress himself as a Jew, another as the Devil: they would begin by kissing each other, and end by seizing each other by the hair . . . God be with them! you laughed till you held your sides. They dressed themselves in Turkish and Tatar garments. All upon them glowed like a conflagration, . . . and then they began to joke and play pranks. . . . Well, then away with the saints!

An amusing thing happened to my grandfather's aunt, who was at this wedding. She was dressed in a voluminous Tatar robe, and, wineglass in hand, was entertaining the company. The Evil One instigated one man to pour vodka over her from behind. Another, at the same moment, evidently not by accident, struck a light, and touched it to her; . . . the flame flashed up; poor aunt, in terror, flung her robe from her, before them all. . . . Screams, laughter, jests, arose, as if at a fair. In a word, the old folks could not recall so merry a wedding.

Pidórka and Petrus began to live like a gentleman and lady. There was plenty of every thing, and every thing was handsome. . . . But honest people shook their heads when they looked at their way of living. "From the Devil no good can come," they unanimously agreed. "Whence, except from the tempter of orthodox people, came this wealth? Where else could he get such a lot of gold? Why, on the very day that he got rich, did Basavriuk vanish as if into thin air?" Say, if you can, that people imagine things! In fact, a month had not passed, and no one would have recognized Petrus. Why, what had happened to him? God knows. He sits in one spot, and says no word to any one: he thinks continually, and seems to be trying to recall something. When Pidórka succeeds in getting him to speak, he seems to forget himself, carries on a conversation, and even grows cheerful; but if he inadvertently glances at the sacks, "Stop, stop! I have forgotten," he cries, and again plunges into revery, and again strives to recall something. Sometimes when he has sat long in a place, it seems to him as though it were coming, just coming back to mind, . . . and again all fades away. It seems as if he is sitting in the tavern: they bring him vodka; vodka stings him; vodka is repulsive to him. Some one comes along, and strikes him on the shoulder; . . . but beyond that every thing is veiled in darkness before him. The perspiration streams down his face, and he sits exhausted in the same place.

What did not Pidórka do? She consulted the sorceress; and they poured out fear, and brewed stomach ache[1]—but all to no avail. And so the summer passed. Many a Cossack had mowed and reaped: many a Cossack, more enterprising than the rest, had set off upon an expedition. Flocks of ducks were

---

[1]"To pour out fear," is done with us in case of fear; when it is desired to know what caused it, melted lead or wax is poured into water, and the object whose form it assumes is the one which frightened the sick person; after this, the fear departs. *Sónyashnitza* is brewed for giddiness, and pain in the bowels. To this end, a bit of stump is burned, thrown into a jug, and turned upside down into a bowl filled with water, which is placed on the patient's stomach: after an incantation, he is given a spoonful of this water to drink.

already crowding our marshes, but there was not even a hint of improvement.

It was red upon the steppes. Ricks of grain, like Cossacks' caps, dotted the fields here and there. On the highway were to be encountered wagons loaded with brushwood and logs. The ground had become more solid, and in places was touched with frost. Already had the snow begun to besprinkle the sky, and the branches of the trees were covered with rime like rabbit-skin. Already on frosty days the red-breasted finch hopped about on the snow-heaps like a foppish Polish nobleman, and picked out grains of corn; and children, with huge sticks, chased wooden tops upon the ice; while their fathers lay quietly on the stove, issuing forth at intervals with lighted pipes in their lips, to growl, in regular fashion, at the orthodox frost, or to take the air, and thresh the grain spread out in the barn. At last the snow began to melt, and the ice rind slipped away; but Petró remained the same; and, the longer it went on, the more morose he grew. He sat in the middle of the cottage as though nailed to the spot, with the sacks of gold at his feet. He grew shy, his hair grew long, he became terrible; and still he thought of but one thing, still he tried to recall something, and got angry and ill-tempered because he could not recall it. Often, rising wildly from his seat, he gesticulates violently, fixes his eyes on something as though desirous of catching it: his lips move as though desirous of uttering some long-forgotten word—and remain speechless. Fury takes possession of him: he gnaws and bites his hands like a man half crazy, and in his vexation tears out his hair by the handful, until, calming down, he falls into forgetfulness, as it were, and again begins to recall, and is again seized with fury and fresh tortures. . . . What visitation of God is this?

Pidórka was neither dead nor alive. At first it was horrible to her to remain alone in the cottage; but, in course of time, the poor woman grew accustomed to her sorrow. But it was impossible to recognize the Pidórka of former days. No blush, no smile: she was thin and worn with grief, and had wept her bright eyes away. Once, some one who evidently took pity on her, advised her to go to the witch who dwelt in the Bear's ravine, and enjoyed the reputation of being able to cure every disease in the world. She determined to try this last remedy: word by word she persuaded the old woman to come to her. This was St. John's Eve, as it chanced. Petró lay insensible on the bench, and did not observe the new-comer. Little by little he rose, and looked about him. Suddenly he trembled in every limb, as though he were on the scaffold: his hair rose upon his head, . . . and he laughed such a laugh as pierced Pidórka's heart with fear. "I have remembered, remembered!" he cried in terrible joy; and, swinging a hatchet round his head, he flung it at the old woman with all his might. The hatchet penetrated the oaken door two *vershok* (three inches and a half). The old woman disappeared; and a child of seven in a white blouse, with covered head, stood in the middle of the cottage. . . . The sheet flew off. "Ivas!" cried Pidórka, and ran to him; but the apparition became covered from head to foot with blood, and illumined the whole room with red light. . . . She ran into the passage in her terror, but, on recovering herself a little, wished to help him; in vain! the door had slammed to behind her so securely that she could not open it. People ran up, and began to knock: they broke in the door, as though there were but one mind among them. The whole cottage was full of smoke; and just in the middle, where Petrus had stood, was a heap of ashes, from which smoke was still rising. They flung themselves upon the sacks: only broken potsherds lay there instead of ducats. The Cossacks stood with staring eyes and open mouths, not daring to move a hair, as if rooted to the earth, such terror did this wonder inspire in them.

I do not remember what happened next. Pidórka took a vow to go upon a pilgrimage, collected the property left her by her father, and in a few days it was as if she had never been in the village. Whither she had gone, no one could tell. Officious old women would have despatched her to the same place whither Petró had gone; but a Cossack from Kief reported that he had seen, in a cloister, a nun withered to a mere skeleton, who prayed unceasingly; and her fellow-villagers recognized her as Pidórka, by all the signs—that no one had ever heard her utter a word; that she had come on foot, and had brought a frame for the ikon of God's mother, set with such brilliant stones that all were dazzled at the sight.

But this was not the end, if you please. On the same day that the Evil One made way with Petrus, Basavriuk appeared again; but all fled from him. They knew what sort of a bird he was—none else than Satan, who had assumed human form in order to unearth treasures; and, since treasures do not yield to unclean hands, he seduced the young. That same year, all deserted their earth huts, and collected in a village; but, even there, there was no peace, on account of that accursed Basavriuk. My late grandfather's aunt said that he was particularly angry with her, because she had abandoned her former tavern, and tried with all his might to revenge himself upon her. Once the village elders were assembled in the tavern, and, as the saying goes, were arranging the precedence at the table, in the middle of which was placed a small roasted lamb, shame to say. They chattered about this, that, and the other—among the rest about various marvels and strange things. Well, they saw something; it would have been nothing if only one had seen it, but all saw it; and it was this: the sheep raised his head; his goggling eyes became alive and sparkled; and the black, bristling mustache, which appeared for one instant, made a significant gesture at those present. All, at once, recognized Basavriuk's countenance in the sheep's head: my grandfather's aunt thought it was on the point of asking for vodka. . . . The worthy elders seized their hats, and hastened home.

Another time, the church starost[1] himself, who was fond of an occasional private interview with my grandfather's brandy-glass, had not succeeded in getting to the bottom twice, when he beheld the glass bowing very low to him. "Satan take you, let us make the sign of the cross over you!" . . . And the same marvel happened to his better half. She had just begun to mix the dough in a huge kneading-trough, when suddenly the trough sprang up. "Stop, stop! where are you going?" Putting its arms akimbo, with dignity, it went skipping all about the cottage. . . . You may laugh, but it was no laughing-matter to our grandfathers. And in vain did Father Athanasii go through all the village with holy water, and chase the Devil through all the streets with his brush; and my

[1] Elder.

late grandfather's aunt long complained, that, as soon as it was dark, some one came knocking at her door, and scratching at the wall.

Well! All appears to be quiet now, in the place where our village stands; but it was not so very long ago—my father was still alive—that I remember how a good man could not pass the ruined tavern, which a dishonest race had long managed for their own interest. From the smoke-blackened chimneys, smoke poured out in a pillar, and rising high in the air, as if to take an observation, rolled off like a cap, scattering burning coals over the steppe; and Satan (the son of a dog should not be mentioned) sobbed so pitifully in his lair, that the startled ravens rose in flocks from the neighboring oak-wood, and flew through the air with wild cries.

No. 1 Branch Line: The Signalman

[**CHARLES DICKENS**]

As significant a social event as the French Revolution was the Industrial one. Factories sprung up around European cities (as did unbelievably frightful slums to house the hapless workers who manned, and womanned them), railroads sped populations from one country to another, and steamships plied rivers and oceans. On the one hand, the stage was being set for the origins of the technological upheaval which continues into our own time; on the other, the miseries of the urban proletariat would eventually spawn first Communism, and then eventually Fascism and Nazism—three "isms" which would produce man-made horrors of their own.

On the supernatural front, the mid-19th century saw an Occult revival, which expressed itself in such movements as Spiritualism. In the realm of fiction, writers moved their locations from the past and the rural present to settings encompassing the new world of technology.

One such writer who was fully at home with the new develop-

ments (and eloquent in denouncing their resulting evils) was Charles Dickens. Although his "Christmas Carol" is one of the best-known ghost stories ever written, the following makes skillful use of an industrialized setting, while delivering the traditional chills.

"Halloa! Below there!"

When he heard a voice thus calling to him, he was standing at the door of his box, with a flag in his hand, furled round its short pole. One would have thought, considering the nature of the ground, that he could not have doubted from what quarter the voice came; but instead of looking up to where I stood on the top of the steep cutting nearly over his head, he turned himself about, and looked down the Line. There was something remarkable in his manner of doing so, though I could not have said for my life what. But I know it was remarkable enough to attract my notice, even though his figure was foreshortened and shadowed, down in the deep trench, and mine was high above him, so steeped in the glow of an angry sunset, that I had shaded my eyes with my hand before I saw him at all.

"Halloa! Below!"

From looking down the Line, he turned himself about again, and, raising his eyes, saw my figure high above him.

"Is there any path by which I can come down and speak to you?"

He looked up at me without replying, and I looked down at him without pressing him too soon with a repetition of my idle question. Just then there came a vague vibration in the earth and air, quickly changing into a violent pulsation, and an oncoming rush that caused me to start back, as though it had force to draw me down. When such vapour as rose to my height from this rapid train had passed me, and was skimming away over the landscape, I looked down again, and saw him refurling the flag he had shown while the train went by.

I repeated my inquiry. After a pause, during which he seemed to regard me with fixed attention, he motioned with his rolled-up flag towards a point on my level, some two or three hundred yards distant. I called down to him, "All right!" and made for that point. There, by dint of looking closely about me, I found a rough zigzag descending path notched out, which I followed.

The cutting was extremely deep, and unusually precipitate. It was made through a clammy stone, that became oozier and wetter as I went down. For these reasons, I found the way long enough to give me time to recall a singular air of reluctance or compulsion with which he had pointed out the path.

When I came down low enough upon the zigzag descent to see him again, I saw that he was standing between the rails on the way by which the train had lately passed, in an attitude as if he were waiting for me to appear. He had his left hand at his chin, and that left elbow rested on his right hand, crossed over his breast. His attitude was one of such expectation and watchfulness that I stopped a moment, wondering at it.

I resumed my downward way, and stepping out upon the level of the railroad, and drawing nearer to him, saw that he was a dark sallow man, with a dark beard and rather heavy eyebrows. His post was in as solitary and dismal a place as ever I saw. On either side, a dripping-wet wall of jagged stone, excluding all view but a strip of sky; the perspective one way only a crooked prolongation of this great dungeon; the shorter perspective in the other direction terminating in a gloomy red light, and the gloomier entrance to a black tunnel, in whose massive architecture there was a barbarous, depressing, and forbidding air. So little sunlight ever found its way to this spot, that it had an earthy, deadly smell; and so much cold wind rushed through it, that it struck chill in me, as if I had left the natural world.

Before he stirred, I was near enough to him to have touched him. Not even then removing his eyes from mine, he stepped back one step, and lifted his hand.

This was a lonesome post to occupy (I said), and it had riveted my attention when I looked down from up yonder. A visitor was a rarity, I should suppose; not an unwelcome rarity, I hoped? In me, he merely saw a man who had been shut up within narrow limits all his life, and who, being at last set free, had a newly-awakened interest in these great works. To such purpose I spoke to him; but I am far from sure of the terms I used; for, besides that I am not happy in opening any conversation, there was something in the man that daunted me.

He directed a most curious look towards the red light near the tunnel's mouth, and looked all about it, as if something were missing from it, and then looked at me.

That light was part of his charge? Was it not?

He answered in a low voice, "Don't you know it is?"

The monstrous thought came into my mind, as I perused the fixed eyes and the saturnine face, that this was a spirit, not a man. I have speculated since, whether there may have been infection in his mind.

In my turn I stepped back. But in making the action, I detected in his eyes some latent fear of me. This put the monstrous thought to flight.

"You look at me," I said, forcing a smile, "as if you had a dread of me."

"I was doubtful," he returned, "whether I had seen you before."

"Where?"

He pointed to the red light he had looked at.

"There?" I said.

Intently watchful of me, he replied (but without sound), "Yes."

"My good fellow, what should I do there? However, be that as it may, I never was there, you may swear."

"I think I may," he replied. "Yes; I am sure I may."

His manner cleared, like my own. He replied to my remarks with readiness, and in well-chosen words. Had he much to do there? Yes; that was to say, he had enough responsibility to bear; but exactness and watchfulness were what was required of him, and of actual work—manual labour—he had next to none. To change that signal, to trim those lights, and to turn this iron handle now and then, was all he had to do under that head. Regarding those many long and lonely hours of which I seemed to make so much, he could only say that the routine of his life had shaped itself into that form, and he had grown used to it. He had taught himself a language down here—if only to know it by sight, and to have formed his own crude ideas of its pronunciation, could be called learning it. He had also worked at fractions and decimals, and tried a little algebra; but he was, and had been as a boy, a poor hand at figures. Was it necessary for him when on duty always to remain in that channel of damp air, and could he never rise into the sunshine from between those high stone walls? Why, that depended upon times and circumstances. Under some conditions there would be less upon the Line than under others, and the same held good as to certain hours of the day and night. In bright weather, he did choose occasions for getting a little above these lower shadows; but, being at all times liable to be called by his electric bell, and at such times listening for it with redoubled anxiety, the relief was less than I would suppose.

He took me into his box, where there was a fire, a desk for an official book in which he had to make certain entries, a telegraphic instrument with its dial, face, and needles, and the little bell of which he had spoken. On my trusting that he would excuse the remark that he had been well educated, and (I hoped I might say without offence), perhaps educated above that station, he observed that instances of slight incongruity in such wise would rarely be found wanting among large bodies of men, that he had heard it was so in workhouses, in the police force, even in that last desperate resource, the army;

and that he knew it was so, more or less, in any great railway staff. He had been, when young (if I could believe it, sitting in that hut—he scarcely could), a student of natural philosophy, and had attended lectures; but he had run wild, misused his opportunities, gone down, and never risen again. He had no complaint to offer about that. He had made his bed, and he lay upon it. It was far too late to make another.

All that I have here condensed he said in a quiet manner, with his grave dark regards divided between me and the fire. He threw in the word, "Sir," from time to time, and especially when he referred to his youth—as though to request me to understand that he claimed to be nothing but what I found him. He was several times interrupted by the little bell, and had to read off messages, and send replies. Once he had to stand without the door, and display a flag as a train passed, and make some verbal communication to the driver. In the discharge of his duties, I observed him to be remarkably exact and vigilant, breaking off his discourse at a syllable, and remaining silent until what he had to do was done.

In a word, I should have set this man down as one of the safest of men to be employed in that capacity, but for the circumstance that while he was speaking to me he twice broke off with a fallen colour, turned his face towards the little bell when it did *not* ring, opened the door of the hut (which was kept shut to exclude the unhealthy damp), and looked out towards the red light near the mouth of the tunnel. On both of those occasions, he came back to the fire with the inexplicable air upon him which I had remarked, without being able to define, when we were so far asunder.

Said I, when I rose to leave him, "You almost make me think that I have met with a contented man."

(I am afraid I must acknowledge that I said it to lead him on.)

"I believe I used to be so," he rejoined, in the low voice in which he had first spoken, "but I am troubled, Sir, I am troubled."

He would have recalled the words if he could. He had said them, however, and I took them up quickly.

"With what? What is your trouble?"

"It is very difficult to impart, Sir. It is very, very difficult to speak of. If ever you make me another visit, I will try to tell you."

"But I expressly intend to make you another visit. Say, when shall it be?"

"I go off early in the morning, and I shall be on again at ten tomorrow night, Sir."

"I will come at eleven."

He thanked me, and went out at the door with me. "I'll show my white light, Sir," he said, in his peculiar low voice, "till you have found the way up. When you have found it, don't call out! And when you are at the top, don't call out!"

His manner seemed to make the place strike colder to me, but I said no more than, "Very well."

"And when you come down tomorrow night, don't call out! Let me ask you a parting question. What made you cry, 'Halloa! Below there!' to-night?"

"Heaven knows," said I, "I cried something to that effect—"

"Not to that effect, Sir. Those were the very words. I know them well."

"Admit those were the very words. I said them, no doubt, because I saw you below."

"For no other reason?"

"What other reason could I possibly have?"

"You had no feeling that they were conveyed to you in any supernatural way?"

"No."

He wished me good night, and held up his light. I walked by the side of the down Line of rails (with a very disagreeable sensation of a train coming behind me) until I found the path. It was easier to mount than to descend, and I got back to my inn without any adventure.

Punctual to my appointment, I placed my foot on the first notch of the zigzag next night, as the distant clocks were striking eleven. He was waiting for me at the bottom, with his white light on. "I have not called out," I said, when we came close together; "may I speak now?"

"By all means, Sir."

"Good night, then, and here's my hand."

"Good night, Sir, and here's mine." With that we walked side by side to his box, entered it, closed the door, and sat down by the fire.

"I have made up my mind, Sir," he began, bending forward as soon as we were seated, and speaking in a tone but a little above a whisper, "that you shall not have to ask me twice what troubles me. I took you for some one else yesterday evening. That troubles me."

"That mistake?"

"No. That some one else."

"Who is it?"

"I don't know."

"Like me?"

"I don't know. I never saw the face. The left arm is across the face, and the right arm is waved—violently waved. This way."

I followed his action with my eyes, and it was the action of an arm gesticulating, with the utmost passion and vehemence, "For God's sake, clear the way!"

"One moonlight night," said the man, "I was sitting here, when I heard a voice cry, 'Halloa! Below there!' I started up, looked from that door, and saw this someone else standing by the red light near the tunnel, waving as I just now showed you. The voice seemed hoarse with shouting, and it cried, 'Look out! Look out!' And then again, 'Halloa! Below there! Look out!' I caught up my lamp, turned it on red, and ran towards the figure, calling, 'What's wrong? What has happened? Where?' It stood just outside the blackness of the tunnel. I advanced so close upon it that I wondered at its keeping the sleeve across its eyes. I ran right up at it, and had my hand stretched out to pull the sleeve away, when it was gone."

"Into the tunnel?' said I.

"No. I ran on into the tunnel, five hundred yards. I stopped, and held my lamp above my head, and saw the figures of the measured distance, and saw the wet stains stealing down the walls and trickling through the arch. I ran out again faster than I had run in (for I had a mortal abhorrence of the place upon me), and I looked all round the red light with my own red light, and I went up the iron ladder to the gallery atop of it, and I came down again, and ran back here. I telegraphed both ways. 'An alarm has been given. Is anything wrong?' The answer came back, both ways, 'All well.' "

Resisting the slow touch of a frozen finger tracing out my spine, I showed him how that this figure must be a deception of his sense of sight; and how that figures, originating in disease of the delicate nerves that minister to the functions of the eye, were known to have often troubled patients, some of whom had become conscious of the nature of their affliction, and had even proved it by experiments upon themselves. "As to an imaginary cry," said I, "do but listen for a moment to the wind in this unnatural valley while we speak so low, and to the wild harp it makes of the telegraph wires."

That was all very well, he returned, after we had sat listening for a while, and he ought to know something of the wind and the wires—he who so often passed long winter nights there, alone and watching. But he would beg to remark that he had not finished.

I asked his pardon, and he slowly added these words, touching my arm—

"Within six hours after the appearance, the memorable accident on this Line happened, and within ten hours the dead and wounded were brought along through the tunnel over the spot where the figure had stood."

A disagreeable shudder crept over me, but I did my best against it. It was not to be denied, I rejoined, that this was a remarkable coincidence, calculated deeply to impress his mind. But it was unquestionable that remarkable coincidences did continually occur, and they must be taken into account in dealing with such a subject. Though to be sure I must admit, I added (for I thought I saw that he was going to bring the objection to bear upon me), men of common sense did not allow much for coincidences in making the ordinary calculations of life.

He again begged to remark that he had not finished.

I again begged his pardon for being betrayed into interruptions.

"This," he said, again laying his hand upon my arm, and glancing over his shoulder with hollow eyes, "was just a year ago. Six or seven months passed, and I had recovered from the surprise and shock, when one morning, as the day was breaking, I, standing at the door, looked towards the red light, and saw the spectre again." He stopped, with a fixed look at me.

"Did it cry out?"

"No. It was silent."

"Did it wave its arm?"

"No. It leaned against the shaft of the light, with both hands before the face. Like this."

Once more I followed his action with my eyes. It was an action of mourning. I have seen such an attitude on stone figures on tombs.

"Did you go up to it?"

"I came in and sat down, partly to collect my

thoughts, partly because it had turned me faint. When I went to the door again, daylight was above me, and the ghost was gone."

"But nothing followed? Nothing came of this?"

He touched me on the arm with his forefinger twice or thrice, giving a ghastly nod each time—

"That very day, as a train came out of the tunnel, I noticed, at a carriage window on my side, what looked like a confusion of hands and heads, and something waved. I saw it just in time to signal the driver, Stop! He shut off, and put his brake on, but the train drifted past here a hundred and fifty yards or more. I ran after it, and, as I went along, heard terrible screams and cries. A beautiful young lady had died instantaneously in one of the compartments, and was brought back in here, and laid down on this floor between us."

Involuntarily I pushed my chair back, as I looked from the boards at which he pointed to himself.

"True, Sir. True. Precisely as it happened, so I tell it you."

I could think of nothing to say, to any purpose, and my mouth was very dry. The wind and the wires took up the story with a long lamenting wail.

He resumed, "Now, Sir, mark this, and judge how my mind is troubled. The spectre came back a week ago. Ever since, it has been there, now and again, by fits and starts."

"At the light?"

"At the Danger-light."

"What does it seem to do?"

He repeated, if possible with increased passion and vehemence, that former gesticulation of "For God's sake, clear the way!"

Then he went on. "I have no peace or rest for it. It calls to me, for many minutes together, in an agonised manner, 'Below there! Look out! Look out!' It stands waving to me. It rings my little bell—"

I caught at that. "Did it ring your bell yesterday evening when I was here, and you went to the door?"

"Twice."

"Why, see," said I, "how your imagination misleads you. My eyes were on the bell, and my ears were open to the bell, and if I am a living man, it did not ring at those times. No, nor at any other time, except when it was rung in the natural course of physical things by the station communicating with you."

He shook his head. "I have never made a mistake as to that yet, Sir. I have never confused the spectre's ring with the man's. The ghost's ring is a strange vibration in the bell that it derives from nothing else, and I have not asserted that the bell stirs to the eye. I don't wonder that you failed to hear it. But I heard it."

"And did the spectre seem to be there when you looked out?"

"It *was* there."

"Both times?"

He repeated firmly: "Both times."

"Will you come to the door with me, and look for it now?"

He bit his under lip as though he were somewhat unwilling, but arose. I opened the door, and stood on the step, while he stood in the doorway. There was the Danger-light. There was the dismal mouth of the tunnel. There were the high, wet stone walls of the cutting. There were the stars above them.

"Do you see it?" I asked him, taking particular note of his face. His eyes were prominent and strained, but not very much more so, perhaps than my own had been when I had directed them earnestly towards the same spot.

"No," he answered. "It is not there."

"Agreed," said I.

We went in again, shut the door, and resumed our seats. I was thinking how best to improve this advantage, if it might be called one, when he took up the conversation in such a matter-of-course way, so assuming that there could be no serious question of fact between us, that I felt myself placed in the weakest of positions.

"By this time you will fully understand, Sir," he

said, "that what troubles me so dreadfully is the question, What does the spectre mean?"

I was not sure, I told him, that I did fully understand.

"What is its warning against?" he said, ruminating, with his eyes on the fire, and only by times turning them on me. "What is the danger? Where is the danger? There is danger overhanging somewhere on the Line. Some dreadful calamity will happen. It is not to be doubted this third time, after what has gone before. But surely this is a cruel haunting of me. What can I do?"

He pulled out his handkerchief, and wiped the drops from his heated forehead.

"If I telegraph Danger, on either side of me, or on both, I can give no reason for it," he went on, wiping the palms of his hands. "I should get into trouble and do no good. They would think I was mad. This is the way it would work—Message: 'Danger! Take care!' Answer: 'What Danger? Where?' Message: 'Don't know. But, for God's sake, take care!' They would displace me. What else could they do?"

His pain of mind was most pitiable to see. It was the mental torture of a conscientious man, oppressed beyond endurance by an unintelligible responsibility involving life.

"When it first stood under the Danger-light," he went on, putting his dark hair back from his head, and drawing his hands outward across and across his temples in an extremity of feverish distress, "why not tell me where that accident was to happen—if it must happen? Why not tell me how it could be averted—if it could have been averted? When on its second coming it hid its face, why not tell me, instead, 'She is going to die. Let them keep her at home'? If it came, on those two occasions, only to show me that its warnings were true, and so to prepare me for the third, why not warn me plainly now? And I, Lord help me! A mere poor signalman on this solitary station! Why not go to somebody with credit to be believed, and power to act?"

When I saw him in this state, I saw that for the poor man's sake, as well as for the public safety, what I had to do for the time was to compose his mind. Therefore, setting aside all question of reality or unreality between us, I represented to him that whoever thoroughly discharged his duty must do well, and that at least it was his comfort that he understood his duty, though he did not understand these confounding Appearances. In this effort I succeeded far better than in the attempt to reason him out of his conviction. He became calm; the occupations incidental to his post as the night advanced began to make larger demands on his attention: and I left him at two in the morning. I had offered to stay through the night, but he would not hear of it.

That I more than once looked back at the red light as I ascended the pathway, that I did not like the red light, and that I should have slept but poorly if my bed had been under it, I see no reason to conceal. Nor did I like the two sequences of the accident and the dead girl. I see no reason to conceal that either.

But what ran most in my thoughts was the consideration how ought I to act, having become the recipient of this disclosure? I had proved the man to be intelligent, vigilant, painstaking, and exact; but how long might he remain so, in his state of mind? Though in a subordinate position, still he held a most important trust, and would I (for instance) like to stake my own life on the chances of his continuing to execute it with precision?

Unable to overcome a feeling that there would be something treacherous in my communicating what he had told me to his superiors in the Company, without first being plain with himself and proposing a middle course to him, I ultimately resolved to offer to accompany him (otherwise keeping his secret for the present) to the wisest medical practitioner we could hear of in those parts, and to take his opinion. A change in his time of duty would come round next night, he had apprised me, and he would be off an hour or two after sunrise, and on again soon after sunset. I had appointed to return accordingly.

Next evening was a lovely evening, and I walked

out early to enjoy it. The sun was not yet quite down when I traversed the field-path near the top of the deep cutting. I would extend my walk for an hour, I said to myself, half an hour on and half an hour back, and it would then be time to go to my signalman's box.

Before pursuing my stroll, I stepped to the brink and mechanically looked down, from the point from which I had first seen him. I cannot describe the thrill that seized upon me, when, close at the mouth of the tunnel, I saw the appearance of a man, with his left sleeve across his eyes, passionately waving his right arm.

The nameless horror that oppressed me passed in a moment, for in a moment I saw that this appearance of a man was a man indeed, and that there was a little group of other men, standing at a short distance, to whom he seemed to be rehearsing the gesture he made. The Danger-light was not yet lighted. Against its shaft a little low hut, entirely new to me, had been made of some wooden supports and tarpaulin. It looked no bigger than a bed.

With an irresistible sense that something was wrong—with a flashing self-reproachful fear that fatal mischief had come of my leaving the man there, and causing no one to be sent to overlook or correct what he did—I descended the notched path with all the speed I could make.

"What is the matter?" I asked the men.

"Signalman killed this morning, Sir."

"Not the man belonging to that box?"

"Yes, Sir."

"Not the man I know?"

"You will recognize him, Sir, if you knew him," said the man who spoke for the others, solemnly uncovering his own head, and raising an end of the tarpaulin, "for his face is quite composed."

"O, how did this happen, how did this happen?" I asked, turning from one to another as the hut closed in again.

"He was cut down by an engine, Sir. No man in England knew his work better. But somehow he was not clear of the outer rail. It was just at broad day. He had struck the light, and had the lamp in his hand. As the engine came out of the tunnel, his back was towards her, and she cut him down. That man drove her, and was showing how it happened. Show the gentleman, Tom."

The man, who wore a rough dark dress, stepped back to his former place at the mouth of the tunnel.

"Coming round the curve in the tunnel, Sir," he said, "I saw him at the end, like as if I saw him down a perspective-glass. There was no time to check speed, and I knew him to be very careful. As he didn't seem to take heed of the whistle, I shut it off when we were running down upon him, and called to him as loud as I could call."

"What did you say?"

"I said, 'Below there! Look out! Look out! For God's sake, clear the way!'"

I started.

"Ah! it was a dreadful time, Sir. I never left off calling to him. I put this arm before my eyes not to see, and I waved this arm to the last; but it was no use."

Without prolonging the narrative to dwell on any one of its curious circumstances more than on any other, I may, in closing it, point out the coincidence that the warning of the engine-driver included, not only the words which the unfortunate signalman had repeated to me as haunting him, but also the words which I myself—not he—had attached, and that only in my own mind, to the gesticulation he had imitated.

The Mark of the Beast

[RUDYARD KIPLING]

Although Europe had been expanding overseas since the 15th century, the 19th was the colonial century par excellence. While most of the Spanish and Portuguese Empires in Latin America followed the lead of the United States (becoming independent in the first two decades of the century), most of the rest of the world was partitioned between older colonies of those two nations, and the British, French, Dutch, and newcoming Italians, Germans, and Belgians. In all of these countries, the colonial experience and interaction with alien cultures had a tremendous effect on the arts—particularly literature. Supernatural horrors drawn from the exotic settings of Australia, India, and elsewhere became very popular.

Kipling, regarded as the preeminent chronicler of Imperialism, also wrote a number of ghost and other weird tales. While some of these were set in the England of his forebears, many took place in the India of his birth. Here, a cautionary tale about interfering with native customs.

Your Gods and my Gods—
do you or I know which are the stronger?
Native Proverb

East of Suez, some hold, the direct control of Providence ceases; Man being there handed over to the power of the Gods and Devils of Asia, and the Church of England, Providence only exercising an occasional and modified supervision in the case of Englishmen.

This theory accounts for some of the more unnecessary horrors of life in India: it may be stretched to explain my story.

My friend Strickland of the Police, who knows as much of the natives as is good for any man, can bear witness to the facts of the case. Dumoise, our doctor, also saw what Strickland and I saw. The inference which he drew from the evidence was entirely incorrect.

When Fleete came to India he owned a little money and some land in the Himalayas, near a place called Dharmsala. Both properties had been left him by an uncle, and he came out to finance them. He was a big, heavy, genial, and inoffensive man. His knowledge of natives was, of course, limited, and he complained of the difficulties of the language.

He rode in from his place in the hills to spend

New Year in the station, and he stayed with Strickland. On New Year's Eve there was a big dinner at the club, and the night was excusably wet. When men foregather from the uttermost ends of the Empire, they have a right to be riotous. The frontier had sent down a contingent o' Catch-'em-Alive-O's who had not seen twenty white faces a year, and were used to ride fifteen miles to dinner at the next fort at the risk of a Khyberee bullet where their drinks should lie. They profited by their new security, for they tried to play pool with a curled-up hedgehog found in the garden, and one of them carried the marker round the room in his teeth. Half a dozen planters had come in from the south and were talking "horse" to the Biggest Liar in Asia, who was trying to cap all their stories at once. Everybody was there, and there was a general closing up of ranks and taking stock of our losses in dead or disabled that had fallen during the past year. It was a very wet night, and I remember that we sang "Auld Lang Syne" with our feet in the Polo Championship Cup, and our heads among the stars, and swore that we were all dear friends. Then some of us went away and annexed Burma, and some tried to open up the Sudan and were opened up by Fuzzies in that cruel scrub outside Suakin, and some found stars and medals, and some were married, which was bad, and some did other things which were worse, and others of us stayed in our chains and strove to make money on insufficient experiences.

Fleete began the night with sherry and bitters, drank champagne steadily up to the dessert, then raw, rasping Capri with all the strength of whisky, took Benedictine with his coffee, four or five whiskies and sodas to improve his pool strokes, beer and bones at half-past two, winding up with old brandy. Consequently, when he came out, at half-past three in the morning, into fourteen degrees of frost, he was very angry with his horse for coughing, and tried to leapfrog into the saddle. The horse broke away and went to his stables; so Strickland and I formed a Guard of Dishonour to take Fleete home.

Our road lay through the bazaar, close to a little temple of Hanuman, the Monkey-god, who is a leading divinity worthy of respect. All gods have good points, just as have all priests. Personally, I attach much importance to Hanuman, and am kind to his people—the great gray apes of the hills. One never knows when one may want a friend.

There was a light in the temple, and as we passed, we could hear voices of men chanting hymns. In a native temple, the priests rise at all hours of the night to do honour to their god. Before we could stop him, Fleete dashed up the steps, patted two priests on the back, and was gravely grinding the ashes of his cigar butt into the forehead of the red stone image of Hanuman. Strickland tried to drag him out, but he sat down and said solemnly:

"Shee that? Mark of the B—beasht! *I* made it. Ishn't it fine?"

In half a minute the temple was alive and noisy, and Strickland, who knew what came of polluting gods, said that things might occur. He, by virtue of his official position, long residence in the country, and weakness for going among the natives, was known to the priests and he felt unhappy. Fleete sat on the ground and refused to move. He said that "good old Hanuman" made a very soft pillow.

Then, without any warning, a Silver Man came out of a recess behind the image of the god. He was perfectly naked in that bitter, bitter cold, and his body shone like frosted silver, for he was what the Bible calls "a leper as white as snow." Also he had no face, because he was a leper of some years' standing and his disease was heavy upon him. We two stooped to haul Fleete up, and the temple was filling and filling with folk who seemed to spring from the earth, when the Silver Man ran in under our arms, making a noise exactly like the mewing of an otter, caught Fleete round the body and dropped his head on Fleete's breast before we could wrench him away. Then he retired to a corner and sat mewing while the crowd blocked all the doors.

The priests were very angry until the Silver Man touched Fleete. That nuzzling seemed to sober them.

At the end of a few minutes' silence one of the priests came to Strickland and said, in perfect English, "Take your friend away. He has done with Hanuman, but Hanuman has not done with him."

The crowd gave room and we carried Fleete into the road.

Strickland was very angry. He said that we might all three have been knifed, and that Fleete should thank his stars that he had escaped without injury.

Fleete thanked no one. He said that he wanted to go to bed. He was gorgeously drunk.

We moved on, Strickland silent and wrathful, until Fleete was taken with violent shivering fits and sweating. He said that the smells of the bazaar were overpowering, and he wondered what slaughter-houses were permitted so near English residences. "Can't you smell the blood?" said Fleete.

We put him to bed at last, just as the dawn was breaking, and Strickland invited me to have another whisky and soda. While we were drinking he talked of the trouble in the temple, and admitted that it baffled him completely. Strickland hates being mystified by natives, because his business in life is to overmatch them with their own weapons. He has not yet succeeded in doing this, but in fifteen or twenty years he will have made some small progress.

"They should have mauled us," he said, "instead of mewing at us. I wonder what they meant. I don't like it one little bit."

I said that the Managing Committee of the temple would in all probability bring a criminal action against us for insulting their religion. There was a section of the Indian Penal Code which exactly met Fleete's offense. Strickland said he only hoped and prayed that they would do this. Before I left I looked into Fleete's room, and saw him lying on his right side, scratching his left breast. Then I went to bed cold, depressed, and unhappy, at seven o'clock in the morning.

At one o'clock I rode over to Strickland's house to inquire after Fleete's head. I imagined that it would be a sore one. Fleete was breakfasting and seemed unwell. His temper was gone, for he was abusing the cook for not supplying him with an undone chop. A man who can eat raw meat after a wet night is a curiosity. I told Fleete this and he laughed.

"You breed queer mosquitoes in these parts," he said. "I've been bitten to pieces, but only in one place."

"Let's have a look at the bite," said Strickland. "It may have gone down since this morning."

While the chops were being cooked, Fleete opened his shirt and showed us, just over his left breast, a mark, the perfect double of the black rosettes—the five or six irregular blotches arranged in a circle—on a leopard's hide. Strickland looked and said, "It was only pink this morning. It's grown black now."

Fleete ran to a glass.

"By jove!" he said, "this is nasty. What is it?"

We could not answer. Here the chops came in, all red and juicy, and Fleete bolted three in a most offensive manner. He ate on his right grinders only, and threw his head over his right shoulder as he snapped the meat. When he had finished, it struck him that he had been behaving strangely, for he said apologetically, "I don't think I ever felt so hungry in my life. I've bolted like an ostrich."

After breakfast Strickland said to me, "Don't go. Stay here, and stay for the night."

Seeing that my house was not three miles from Strickland's, this request was absurd. But Strickland insisted, and was going to say something when Fleete interrupted by declaring in a shamefaced way that he felt hungry again. Strickland sent a man to my house to fetch over my bedding and a horse, and we three went down to Strickland's stables to pass the hours until it was time to go out for a ride. The man who has a weakness for horses never wearies of inspecting them; and when two men are killing time in this way they gather knowledge and lies the one from the other.

There were five horses in the stables, and I shall never forget the scene as we tried to look them over. They seemed to have gone mad. They reared and screamed and nearly tore up their pickets; they sweated and shivered and lathered and were distraught with fear. Strickland's horses used to know him as well as his dogs; which made the matter more curious. We left the stable for fear of the brutes throwing themselves in panic. Then Strickland turned back and called me. The horses were still frightened, but they let us "gentle" and make much of them, and put their heads in our bosoms.

"They aren't afraid of *us*," said Strickland. "D'you know, I'd give three months' pay if *Outrage* here could talk."

But *Outrage* was dumb and could only cuddle up to his master and blow out his nostrils, as is the custom of horses when they wish to explain things but can't. Fleete came up when we were in the stalls, and as soon as the horses saw him, their fright broke out afresh. It was all that we could do to escape from the place unkicked. Strickland said, "They don't seem to love you, Fleete."

"Nonsense," said Fleete; "my mare will follow me like a dog." He went to her; she was in a loose box;

but as he slipped the bars she plunged, knocked him down, and broke away into the garden. I laughed, but Strickland was not amused. He took his moustache in both fists and pulled at it till it nearly came out. Fleete, instead of going off to chase his property, yawned, saying that he felt sleepy. He went to the house to lie down, which was a foolish way of spending New Year's Day.

Strickland sat with me in the stables and asked if I had noticed anything peculiar in Fleete's manner. I said that he ate his food like a beast; but that this might have been the result of living alone in the hills out of the reach of society as refined and elevating as ours for instance. Strickland was not amused. I do not think that he listened to me, for his next sentence referred to the mark on Fleete's breast, and I said that it might have been caused by blister flies, or that it was possibly a birthmark newly born and now visible for the first time. We both agreed that it was unpleasant to look at, and Strickland found occasion to say that I was a fool.

"I can't tell you what I think now," said he, "because you would call me a madman; but you must stay with me for the next few days, if you can. I want you to watch Fleete, but don't tell me what you think till I have made up my mind."

"But I am dining out tonight," I said.

"So am I," said Strickland, "and so is Fleete. At least if he doesn't change his mind."

We walked about the garden smoking, but saying nothing—because we were friends, and talking spoils good tobacco—till our pipes were out. Then we went to wake up Fleete. He was wide awake and fidgeting about his room.

"I say, I want some more chops," he said. "Can I get them?"

We laughed and said, "Go and change. The ponies will be round in a minute."

"All right," said Fleete. "I'll go when I get the chops—underdone ones, mind."

He seemed to be quite in earnest. It was four o'clock, and we had had breakfast at one; still, for a long time, he demanded those underdone chops. Then he changed into riding clothes and went out into the veranda. His pony—the mare had not been caught—would not let him come near. All three horses were unmanageable mad with fear—and finally Fleete said that he would stay at home and get something to eat. Strickland and I rode out wondering. As we passed the temple of Hanuman, the Silver Man came out and mewed at us.

"He is not one of the regular priests of the temple," said Strickland. "I think I should peculiarly like to lay my hands on him."

There was no spring in our gallop on the race-course that evening. The horses were stale, and moved as though they had been ridden out.

"The fright after breakfast has been too much for them," said Strickland.

That was the only remark he made through the remainder of the ride. Once or twice I think he swore to himself; but that did not count.

We came back in the dark at seven o'clock, and saw that there were no lights in the bungalow. "Careless ruffians my servants are!" said Strickland.

My horse reared at something on the carriage drive, and Fleete stood up under its nose.

"What are you doing, groveling about the garden?" said Strickland.

But both horses bolted and nearly threw us. We dismounted by the stables and returned to Fleete, who was on his hands and knees under the orange bushes.

"What the devil's wrong with you?" said Strickland.

"Nothing, nothing in the world," said Fleete, speaking very quickly and thickly. "I've been gardening—botanizing you know. The smell of the earth is delightful. I think I'm going for a walk—a long walk—all night."

Then I saw that there was something excessively

out of order somewhere, and I said to Strickland, "I am not dining out."

"Bless you!" said Strickland. "Here, Fleete, get up. You'll catch fever there. Come in to dinner and let's have the lamps lit. We'll all dine at home."

Fleete stood up unwillingly, and said, "No lamps—no lamps. It's much nicer here. Let's dine outside and have some more chops—lots of 'em and underdone—bloody ones with gristle."

Now a December evening in Northern India is bitterly cold, and Fleete's suggestion was that of a maniac.

"Come in," said Strickland sternly. "Come in at once."

Fleete came, and when the lamps were brought, we saw that he was literally plastered with dirt from head to foot. He must have been rolling in the garden. He shrank from the light and went to his room. His eyes were horrible to look at. There was a green light behind them, not in them, if you understand, and the man's lower lip hung down.

Strickland said, "There is going to be trouble—big trouble—tonight. Don't you change your riding things."

We waited and waited for Fleete's reappearance, and ordered dinner in the meantime. We could hear him moving about his own room, but there was no light there. Presently from the room came the long-drawn howl of a wolf.

People write and talk lightly of blood running cold and hair standing up and things of that kind. Both sensations are too horrible to be trifled with. My heart stopped as though a knife had been driven through it, and Strickland turned as white as the tablecloth.

The howl was repeated, and was answered by another howl far across the fields.

That set the gilded roof on the horror. Strickland dashed into Fleete's room. I followed, and we saw Fleete getting out of the window. He made beast noises in the back of his throat. He could not answer us when we shouted at him. He spat.

I don't quite remember what followed, but I think that Strickland must have stunned him with the long bootjack or else I should never have been able to sit on his chest. Fleete could not speak, he could only snarl, and his snarls were those of a wolf, not of a man. The human spirit must have been giving way all day and have died out with the twilight. We were dealing with a beast that had once been Fleete.

The affair was beyond any human and rational experience. I tried to say "Hydrophobia," but the word wouldn't come, because I knew that I was lying.

We bound this beast with leather thongs of the

punkah-rope, and tied its thumbs and big toes together, and gagged it with a shoehorn, which makes a very efficient gag if you know how to arrange it. Then we carried it into the dining room, and sent a man to Dumoise, the doctor, telling him to come over at once. After we had despatched the messenger and were drawing breath, Strickland said, "It's no good. This isn't any doctor's work." I, also, knew that he spoke the truth.

The beast's head was free, and it threw it about from side to side. Any one entering the room would have believed that we were curing a wolf's pelt. That was the most loathsome accessory of all.

Strickland sat with his chin in the heel of his fist, watching the beast as it wriggled on the ground, but saying nothing. The shirt had been torn open in the scuffle and showed the black rosette mark on the left breast. It stood out like a blister.

In the silence of the watching we heard something without mewing like a she-otter. We both rose to our feet, and, I answer for myself, not Strickland, felt sick—actually and physically sick. We told each other, as did the men in *Pinafore*, that it was the cat.

Dumoise arrived, and I never saw a little man so unprofessionally shocked. He said that it was a heart-rending case of hydrophobia, and that nothing could be done. At least any palliative measures would only prolong the agony. The beast was foaming at the mouth. Fleete, as we told Dumoise, had been bitten by dogs once or twice. Any man who keeps half a dozen terriers must expect a nip now and again. Dumoise could offer no help. He could only certify that Fleete was dying of hydrophobia. The beast was then howling, for it had managed to spit out the shoehorn. Dumoise said that he would be ready to certify to the cause of death, and that the end was certain. He was a good little man, and he offered to remain with us; but Strickland refused the kindness. He did not wish to poison Dumoise's New Year. He would only ask him not to give the real cause of Fleete's death to the public.

So Dumoise left, deeply agitated; and as soon as the noise of the cartwheels had died away, Strickland told me, in a whisper, his suspicions. They were so wildly improbable that he dared not say them out loud; and I, who entertained all Strickland's beliefs, was so ashamed of owning to them that I pretended to disbelieve.

"Even if the Silver Man had bewitched Fleete for polluting the image of Hanuman, the punishment could not have fallen so quickly."

As I was whispering this the cry outside the house rose again, and the beast fell into a fresh paroxysm of struggling till we were afraid that the thongs that held it would give way.

"Watch!" said Strickland. "If this happens six

times I shall take the law into my own hands. I order you to help me."

He went into his room and came out in a few minutes with the barrels of an old shotgun, a piece of fishing line, some thick cord, and his heavy wooden bedstead. I reported that convulsions had followed the cry by two seconds in each case, and the beast seemed perceptibly weaker.

Strickland muttered, "But he can't take away the life! He can't take away the life!"

I said, though I knew that I was arguing against myself, "It may be a cat. It must be a cat. If the Silver Man is responsible, why does he dare to come here?"

Strickland arranged the wood on the hearth, put the gun barrels into the glow of the fire, spread the twine on the table and broke a walking stick in two. There was one yard of fishing line, gut, lapped with wire, such as is used for *mahseer*-fishing, and he tied the two ends together in a loop.

Then he said, "How can we catch him? He must be taken alive and unhurt."

I said that we must trust in Providence, and go out softly with polo sticks into the shrubbery at the front of the house. The man or animal that made the cry was evidently moving round the house as regularly as a night watchman. We could wait in the bushes till he came by and knock him over.

Strickland accepted this suggestion, and we slipped

out from a bathroom window into the front veranda and then across the carriage drive into the bushes.

In the moonlight we could see the leper coming round the corner of the house. He was perfectly naked, and from time to time he mewed and stopped to dance with his shadow. It was an unattractive sight, and thinking of poor Fleete, brought to such degradation by so foul a creature, I put away my doubts and resolved to help Strickland from the heated gun barrels to the loop of twine—from the loins to the head and back again—with all tortures that might be needful.

The leper halted in the front porch for a moment and we jumped out on him with the sticks. He was wonderfully strong, and we were afraid that he might escape or be fatally injured before we caught him. We had an idea that lepers were frail creatures, but this proved to be incorrect. Strickland knocked his legs from under him and I put my foot on his neck. He mewed hideously, and even through my riding boots I could feel that his flesh was not the flesh of a clean man.

He struck at us with his hand and feet stumps. We looped the lash of a dog whip round him, under the armpits, and dragged him backwards into the hall and so into the dining room where the beast lay. There we tied him with trunk straps. He made no attempt to escape, but mewed.

When we confronted him with the beast the scene was beyond description. The beast doubled back-wards into a bow as though he had been poisoned with strychnine, and moaned in the most pitiable fashion. Several other things happened also, but they cannot be put down here.

"I think I was right," said Strickland. "Now we will ask him to cure this case."

But the leper only mewed. Strickland wrapped a towel round his hand and took the gun barrels out of the fire. I put the half of the broken walking stick through the loop of fishing line and buckled the leper comfortably to Strickland's bedstead. I under-stood then how men and women and little children can endure to see a witch burnt alive; for the beast was moaning on the floor, and though the Silver Man had no face, you could see horrible feelings passing through the slab that took its place, exactly as waves of heat play across red-hot iron—gun barrels for instance.

Strickland shaded his eyes with his hands for a moment and we got to work. This part is not to be printed.

The dawn was beginning to break when the leper spoke. His mewings had not been satisfactory up to that point. The beast had fainted from exhaustion and the house was very still. We unstrapped the leper and told him to take away the evil spirit. He crawled to the beast and laid his hand upon the left breast. That was all. Then he fell face down and whined, drawing in his breath as he did so.

We watched the face of the beast, and saw the soul of Fleete coming back into the eyes. Then a sweat broke out on the forehead and the eyes—they were human eyes—closed. We waited for an hour but Fleete still slept. We carried him to his room and bade the leper go, giving him the bedstead, and the sheet on the bedstead to cover his nakedness, the gloves and the towels with which we had touched him, and the whip that had been hooked round his body. He put the sheet about him and went out into the early morning without speaking or mewing.

Strickland wiped his face and sat down. A night gong, far away in the city, made seven o'clock.

"Exactly four-and-twenty hours!" said Strickland. "And I've done enough to ensure my dismissal from the service, besides permanent quarters in a lunatic asylum. Do you believe that we are awake?"

The red-hot gun barrel had fallen to the floor and was singeing the carpet. The smell was entirely real.

That morning at eleven we two together went to wake up Fleete. We looked and saw that the black leopard-rosette on his chest had disappeared. He was very drowsy and tired, but as soon as he saw us, he said, "Oh! Confound you fellows. Happy New Year to you. Never mix your liquors. I'm nearly dead."

"Thanks for your kindness, but you're over time," said Strickland. "Today is the morning of the second. You've slept the clock round with a vengeance."

The door opened, and little Dumoise put his head in. He had come on foot, and fancied that we were laying out Fleete.

"I've brought a nurse," said Dumoise. "I suppose that she can come in for what is necessary."

"By all means," said Fleete cheerfully, sitting up in bed. "Bring on your nurses."

Dumoise was dumb. Strickland led him out and explained that there must have been a mistake in the diagnosis. Dumoise remained dumb and left the house hastily. He considered that his professional reputation had been injured, and was inclined to make a personal matter of the recovery. Strickland went out too. When he came back, he said that he had been to call on the Temple of Hanuman to offer redress for the pollution of the god, and had been solemnly assured that no white man had ever touched the idol and that he was an incarnation of all the virtues laboring under a delusion. "What do you think?" said Strickland.

I said, " 'There are more things . . . ' "

But Strickland hates that quotation. He says that I have worn it threadbare.

One other curious thing happened which frightened me as much as anything in all the night's work. When Fleete was dressed he came into the dining room and sniffed. He had a quaint trick of moving his nose when he sniffed. "Horrid doggy smell, here," said he. "You should really keep those terriers of yours in better order. Try sulfur, Strick."

But Strickland did not answer. He caught hold of the back of a chair, and, without warning, went into an amazing fit of hysterics. It is terrible to see a strong man overtaken with hysteria. Then it struck me that we had fought for Fleete's soul with the Silver Man in that room, and had disgraced ourselves as Englishmen for ever, and I laughed and gasped and gurgled just as shamefully as Strickland, while Fleete thought that we had both gone mad. We never told him what we had done.

Some years later, when Strickland had married and was a church-going member of society for his wife's sake, we reviewed the incident dispassionately, and Strickland suggested that I should put it before the public.

I cannot myself see that this step is likely to clear up the mystery; because, in the first place, no one will believe a rather unpleasant story, and, in the second, it is well known to every right-minded man that the gods of the heathen are stone and brass, and any attempt to deal with them otherwise is justly condemned.

Gabriel-Ernest

[SAKI (H. H. MUNRO)]

Saki, in many ways, serves as a sort of satiric parallel to Kipling, although his birth was in Burma, rather than India (his pen-name was taken from the name of the cup-bearer in the Rubaiyat of Omar Khayam). Better known in his day for humorous tales, he nevertheless turned out a number of highly effective horror pieces; this one is a nasty turn on the werewolf legend.

"There is a wild beast in your woods," said the artist Cunningham, as he was being driven to the station. It was the only remark he had made during the drive, but as Van Cheele had talked incessantly his companion's silence had not been noticeable.

"A stray fox or two and some resident weasels. Nothing more formidable," said Van Cheele. The artist said nothing.

"What did you mean about a wild beast?" said Van Cheele later, when they were on the platform.

"Nothing. My imagination. Here is the train,"said Cunningham.

That afternoon Van Cheele went for one of his frequent rambles through his woodland property. He had a stuffed bittern in his study, and knew the names of quite a number of wild flowers, so his aunt had possibly some justification in describing him as a great naturalist. At any rate, he was a great walker. It was his custom to take mental notes of everything he saw during his walks, not so much for the purpose of assisting contemporary science as to provide topics for conversation afterwards. When the blue-bells began to show themselves in flower he made a point of informing every one of the fact; the season of the year might have warned his hearers of the likelihood of such an occurrence, but at least they felt that he was being absolutely frank with them.

What Van Cheele saw on this particular afternoon was, however, something far removed from his ordinary range of experience. On a shelf of smooth stone overhanging a deep pool in the hollow of an oak coppice a boy of about sixteen lay asprawl, drying his wet brown limbs luxuriously in the sun. His wet hair, parted by a recent dive, lay close to his head, and his light-brown eyes, so light that there was an almost tigerish gleam in them, were turned towards Van Cheele with a certain lazy watchfulness. It was an unexpected apparition, and Van Cheele found himself engaged in the novel process of thinking before he spoke. Where on earth could this wild-looking boy hail from? The miller's wife had lost a child some two months ago, supposed to have been swept away by the mill-race, but that had been a mere baby, not a half-grown lad.

"What are you doing there?" he demanded.

"Obviously, sunning myself," replied the boy.

"Where do you live?"

"Here, in these woods."

"You can't live in the woods," said Van Cheele.

"They are very nice woods," said the boy, with a touch of patronage in his voice.

"But where do you sleep at night?"

"I don't sleep at night; that's my busiest time."

Van Cheele began to have an irritated feeling that he was grappling with a problem that was eluding him.

"What do you feed on?" he asked.

"Flesh," said the boy, and he pronounced the word with slow relish, as though he were tasting it.

"Flesh! What flesh?"

"Since it interests you, rabbits, wild-fowl, hares, poultry, lambs in their season, children when I can get any; they're usually too well locked in at night, when I do most of my hunting. It's quite two months since I tasted child-flesh."

Ignoring the chaffing nature of the last remark, Van Cheele tried to draw the boy on the subject of possible poaching operations.

"You're talking rather through your hat when you speak of feeding on hares." (Considering the nature of the boy's toilet, the simile was hardly an apt one.) "Our hillside hares aren't easily caught."

"At night I hunt on four feet," was the somewhat cryptic response.

"I suppose you mean that you hunt with a dog?" hazarded Van Cheele.

The boy rolled slowly over on to his back, and laughed a weird low laugh, that was pleasantly like a chuckle and disagreeably like a snarl.

"I don't fancy any dog would be very anxious for my company, especially at night."

Van Cheele began to feel that there was something positively uncanny about the strange-eyed, strange-tongued youngster.

"I can't have you staying in these woods," he declared authoritatively.

"I fancy you'd rather have me here than in your house," said the boy.

The prospect of this wild, nude animal in Van

Cheele's primly ordered house was certainly an alarming one.

"If you don't go I shall have to make you," said Van Cheele.

The boy turned like a flash, plunged into the pool, and in a moment had flung his wet and glistening body half-way up the bank where Van Cheele was standing. In an otter the movement would not have been remarkable; in a boy Van Cheele found it sufficiently startling. His foot slipped as he made an involuntary backward movement and he found himself almost prostrate on the slippery weed-grown bank, with those tigerish yellow eyes not very far from his own. Almost instinctively he half-raised his hand to his throat. The boy laughed again, a laugh in which the snarl had nearly driven out the chuckle, and then, with another of his astonishing lightning movements plunged out of view into a yielding tangle of weed and fern.

"What an extraordinary wild animal!" said Van Cheele as he picked himself up. And then he recalled Cunningham's remark, "There is a wild beast in your woods."

Walking slowly homeward, Van Cheele began to turn over in his mind various local occurrences which might be traceable to the existence of this astonishing young savage.

Something had been thinning the game in the woods lately, poultry had been missing from the farms, hares were growing unaccountably scarcer, and complaints had reached him of lambs being carried off bodily from the hills. Was it possible that this wild boy was really hunting the countryside in company with some clever poacher dog? He had spoken of hunting "four-footed" by night, but then, again, he had hinted strangely at no dog caring to come near him, "especially at night." It was certainly puzzling. And then, as Van Cheele ran his mind over the various depredations that had been committed during the last month or two, he came suddenly to a dead stop, alike in his walk and his speculations. The child missing from the mill two months ago—the accepted theory was that it had tumbled into the mill-race and been swept away; but the mother had always declared she had heard a shriek on the hill side of the house, in the opposite direction from the water. It was unthinkable, of course, but he wished that the boy had not made that uncanny remark about child-flesh eaten two months ago. Such dreadful things should not be said even in fun.

Van Cheele, contrary to his usual wont, did not feel disposed to be communicative about his discovery in the wood. His position as a parish councillor and justice of the peace seemed somehow compromised by the fact that he was harbouring a personal-

ity of such doubtful repute on his property; there
was even a possibility that a heavy bill of damages
for raided lambs and poultry might be laid at his
door. At dinner that night he was quite unusually
silent.

"Where's your voice gone to?" said his aunt.
"One would think you had seen a wolf."

Van Cheele, who was not familiar with the old
saying, thought the remark rather foolish; if he *had*
seen a wolf on his property his tongue would have
been extraordinarily busy with the subject.

At breakfast next morning Van Cheele was conscious that his feeling of uneasiness regarding yesterday's episode had not wholly disappeared, and he
resolved to go by train to the neighbouring cathedral
town, hunt up Cunningham, and learn from him
what he had really seen that had prompted the
remark about a wild beast in the woods. With this
resolution taken, his usual cheerfulness partially
returned, and he hummed a bright little melody as
he sauntered to the morning-room for his customin-
ary cigarette. As he entered the room the melody
made way abruptly for a pious invocation. Gracefully asprawl on the ottoman, in an attitude of
almost exaggerated repose, was the boy of the
woods. He was drier than when Van Cheele had last
seen him, but no other alteration was noticeable in
his toilet.

"How dare you come here?" asked Van Cheele furiously.

"You told me I was not to stay in the woods," said the boy calmly.

"But not to come here. Supposing my aunt should see you!"

And with a view to minimizing that catastrophe Van Cheele hastily obscured as much of his unwelcome guest as possible under the folds of a *Morning Post*. At that moment his aunt entered the room.

"This is a poor boy who has lost his way—and lost his memory. He doesn't know who he is or where he comes from," explained Van Cheele desperately, glancing apprehensively at the waif's face to see whether he was going to add inconvenient candour to his other savage propensities.

Miss Van Cheele was enormously interested.

"Perhaps his underlinen is marked," she suggested.

"He seems to have lost most of that, too," said Van Cheele, making frantic little grabs at the *Morning Post* to keep it in its place.

A naked homeless child appealed to Miss Van Cheele as warmly as a stray kitten or derelict puppy would have done.

"We must do all we can for him," she decided, and in a very short time a messenger, dispatched to the rectory, where a page-boy was kept, had returned with a suit of pantry clothes, and the necessary accessories of shirt, shoes, collar, etc. Clothed, clean, and groomed, the boy lost none of his uncanniness in Van Cheele's eyes, but his aunt found him sweet.

"We must call him something till we know who he really is," she said. "Gabriel-Ernest, I think; those are nice suitable names."

Van Cheele agreed, but he privately doubted whether they were being grafted on to a nice suitable child. His misgivings were not diminished by the fact that his staid and elderly spaniel had bolted out of the house at the first incoming of the boy, and now obstinately remained shivering and yapping at the farther end of the orchard, while the canary, usually as vocally industrious as Van Cheele himself, had put itself on an allowance of frightened cheeps. More than ever he was resolved to consult Cunningham without loss of time.

As he drove off to the station his aunt was arranging that Gabriel-Ernest should help her to entertain the infant members of her Sunday-school class at tea that afternoon.

Cunningham was not at first disposed to be communicative.

"My mother died of some brain trouble," he explained, "so you will understand why I am averse to dwelling on anything of an impossibly fantastic nature that I may see or think that I have seen."

"But what *did* you see?" persisted Van Cheele.

"What I thought I saw was something so extraordinary that no really sane man could dignify it with the credit of having actually happened. I was standing, the last evening I was with you, half-hidden in the hedgegrowth by the orchard gate, watching the dying glow of the sunset. Suddenly I became aware of a naked boy, a bather from some neighbouring pool, I took him to be, who was standing out on the bare hillside also watching the sunset. His pose was so suggestive of some wild faun of Pagan myth that I instantly wanted to engage him as a model, and in another moment I think I should have hailed him. But just then the sun dipped out of view, and all the orange and pink slid out of the landscape, leaving it cold and grey. And at the same moment an astounding thing happened—the boy vanished too!"

"What! vanished away into nothing?" asked Van Cheele excitedly.

"No; that is the dreadful part of it," answered the artist, "on the open hillside where the boy had been standing a second ago, stood a large wolf, blackish in colour, with gleaming fangs and cruel, yellow eyes. You may think—"

But Van Cheele did not stop for anything as futile as thought. Already he was tearing at top speed towards the station. He dismissed the idea of a telegram. "Gabriel-Ernest is a werewolf" was a hopelessly inadequate effort at conveying the situation, and his aunt would think it was a code message to which he had omitted to give her the key. His one hope was that he might reach home before sundown. The cab which he chartered at the other end of the railway journey bore him with what seemed exasperating slowness along the country roads, which were pink and mauve with the flush of the sinking sun. His aunt was putting away some unfinished jams and cake when he arrived.

"Where is Gabriel-Ernest?" he almost screamed.

"He is taking the little Toop child home," said his aunt. "It was getting so late, I thought it wasn't safe to let it go back alone. What a lovely sunset, isn't it?"

But Van Cheele, although not oblivious of the glow in the western sky, did not stay to discuss its beauties. At a speed for which he was scarcely geared he raced along the narrow lane that led to the home of the Toops. On one side ran the swift current of the mill-stream, on the other rose the stretch of bare hillside. A dwindling rim of red sun showed still on the skyline, and the next turning must bring him in view of the ill-assorted couple he was pursuing. Then the colour went suddenly out of things, and a grey light settled itself with a quick shiver over the landscape. Van Cheele heard a shrill wail of fear, and stopped running.

Nothing was ever seen again of the Toop child or Gabriel-Ernest, but the latter's discarded garments were found lying in the road, so it was assumed that the child had fallen into the water, and that the boy had stripped and jumped in, in a vain endeavour to save it. Van Cheele and some workmen who were near by at the time testified as having heard a child scream loudly just near the spot where the clothes were found. Mrs. Toop, who had eleven other children, was decently resigned to her bereavement, but Miss Van Cheele sincerely mourned her lost foundling. It was on her initiative that a memorial brass was put up in the parish church to "Gabriel-Ernest, an unknown boy, who bravely sacrificed his life for another."

Van Cheele gave way to his aunt in most things, but he flatly refused to subscribe to the Gabriel-Ernest memorial.

The Botathen Ghost

[R. S. HAWKER]

Yet another byproduct of Romanticism was the Oxford Movement, which, under its leaders Newman and Pusey, inspired many young English clergymen with the idea of re-Catholicizing the Church of England, by reviving various practices abandoned at the Reformation. Robert Hawker was one of the most unique members of the group.

Given a remote parish on the Cornish coast, he set himself to the task not only of reviving the "Catholic" nature of his parish, but also to resurrecting various folk customs of the area. His deep knowledge of Cornish folklore and history left its mark on the very fine ghost stories he wrote, as in this sample. But this particular piece also foreshadows such works as Henry James' The Turn of the Screw, with its exploration of the effect of the supernatural upon the already strange private world of children.

There was something very painful and peculiar in the position of the clergy in the west of England throughout the seventeenth century. The Church of those days was in a transitory state, and her ministers, like her formularies, embodied a strange mixture of the old belief with the new interpretation. Their wide severance also from the great metropolis of life and manners, the city of London (which in those times was civilized England, much as the Paris of our own day is France), divested the Cornish clergy in particular of all personal access to the master-minds of their age and body. Then, too, the barrier interposed by the rude rough roads of their country, and by their abode in wilds that were almost inaccessible, rendered the existence of a bishop rather a doctrine suggested to their belief than a fact revealed to the actual vision of each in his generation. Hence it came to pass that the Cornish clergyman, insulated within his own limited sphere, often without even the presence of a country squire (and unchecked by the influence of the Fourth Estate—for until the beginning of this nineteenth century, *Flindell's Weekly Miscellany*, distributed from house to house from the pannier of a mule, was the only light of the West), became developed about middle life into an original mind and man, sole and absolute within his parish boundary, eccentric when compared with his brethren in civilized regions, and yet, in German phrase, "a whole and seldom man" in his dominion of souls. He was "the parson," in canonical phrase— that is to say, The Person, the somebody of conse- quence among his own people. These men were not, however, smoothed down into a monotonous aspect of life and manners by this remote and secluded existence. They imbibed, each in his own peculiar circle, the hue of surrounding objects, and were tinged into a distinctive colouring and charac- ter by many a contrast of scenery and people. There was the "light of other days," the curate by the sea- shore, who professed to check the turbulence of the "smugglers' landing" by his presence on the sands, and who "held the lantern" for the guidance of his flock when the nights were dark, as the only proper ecclesiastical part he could take in the proceedings. He was soothed and silenced by the gift of a keg of hollands or a chest of tea. There was the merry min- ister of the mines, whose cure was honeycombed by the underground men. He must needs have been an artist and poet in his way, for he had to enliven his people three or four times a-year, by mastering the arrangements of a "guary," or religious mystery, which was duly performed in the topmost hollow of a green barrow or hill, of which many survive, scooped out into vast amphitheatres and surrounded by benches of turf which held two thousand spectators. Such were the historic plays, "The Creation" and "Noe's Flood," which still exist in the original Celtic as well as the English text, and suggest what critics and antiquaries these Cornish curates, masters of such revels, must have been—for the native language of Cornwall did not lapse into silence until the end of the seventeenth century. Then, moreover, here and there would be one parson more learned than his kind in the mysteries of a deep and thrilling lore of peculiar fascination. He was a man so highly honoured at college for natural gifts and knowledge of learned books which nobody else could read, that when he "took his second orders" the bishop gave him a mantle of scarlet silk to wear upon his shoulders in church, and his lordship had put such power into it that, when the parson had it rightly on, he could "govern any ghost or evil spirit," and even "stop an earthquake."

Such a powerful minister, in combat with supernatural visitations, was one Parson Rudall, of Launceston, whose existence and exploits we gather from the local tradition of his time, from surviving letters and other memoranda, and indeed from his own "diurnal" which fell by chance into the hands of the present writer. Indeed the legend of Parson Rudall and the Botathen Ghost will be recognized by many Cornish people as a local remembrance of their boyhood.

It appears, then, from the diary of this learned master of the grammar school—for such was his office as well as perpetual curate of the parish— "that a pestilential disease did break forth in our town in the beginning of the year AD 1665; yea, and it likewise invaded my school, insomuch that therewithal certain of the chief scholars sickened and died." "Among others who yielded to the malign influence was Master John Eliot, the eldest son and the worshipful heir of Edward Eliot, Esquire, of Trebursey, a stripling of sixteen years of age, but of uncommon parts and hopeful ingenuity. At his own especial motion and earnest desire I did consent to preach his funeral sermon." It should be remembered here that, howsoever strange and singular it may sound to us that a mere lad should formally solicit such a performance at the hands of his master, it was in consonance with the habitual usage of those times. The old services for the dead had been abolished by law, and in the stead of sacrament and ceremony, month's mind and year's mind, the sole substitute which survived was the general desire "to partake," as they called it, of a posthumous discourse, replete with lofty eulogy and flattering remembrance of the living and the dead. The diary proceeds:

"I fulfilled my undertaking, and preached over the coffin in the presence of a full assemblage of mourners and lachrymose friends. An ancient gentleman, who was then and there in the church, a Mr Bligh, of Botathen, was much affected with my discourse, and he was heard to repeat to himself certain parentheses therefrom, especially a phrase from Maro Virgilius, which I had applied to the deceased youth, '*Et puer ipse fuit cantari dignus.*'

"The cause wherefore this old gentleman was moved by my applications was this: He had a first-born and only son—a child who, but a very few months before, had been not unworthy the character I drew of young Master Eliot, but who, by some strange accident, had of late quite fallen away from his parents' hopes, and become moody, and sullen, and distraught. When the funeral obsequies were over, I had no sooner come out of church than I was accosted by this aged parent, and he besought me incontinently, with a singular energy, that I would resort with him forthwith to his abode at Botathen that very night; nor could I have delivered myself from his importunity, had not Mr Eliot urged his claim to enjoy my company at his own house. Hereupon I got loose, but not until I had pledged a fast assurance that I would pay him, faithfully, an early visit the next day."

"The Place," as it was called, of Botathen, where

old Mr Bligh resided, was a low-roofed gabled
manor-house of the fifteenth century, walled and
mullioned, and with clustered chimneys of dark-
grey stone from the neighbouring quarries of
Ventor-gan. The mansion was flanked by a pleasance
or enclosure in one space, of garden and lawn, and it
was surrounded by a solemn grove of stag-horned
trees. It had the sombre aspect of age and of solitude, and looked the very scene of strange and
supernatural events. A legend might well belong to
every gloomy glade around, and there must surely be
a haunted room somewhere within its walls. Hither,
according to his appointment, on the morrow, Parson Rudall betook himself. Another clergyman, as it
appeared, had been invited to meet him, who, very
soon after his arrival, proposed a walk together in the
pleasance, on the pretext of showing him, as a
stranger, the walks and trees, until the dinner-bell
should strike. There, with much prolixity; and with
many a solemn pause, his brother minister proceeded
to "unfold the mystery."

A singular infelicity, he declared, had befallen
young Master Bligh, once the hopeful heir of his
parents and of the lands of Botathen. Whereas he
had been from childhood a blithe and merry boy,
"the gladness," like Isaac of old, of his father's age,
he had suddenly, and of late, become morose and
silent—nay, even austere and stern—dwelling apart,

always solemn, often in tears. The lad had at first repulsed all questions as to the origin of this great change, but of late he had yielded to the importune researches of his parents, and had disclosed the secret cause. It appeared that he resorted every day, by a pathway across the fields, to this very clergyman's house, who had charge of his education, and grounded him in the studies suitable to his age. In the course of his daily walk he had to pass a certain heath or down where the road wound along through tall blocks of granite with open spaces of grassy sward between. There in a certain spot, and always in one and the same place, the lad declared that he encountered, every day, a woman with a pale and troubled face, clothed in a long loose garment of frieze, with one hand always stretched forth, and the other pressed against her side. Her name, he said, was Dorothy Dinglet, for he had known her well from his childhood, and she often used to come to his parents' house; but that which troubled him was, that she had now been dead three years, and he himself had been with the neighbours at her burial; so that, as the youth alleged, with great simplicity, since he had seen her body laid in the grave, this that he saw every day must needs be her soul or ghost. "Questioned again and again," said the clergyman, "he never contradicts himself; but he relates the same and the simple tale as a thing that cannot be gain-said.

Indeed, the lad's observance is keen and calm for a
boy of his age. The hair of the appearance, sayeth he,
is not like anything alive, but it is so soft and light
that it seemeth to melt away while you look; but her
eyes are set, and never blink—no, not when the sun
shineth full upon her face. She maketh no steps, but
seemeth to swim along the top of the grass; and her
hand, which is stretched out alway, seemeth to point
at something far away, out of sight. It is her contin-
ual coming; for she never faileth to meet him, and to
pass on, that hath quenched his spirits; and although
he never seeth her by night, yet cannot he get his
natural rest.

"Thus far the clergyman; whereupon the dinner-
clock did sound, and we went into the house. After
dinner, when young Master Bligh had withdrawn
with his tutor, under excuse of their books, the parents did forthwith beset me as to my thoughts about
their son. Said I, warily, 'The case is strange but by
no means impossible. It is one that I will study, and
fear not to handle, if the lad will be free with me,
and fulfil all that I desire.' The mother was over-
joyed, but I perceived that old Mr Bligh turned pale,
and was downcast with some thought which, however, he did not express. Then they bade that Master
Bligh should be called to meet me in the pleasance
forthwith. The boy came, and he rehearsed to me his
tale with an open countenance, and, withal, a pretty

modesty of speech. Verily he seemed *ingenui vultus puer ingenuique pudoris*. Then I signified to him my purpose. 'Tomorrow,' said I, 'we will go together to the place; and if, as I doubt not, the woman shall appear, it will be for me to proceed according to knowledge, and by rules laid down in my books.' "

The unaltered scenery of the legend still survives, and, like the field of the forty footsteps in another history, the place is still visited by those who take interest in the supernatural tales of old. The pathway leads along a moorland waste, where large masses of rock stand up here and there from the grassy turf, and clumps of heath and gorse weave their tapestry of golden and purple garniture on every side. Amidst all these, and winding along between the rocks, is a natural footway worn by the scant, rare tread of the village traveller. Just midway, a somewhat larger stretch than usual of green sod expands, which is skirted by the path, and which is still identified as the legendary haunt of the phantom, by the name of Parson Rudall's Ghost.

But we must draw the record of the first interview between the minister and Dorothy from his own words. "We met," thus he writes, "in the pleasance very early, and before any others in the house were awake; and together the lad and myself proceeded towards the field. The youth was quite composed, and carried his Bible under his arm, from whence he read to me verses, which he said he had lately picked out, to have always in his mind. These were Job vii. 14, 'Thou scarest me with dreams, and terrifiest me through visions,' and Deuteronomy xxviii. 67, 'In the morning thou shalt say, Would to God it were evening, and in the evening thou shalt say, Would to God it were morning; for the fear of thine heart wherewith thou shalt fear, and for the sight of thine eyes which thou shalt see.'

"I was much pleased with the lad's ingenuity in these pious applications, but for mine own part I was somewhat anxious and out of cheer. For aught I knew this might be a *dœmonium meridianum*, the most stubborn spirit to govern and guide that any man can meet, and the most perilous withal. We had hardly reached the accustomed spot, when we both saw her at once gliding towards us; punctually as the ancient writers describe the motion of their 'lemures, which swoon along the ground, neither marking the sand nor bending the herbage.' The aspect of the woman was exactly that which had been related by the lad. There was the pale and stony face, the strange and misty hair, the eyes firm and fixed, that gazed, yet not on us, but on something that they saw far, far away; one hand and arm stretched out, and the other grasping the girdle of her waist. She floated along the field like a sail upon a stream, and glided past the spot where we stood, pausingly. But so deep was the awe that overcame me, as I stood there in the light of day, face to face with a human soul separate from her bones and flesh, that my heart and purpose both failed me. I had resolved to speak to the spectre in the appointed form of words, but I did not. I stood like one amazed and speechless, until she had passed clean out of sight. One thing remarkable came to pass. A spaniel dog, the favourite of young Master Bligh, had followed us, and lo! when the woman drew nigh, the poor creature began to yell and bark piteously, and ran backward and away, like a thing dismayed and appalled. We returned to the house, and after I had said all that I could to pacify the lad, and to soothe the aged people, I took my leave for that time, with a promise that when I had fulfilled certain business elsewhere, which I then alleged, I would return and take orders to assuage these disturbances and their cause.

"*January* 7, 1665. At my own house, I find, by my books, what is expedient to be done; and then Apage, Sathanas!

"*January* 9, 1665. This day I took leave of my wife and family, under pretext of engagements elsewhere, and made my secret journey to our diocesan city, wherein the good and venerable bishop then abode.

"*January* 10. *Deo gratias*, in safe arrival in Exeter; craved and obtained immediate audience of his lordship; pleading it was for counsel and admonition on a weighty and pressing cause; called to the presence; made obeisance; then and by command stated my case—the Botathen perplexity—which I moved with strong and earnest instances and solemn assev-erations of that which I had myself seen and heard. Demanded by his lordship, what was the succour that I had come to entreat at his hands. Replied, licence for my exorcism, that so I might, ministeri-ally, allay this spiritual visitant, and thus render to the living and the dead release from this surprise. 'But,' said our bishop, 'on what authority do you allege that I am entrusted with faculty so to do? Our Church, as is well known, hath abjured certain branches of her ancient power, on grounds of per-version and abuse.' 'Nay, my lord,' I humbly answered, 'under favour, the seventy-second of the canons ratified and enjoined on us, the clergy, anno Domini 1604, doth expressly provide, that "no min-ister, *unless he hath* the licence of his diocesan bishop, shall essay to exorcise a spirit, evil or good." There-fore it was,' I did here mildly allege, 'that I did not presume to enter on such a work without lawful privilege under your lordship's hand and seal.' Here-upon did our wise and learned bishop, sitting in his chair, condescend upon the theme at some length with many gracious interpretations from ancient writers and from Holy Scriptures, and I did humbly

rejoin and reply, till the upshot was that he did call in
his secretary and command him to draw the afore-
said faculty, forthwith and without further delay,
assigning him a form, insomuch that the matter was
incontinently done; and after I had disbursed into
the secretary's hands certain moneys for signitary
purposes, as the manner of such officers hath always
been, the bishop did himself affix his signature under
the *sigillum* of his see, and deliver the document into
my hands. When I knelt down to receive his benediction, he softly said, 'Let it be secret, Mr R. Weak
brethren! Weak brethren!' "

This interview with the bishop, and the success
with which he vanquished his lordship's scruples,
would seem to have confirmed Parson Rudall very
strongly in his own esteem, and to have invested him
with that courage which he evidently lacked at his
first encounter with the ghost.

The entries proceed: "*January* 11, 1665. Therewithal did I hasten home and prepare my instru-
ments, and cast my figures for the onset of the next
day. Took out my ring of brass, and put it on the
index-finger of my right hand, with the *scutum
Davidis* traced thereon.

"*January* 12, 1665. Rode into the gateway at Botathen, armed at all points, but not with Saul's armour,
and ready. There is danger from the demons, but so
there is in the surrounding air every day. At early

morning then, and alone—for so the usage ordains—
I betook me towards the field. It was void, and I had
thereby due time to prepare. First I paced and measured out my circle on the grass. Then I did mark my
pentacle in the very midst, and at the intersection of
the five angles I did set up and fix my crutch of *raun*
[rowan]. Lastly, I took my station south, at the true
line of the meridian, and stood facing due north. I
waited and watched for a long time. At last there was
a kind of trouble in the air, a soft and rippling sound,
and all at once the shape appeared, and came on
towards me gradually. I opened my parchment-scroll,
and read aloud the command. She paused, and
seemed to waver and doubt; stood still; then I
rehearsed the sentence again, sounding out every syllable like a chant. She drew near my ring, but halted
at first outside, on the brink. I sounded again, and
now at the third time I gave the signal in Syriac—the
speech which is used, they say, where such ones
dwell and converse in thoughts that glide.

"She was at last obedient, and swam into the midst
of the circle, and there stood still, suddenly. I saw,
moreover, that she drew back her pointing hand. All
this while I do confess that my knees shook under
me, and the drops of sweat ran down my flesh like
rain. But now, although face to face with the spirit,
my heart grew calm, and my mind was composed. I
knew that the pentacle would govern her, and the

ring must bind, until I gave the word. Then I called to mind the rule laid down of old, that no angel or fiend, no spirit, good or evil, will ever speak until they have been first spoken to. *N.B.* This is the great law of prayer. God Himself will not yield reply until man hath made vocal entreaty, once and again. So I went on to demand, as the books advise; and the phantom made answer, willingly. Questioned wherefore not at rest. Unquiet, because of a certain sin. Asked what, and by whom. Revealed it; but it is *sub sigillo*, and therefore *nefas dictu*; more anon. Enquired, what sign she could give that she was a true spirit and not a false fiend. Stated, before next Yule-tide a fearful pestilence would lay waste the land and myriads of souls would be loosened from their flesh, until, as she piteously said, 'our valleys will be full.' Asked again, why she so terrified the lad. Replied: 'It is the law: we must seek a youth or a maiden of clean life, and under age, to receive messages and admonitions.' We conversed with many more words, but it is not lawful for me to set them down. Pen and ink would degrade and defile the thoughts she uttered, and which my mind received that day. I broke the ring and she passed, but to return once more next day. At even-song, a long discourse with that ancient transgressor, Mr B. Great horror and remorse; entire atonement and penance; whatsoever I enjoin; full acknowledgement before pardon.

"*January* 13, 1665. At sunrise I was again in the field. She came in at once, and, as it seemed, with freedom. Enquired if she knew my thoughts, and what I was going to relate? Answered, 'Nay, we only know what we perceive and hear; we cannot see the heart.' Then I rehearsed the penitent words of the man she had come up to denounce, and the satisfaction he would perform. Then said she, 'Peace in our midst.' I went through the proper forms of dismissal, and fulfilled all as it was set down and written in my memoranda; and then, with certain fixed rites, I did dismiss that troubled ghost, until she peacefully withdrew, gliding towards the west. Neither did she ever afterward appear, but was allayed until she shall come in her second flesh to the valley of Armageddon on the last day."

These quaint and curious details from the "diurnal" of a simple-hearted clergyman of the seventeenth century appear to betoken his personal persuasion of the truth of what he saw and said, although the statements are strongly tinged with what some may term the superstition, and others the excessive belief, of those times. It is a singular fact, however, that the canon which authorizes exorcism under episcopal licence is still a part of the ecclesiastical law of the Anglican Church, although it might have a singular effect on the nerves of certain of our bishops if their clergy were to resort to them for the faculty which Parson Rudall obtained. The general facts stated in his diary are to this day matters of belief in that neighbourhood; and it has been always accounted a strong proof of the veracity of the Parson and the Ghost, that the plague, fatal to so many thousands, did break out in London at the close of that very year. We may well excuse a triumphant entry, on a subsequent page of the "diurnal," with the date of July 10, 1665: "How sorely must the infidels and heretics of this generation be dismayed when they know that this Black Death, which is now swallowing its thousands in the streets of the great city, was foretold six months agone, under the exorcisms of a country minister, by a visible and suppliant ghost! And what pleasures and improvements do such deny themselves who scorn and avoid all opportunity of intercourse with souls separate, and the spirits, glad and sorrowful, which inhabit the unseen world!"

Thurnley Abbey

[PERCEVAL LANDON]

The growth of technology—most particularly of the gas and then electric light—could not help but have an effect on the weird tale. A great consciousness of "this modern age" grew up in the culture, and so among writers. In this chilling story from the pen of a correspondent for the Times, *modernity collides with the supernatural, but not to the former's advantage.*

Three years ago I was on my way out to the East, and as an extra day in London was of some importance, I took the Friday evening mail-train to Brindisi instead of the usual Thursday morning Marseilles express. Many people shrink from the long forty-eight-hour train journey through Europe, and the subsequent rush across the Mediterranean on the nineteen-knot *Isis* or *Osiris*; but there is really very little discomfort on either the train or the mail-boat, and unless there is actually nothing for me to do, I always like to save the extra day and a half in London before I say goodbye to her for one of my longer tramps. This time—it was early, I remember, in the shipping season, probably about the beginning of September—there were few passengers, and I had a compartment in the P. & O. Indian express to myself all the way from Calais. All Sunday I watched the blue waves dimpling the Adriatic, and the pale rosemary along the cuttings; the plain white towns, with their flat roofs and their bold "duomos," and the grey-green gnarled olive orchards of Apulia. The journey was just like any other. We ate in the dining-car as often and as long as we decently could. We slept after luncheon; we dawdled the afternoon away with yellow-backed novels; sometimes we exchanged platitudes in the smoking-room, and it was there that I met Alastair Colvin.

Colvin was a man of middle height, with a res-olute, well-cut jaw; his hair was turning grey; his moustache was sun-whitened, otherwise he was clean-shaven—obviously a gentleman, and obviously also a preoccupied man. He had no great wit. When spoken to, he made the usual remarks in the right way, and I dare say he refrained from banalities only because he spoke less than the rest of us; most of the time he buried himself in the Wagon-lit Company's time-table, but seemed unable to concentrate his attention on any one page of it. He found that I had been over the Siberian railway, and for a quarter of an hour he discussed it with me. Then he lost interest in it, and rose to go to his compartment. But he came back again very soon, and seemed glad to pick up the conversation again.

Of course this did not seem to me to be of any importance. Most travellers by train become a trifle infirm of purpose after thirty-six hours' rattling. But Colvin's restless way I noticed in somewhat marked contrast with the man's personal importance and dignity; especially ill suited was it to his finely made large hand with strong, broad, regular nails and its few lines. As I looked at his hand I noticed a long, deep, and recent scar of ragged shape. However, it is absurd to pretend that I thought anything was unusual. I went off at five o'clock on Sunday afternoon to sleep away the hour or two that had still to be got through before we arrived at Brindisi.

Once there, we few passengers transhipped our hand baggage, verified our berths—there were only a score of us in all—and then, after an aimless ramble of half an hour in Brindisi, we returned to dinner at the Hôtel International, not wholly surprised that the town had been the death of Virgil. If I remember rightly, there is a gaily painted hall at the International—I do not wish to advertise anything, but there is no other place in Brindisi at which to await the coming of the mails—and after dinner I was looking with awe at a trellis overgrown with blue vines, when Colvin moved across the room to my table. He picked up *Il Secolo*, but almost immediately gave up the pretence of reading it. He turned squarely to me and said:

"Would you do me a favour?"

One doesn't do favours to stray acquaintances on Continental expresses without knowing something more of them than I knew of Colvin. But I smiled in a noncommittal way, and asked him what he wanted. I wasn't wrong in part of my estimate of him; he said bluntly:

"Will you let me sleep in your cabin on the *Osiris*?" And he coloured a little as he said it.

Now, there is nothing more tiresome than having to put up with a stable-companion at sea, and I asked him rather pointedly:

"Surely there is room for all of us?" I thought that perhaps he had been partnered off with some mangy Levantine, and wanted to escape from him at all hazards.

Colvin, still somewhat confused, said: "Yes; I am in a cabin by myself. But you would do me the greatest favour if you would allow me to share yours."

This was all very well, but, besides the fact that I always sleep better when alone, there had been some recent thefts on board English liners, and I hesitated, frank and honest and self-conscious as Colvin was. Just then the mail-train came in with a clatter and a rush of escaping steam, and I asked him to see me again about it on the boat when we started. He answered me curtly—I suppose he saw the mistrust in my manner—"I am a member of White's." I smiled to myself as he said it, but I remembered in a moment that the man—if he were really what he claimed to be, and I make no doubt that he was — must have been sorely put to it before he urged the fact as a guarantee of his respectability to a total stranger at a Brindisi hotel.

That evening, as we cleared the red and green harbour-lights of Brindisi, Colvin explained. This is his story in his own words.

"When I was travelling in India some years ago, I made the acquaintance of a youngish man in the Woods and Forests. We camped out together for a week, and I found him a pleasant companion. John Broughton was a light-hearted soul when off duty, but a steady and capable man in any of the small emergencies that continually arise in that department. He was liked and trusted by the natives, and though a trifle over-pleased with himself when he escaped to civilization at Simla or Calcutta, Broughton's future was well assured in Government service, when a fair-sized estate was unexpectedly left to him, and he joyfully shook the dust of the Indian plains from his feet and returned to England. For five years he drifted about London. I saw him now and then. We dined together about every eighteen months, and I could trace pretty exactly the gradual sickening of Broughton with a merely idle life. He then set out on a couple of long voyages, returned as restless as before, and at last told me that he had decided to marry and settle down at his place, Thurnley Abbey, which had long been empty. He spoke about looking after the property and standing for his constituency in the usual way. Vivien Wilde, his fiancée, had, I suppose, begun to take him in hand. She was a pretty girl with a deal of fair hair and rather an exclusive manner; deeply religious in a narrow school, she was still kindly and high-spirited, and I thought that Broughton was in luck. He was quite happy and full of information about his future.

"Among other things, I asked him about Thurnley Abbey. He confessed that he hardly knew the place. The last tenant, a man called Clarke, had lived in one wing for fifteen years and seen no one. He had been a miser and a hermit. It was the rarest thing for a light to be seen at the Abbey after dark. Only the barest necessities of life were ordered, and the tenant himself received them at the side-door. His one half-caste manservant, after a month's stay in the house, had abruptly left without warning, and had returned to the Southern States. One thing Broughton complained bitterly about: Clarke had wilfully spread the rumour among the villagers that the Abbey was haunted, and had even condescended to play childish tricks with spirit-lamps and salt in order to scare trespassers away at night. He had been detected in the act of this tomfoolery, but the story spread, and no one, said Broughton, would venture near the house except in broad daylight. The haunt-edness of Thurnley Abbey was now, he said with a grin, part of the gospel of the countryside, but he and his young wife were going to change all that. Would I propose myself any time I liked? I, of course, said I would, and equally, of course, intended to do nothing of the sort without a definite invita-tion.

"The house was put in thorough repair, though not a stick of the old furniture and tapestry were removed. Floors and ceilings were relaid: the roof was made watertight again, and the dust of half a century was scoured out. He showed me some pho-tographs of the place. It was called an Abbey, though as a matter of fact it had been only the infirmary of the long-vanished Abbey of Closter some five miles away. The larger part of this building remained as it had been in pre-Reformation days, but a wing had been added in Jacobean times, and that part of the house had been kept in something like repair by Mr Clarke. He had in both the ground and first floors set a heavy timber door, strongly barred with iron, in the passage between the earlier and the Jacobean parts of the house, and had entirely neglected the former. So there had been a good deal of work to be done.

"Broughton, whom I saw in London two or three times about this period, made a deal of fun over the positive refusal of the workmen to remain after sundown. Even after the electric light had been put into every room, nothing would induce them to remain, though, as Broughton observed, electric light was death on ghosts. The legend of the Abbey's ghosts had gone far and wide, and the men would take no risks. They went home in batches of five and six, and even during the daylight hours there was an inordinate amount of talking between one and another, if either happened to be out of sight of his companion. On the whole, though nothing of any sort or kind had been conjured up even by their heated imaginations during their five months' work upon the Abbey, the belief in the ghosts was rather strengthened than otherwise in Thurnley because of the men's confessed nervousness, and local tradition declared itself in favour of the ghost of an immured nun.

" 'Good old nun!' said Broughton.

"I asked him whether in general he believed in the possibility of ghosts, and, rather to my surprise, he said that he couldn't say he entirely disbelieved in them. A man in India had told him one morning in camp that he believed that his mother was dead in England, as her vision had come to his tent the night before. He had not been alarmed, but had said nothing, and the figure vanished again. As a matter of fact, the next possible dak-walla brought on a telegram announcing the mother's death. 'There the thing was,' said Broughton. But at Thurnley he was practical enough. He roundly cursed the idiotic selfishness of Clarke, whose silly antics had caused all the inconvenience. At the same time, he couldn't refuse to sympathize to some extent with the ignorant workmen. "My own idea,' said he, 'is that if a ghost ever does come in one's way, one ought to speak to it.'

"I agreed. Little as I knew of the ghost world and its conventions, I had always remembered that a spook was in honour bound to wait to be spoken to. It didn't seem much to do, and I felt that the sound of one's own voice would at any rate reassure oneself as to one's wakefulness. But there are few ghosts outside Europe—few, that is, that a white man can see—and I had never been troubled with any. However, as I have said, I told Broughton that I agreed.

"So the wedding took place, and I went to it in a

tall hat which I bought for the occasion, and the new Mrs Broughton smiled very nicely at me afterwards. As it had to happen, I took the Orient Express that evening and was not in England again for nearly six months. Just before I came back I got a letter from Broughton. He asked if I could see him in London or come to Thurnley, as he thought I should be better able to help him than anyone else he knew. His wife sent a nice message to me at the end, so I was reassured about at least one thing. I wrote from Budapest that I would come and see him at Thurnley two days after my arrival in London, and as I sauntered out of the Pannonia into the Kerepesi Utcza to post my letters, I wondered of what earthly service I could be to Broughton. I had been out with him after tiger on foot, and I could imagine few men better able at a pinch to manage their own business. However, I had nothing to do, so after dealing with some small accumulations of business during my absence, I packed a kit-bag and departed to Euston.

"I was met by Broughton's great limousine at Thurnley Road station, and after a drive of nearly seven miles we echoed through the sleepy streets of Thurnley village, into which the main gates of the park thrust themselves, splendid with pillars and spreadeagles and tom-cats rampant atop of them. I never was a herald, but I know that the Broughtons have the right to supporters—Heaven knows why! From the gates a quadruple avenue of beech-trees led inwards for a quarter of a mile. Beneath them a neat strip of fine turf edged the road and ran back until the poison of the dead beech-leaves killed it under the trees. There were many wheel-tracks on the road, and a comfortable little pony trap jogged past me laden with a country parson and his wife and daughter. Evidently there was some garden party going on at the Abbey. The road dropped away to the right at the end of the avenue, and I could see the Abbey across a wide pasturage and a broad lawn thickly dotted with guests.

"The end of the building was plain. It must have been almost mercilessly austere when it was first built, but time had crumbled the edges and toned the stone down to an orange-lichened grey wherever it showed behind its curtain of magnolia, jasmine, and ivy. Further on was the three-storied Jacobean house, tall and handsome. There had not been the slightest attempt to adapt the one to the other, but the kindly ivy had glossed over the touching-point. There was a tall flèche in the middle of the building, surmounting a small bell tower. Behind the house there rose the mountainous verdure of Spanish chestnuts all the way up the hill.

"Broughton had seen me coming from afar, and walked across from his other guests to welcome me before turning me over to the butler's care. This man was sandy-haired and rather inclined to be talkative. He could, however, answer hardly any questions about the house; he had, he said, only been there three weeks. Mindful of what Broughton had told me, I made no enquiries about ghosts, though the room into which I was shown might have justified anything. It was a very large low room with oak beams projecting from the white ceiling. Every inch of the walls, including the doors, was covered with tapestry, and a remarkably fine Italian fourpost bedstead, heavily draped, added to the darkness and dignity of the place. All the furniture was old, well made, and dark. Underfoot there was a plain green pile carpet, the only new thing about the room except the electric light fittings and the jugs and basins. Even the looking-glass on the dressing-table was an old pyramidal Venetian glass set in heavy repoussé frame of tarnished silver.

"After a few minutes' cleaning up, I went downstairs and out upon the lawn, where I greeted my hostess. The people gathered there were of the usual country type, all anxious to be pleased and roundly curious as to the new master of the Abbey. Rather to my surprise, and quite to my pleasure, I rediscovered Glenham, whom I had known well in old days in Barotseland: he lived quite close, as, he remarked with a grin, I ought to have known. 'But,' he added,

'I don't live in a place like this.' He swept his hand to the long, low lines of the Abbey in obvious admiration, and then, to my intense interest, muttered beneath his breath, 'Thank God!' He saw that I had overheard him, and turning to me said decidedly, 'Yes, "thank God" I said, and I meant it. I wouldn't live at the Abbey for all Broughton's money.'

" 'But surely,' I demurred, 'you know that old Clarke was discovered in the very act of setting light to his bug-a-boos?'

"Glenham shrugged his shoulders. 'Yes, I know about that. But there is something wrong with the place still. All I can say is that Broughton is a different man since he has lived here. I don't believe that he will remain much longer. But—you're staying here?—well, you'll hear all about it tonight. There's a big dinner, I understand.' The conversation turned off to old reminiscences, and Glenham soon after had to go.

"Before I went to dress that evening I had twenty minutes' talk with Broughton in his library. There was no doubt that the man was altered, gravely altered. He was nervous and fidgety, and I found him looking at me only when my eye was off him. I naturally asked him what he wanted of me. I told him I would do anything I could, but that I couldn't conceive what he lacked that I could provide. He said with a lustreless smile that there was, however, something, and that he would tell me the following morning. It struck me that he was somehow ashamed of himself, and perhaps ashamed of the part he was asking me to play. However, I dismissed the subject from my mind and went up to dress in my palatial room. As I shut the door a draught blew out the Queen of Sheba from the wall, and I noticed that the tapestries were not fastened to the wall at the bottom. I have always held very practical views about spooks, and it has often seemed to me that the slow waving in firelight of loose tapestry upon a wall would account for ninety-nine per cent of the stories one hears. Certainly the dignified undulation of this lady with her attendants and huntsmen—one of whom was untidily cutting the throat of a fallow deer upon the very steps on which King Solomon, a grey-faced Flemish nobleman with the order of the Golden Fleece, awaited his fair visitor—gave colour to my hypothesis.

"Nothing much happened at dinner. The people were very much like those of the garden party. A young woman next to me seemed anxious to know what was being read in London. As she was far more familiar than I with the most recent magazines and literary supplements, I found salvation in being myself instructed in the tendencies of modern fiction. All true art, she said, was shot through and through with melancholy. How vulgar were the attempts at wit that marked so many modern books! From the beginning of literature it had always been tragedy that embodied the highest attainment of every age. To call such works morbid merely begged the question. No thoughtful man—she looked sternly at me through the steel rim of her glasses—could fail to agree with me. Of course, as one would, I immediately and properly said that I slept with Pett Ridge and Jacobs under my pillow at night, and that if *Jorrocks* weren't quite so large and cornery, I would add him to the company. She hadn't read any of them, so I was saved—for a time. But I remember grimly that she said that the dearest wish of her life was to be in some awful and soul-freezing situation of horror, and I remember that she dealt hardly with the hero of Nat Paynter's vampire story, between nibbles at her brown-bread ice. She was a cheerless soul, and I couldn't help thinking that if there were many such in the neighbourhood, it was not surprising that old Glenham had been stuffed with some nonsense or other about the Abbey. Yet nothing could well have been less creepy than the glitter of silver and glass, and the subdued lights and cackle of conversation all round the dinner-table.

"After the ladies had gone I found myself talking to the rural dean. He was a thin, earnest man, who at once turned the conversation to old Clarke's buf-

fooneries. But, he said, Mr Broughton had introduced such a new and cheerful spirit, not only into
the Abbey, but, he might say, into the whole neighbourhood, that he had great hopes that the ignorant
superstitions of the past were from henceforth des-
tined to oblivion. Thereupon his other neighbour, a
portly gentleman of independent means and position, audibly remarked 'Amen,' which damped the
rural dean, and we talked of partridges past, partridges present, and pheasants to come. At the other
end of the table Broughton sat with a couple of his
friends, red-faced hunting men. Once I noticed that
they were discussing me, but I paid no attention to it
at the time. I remembered it a few hours later.

"By eleven all the guests were gone, and
Broughton, his wife, and I were alone together under
the fine plaster ceiling of the Jacobean drawing-
room. Mrs Broughton talked about one or two of
the neighbours, and then, with a smile, said that she
knew I would excuse her, shook hands with me, and
went off to bed. I am not very good at analysing
things, but I felt that she talked a little uncomfortably
and with a suspicion of effort, smiled rather conven-
tionally, and was obviously glad to go. These things
seem trifling enough to repeat, but I had throughout
the faint feeling that everything was not square.
Under the circumstances, this was enough to set me
wondering what on earth the service could be that I

was to render—wondering also whether the whole business were not some ill-advised jest in order to make me come down from London for a mere shooting-party.

"Broughton said little after she had gone. But he was evidently labouring to bring the conversation round to the so-called haunting of the Abbey. As soon as I saw this, of course I asked him directly about it. He then seemed at once to lose interest in the matter. There was no doubt about it: Broughton was somehow a changed man, and to my mind he had changed in no way for the better. Mrs Broughton seemed no sufficient cause. He was clearly very fond of her, and she of him. I reminded him that he was going to tell me what I could do for him in the morning, pleaded my journey, lighted a candle, and went upstairs with him. At the end of the passage leading into the old house he grinned weakly and said, 'Mind, if you see a ghost, do talk to it; you said you would.' He stood irresolutely a moment and then turned away. At the door of his dressing-room he paused once more: 'I'm here,' he called out, 'if you should want anything. Good night,' and he shut his door.

"I went along the passage to my room, undressed, switched on a lamp beside my bed, read a few pages of *The Jungle Book*, and then, more than ready for sleep, turned the light off and went fast asleep.

"Three hours later I woke up. There was not a breath of wind outside. There was not even a flicker of light from the fireplace. As I lay there, an ash tinkled slightly as it cooled, but there was hardly a gleam of the dullest red in the grate. An owl cried among the silent Spanish chestnuts on the slope outside. I idly reviewed the events of the day, hoping that I should fall off to sleep again before I reached dinner. But at the end I seemed as wakeful as ever. There was no help for it. I must read my *Jungle Book* again till I felt ready to go off, so I fumbled for the pear at the end of the cord that hung down inside the bed, and I switched on the bedside lamp. The sudden glory dazzled me for a moment. I felt under my pillow for my book with half-shut eyes. Then, growing used to the light, I happened to look down to the foot of my bed.

"I can never tell you really what happened then. Nothing I could ever confess in the most abject words could even faintly picture to you what I felt. I know that my heart stopped dead, and my throat shut automatically. In one instinctive movement I crouched back up against the head-boards of the bed, staring at the horror. The movement set my heart going again, and the sweat dripped from every pore. I am not a particularly religious man, but I had always believed that God would never allow any supernatural appearance to present itself to man in such a guise and in such circumstances that harm, either bodily or mental, could result to him. I can only tell you that at that moment both my life and my reason rocked unsteadily on their seats."

The other *Osiris* passengers had gone to bed. Only he and I remained leaning over the starboard railing, which rattled uneasily now and then under the fierce vibration of the over-engined mail-boat. Far over, there were the lights of a few fishing-smacks riding out the night, and a great rush of white combing and seething water fell out and away from us overside. At last Colvin went on:

"Leaning over the foot of my bed, looking at me, was a figure swathed in a rotten and tattered veiling. This shroud passed over the head, but left both eyes and the right side, of the face bare. It then followed the line of the arm down to where the hand grasped the bed-end. The face was not entirely that of a skull, though the eyes and the flesh of the face were totally gone. There was a thin, dry skin drawn tightly over the features, and there was some skin left on the hand. One wisp of hair crossed the forehead. It was perfectly still. I looked at it, and it looked at me, and my brains turned dry and hot in my head. I had still got the pear of the electric lamp in my hand, and I played idly with it; only I dared not turn the light out again. I shut my eyes, only to open them in a hideous terror the same second. The thing had not moved. My heart was thumping, and the sweat cooled me as it evaporated. Another cinder tinkled in the grate, and a panel creaked in the wall.

"My reason failed me. For twenty minutes, or twenty seconds, I was able to think of nothing else but this awful figure, till there came, hurtling through the empty channels of my senses, the remembrance that Broughton and his friends had discussed me furtively at dinner. The dim possibility of its being a hoax stole gratefully into my unhappy mind, and once there, one's pluck came creeping back along a thousand tiny veins. My first sensation was one of blind unreasoning thankfulness that my brain was going to stand the trial. I am not a timid man, but the best of us needs some human handle to steady him in time of extremity, and in this faint but growing hope that after all it might be only a brutal hoax, I found the fulcrum that I needed. At last I moved.

"How I managed to do it I cannot tell you, but with one spring towards the foot of the bed I got within arm's-length and struck out one fearful blow with my fist at the thing. It crumbled under it, and my hand was cut to the bone. With a sickening revulsion after my terror, I dropped half-fainting across the end of the bed. So it was merely a foul trick after all. No doubt the trick had been played many a time before: no doubt Broughton and his friends had had some large bet among themselves as to what I should do when I discovered the gruesome thing. From my state of abject terror I found myself transported into an insensate anger. I shouted curses upon Broughton. I dived rather than climbed over the bed-end on to the sofa. I tore at the robed skeleton—how well the whole thing had been carried out, I thought—I broke the skull against the floor, and stamped upon its dry bones. I flung the head away under the bed, and rent the brittle bones of the trunk in pieces. I snapped the thin thigh-bones across my knee, and flung them in different directions. The shin-bones I set up against a stool and broke with my heel. I raged like a Berserker against the loathly thing, and stripped the ribs from the backbone and slung the breastbone against the cupboard. My fury increased as the work of destruction went on. I tore the frail rotten veil into twenty pieces, and the dust went up over everything, over the clean blotting-paper and the silver inkstand. At last my work was done. There was but a raffle of broken bones and strips of parchment and crumbling wool. Then, picking up a piece of the skull—it was the cheek and temple bone of the right side, I remember—I opened the door and went down the passage to Broughton's dressing-room. I remember still how my sweat-dripping pyjamas clung to me as I walked. At the door I kicked and entered.

"Broughton was in bed. He had already turned the light on and seemed shrunken and horrified. For a moment he could hardly pull himself together. Then I spoke. I don't know what I said. Only I know that from a heart full and over-full with hatred and contempt, spurred on by shame of my own recent cowardice, I let my tongue run on. He answered nothing. I was amazed at my own fluency. My hair still clung lankily to my wet temples, my hand was bleeding profusely, and I must have looked a strange sight. Broughton huddled himself up at the head of the bed just as I had. Still he made no answer, no defence. He seemed preoccupied with something besides my reproaches, and once or twice moistened his lips with his tongue. But he could say nothing though he moved his hands now and then, just as a baby who cannot speak moves its hands.

"At last the door into Mrs Broughton's room opened and she came in, white and terrified. 'What is it? What is it? Oh, in God's name! what is it?' she cried again and again, and then she went up to her husband and sat on the bed in her night-dress, and the two-faced me. I told her what the matter was. I spared her husband not a word for her presence there. Yet he seemed hardly to understand. I told the pair that I had spoiled their cowardly joke for them. Broughton looked up.

" 'I have smashed the foul thing into a hundred pieces," I said. Broughton licked his lips again and his mouth worked. 'By God!' I shouted, 'it would serve you right if I thrashed you within an inch of your life. I will take care that not a decent man or woman of my acquaintance ever speaks to you again. And there,' I added, throwing the broken piece of the skull upon the floor beside his bed, 'there is a souvenir for you, of your damned work tonight!'

"Broughton saw the bone, and in a moment it was his turn to frighten me. He squealed like a hare caught in a trap. He screamed and screamed till Mrs Broughton, almost as bewildered as myself, held on to him and coaxed him like a child to be quiet. But Broughton—and as he moved I thought that ten minutes ago I perhaps looked as terribly ill as he did—thrust her from him, and scrambled out of the bed on to the floor, and still screaming put out his hand to the bone. It had blood on it from my hand. He paid no attention to me whatever. In truth I said nothing. This was a new turn indeed to the horrors of the evening. He rose from the floor with the bone in his hand and stood silent. He seemed to be listening. 'Time, time, perhaps,' he muttered, and almost at the same moment fell at full length on the carpet, cutting his head against the fender. The bone flew from his hand and came to rest near the door. I picked Broughton up, haggard and broken, with blood over his face. He whispered hoarsely and quickly, 'Listen, listen!' We listened.

"After ten seconds' utter quiet, I seemed to hear something. I could not be sure, but at last there was no doubt. There was a quiet sound as of one moving along the passage. Little regular steps came towards us over the hard oak flooring. Broughton moved to where his wife sat, white and speechless, on the bed, and pressed her face into his shoulder.

"Then, the last thing that I could see as he turned the light out, he fell forward with his own head pressed into the pillow of the bed. Something in their company, something in their cowardice, helped me, and I faced the open doorway of the room, which was outlined fairly clearly against the dimly lighted passage. I put out one hand and touched Mrs Broughton's shoulder in the darkness. But at the last moment I too failed. I sank on my knees and put my face in the bed. Only we all heard. The footsteps came to the door, and there they stopped. The piece of bone was lying a yard inside the door. There was a rustle of moving stuff, and the thing was in the room. Mrs Broughton was silent: I could hear Broughton's voice praying, muffled in the pillow: I was cursing my own cowardice. Then the steps moved out again on the oak boards of the passage, and I heard the sounds dying away. In a flash of remorse I went to the door and looked out. At the end of the corridor I thought I saw something that moved away. A moment later the passage was empty. I stood with my forehead against the jamb of the door almost physically sick.

" 'You can turn the light on,' I said, and there was an answering flare. There was no bone at my feet. Mrs Broughton had fainted. Broughton was almost useless, and it took me ten minutes to bring her to. Broughton only said one thing worth remembering. For the most part he went on muttering prayers. But I was glad afterwards to recollect that he had said that thing. He said in a colourless voice, half as a question, half as a reproach, 'You didn't speak to her.'

"We spent the remainder of the night together. Mrs Broughton actually fell off into in a kind of sleep before dawn, but she suffered so horribly in her dreams that I shook her into consciousness again. Never was dawn so long in coming. Three or four times Broughton spoke to himself. Mrs Broughton would then just tighten her hold on his arm, but she could say nothing. As for me, I can honestly say that I grew worse as the hours passed and the light strengthened. The two violent reactions had battered down my steadiness of view, and I felt that the foundations of my life had been built upon the sand. I said nothing, and after binding up my hand with a towel, I did not move. It was better so. They helped me and I helped them, and we all three knew that our reason had gone very near to ruin that night. At last, when the light came in pretty strongly, and the birds outside were chattering and singing, we felt that we must do something. Yet we never moved. You might have thought that we should particularly dislike being found as we were by the servants: yet nothing of that kind mattered a straw, and an over-powering listlessness bound us as we sat, until Chapman, Broughton's man, actually knocked and opened the door. None of us moved. Broughton, speaking hardly and stiffly, said, 'Chapman you can come back in five minutes.' Chapman, was a discreet man, but it would have made no difference to us if he had carried his news to the 'room' at once.

"We looked at each other and I said I must go back. I meant to wait outside till Chapman returned. I simply dared not re-enter my bedroom alone. Broughton roused himself and said that he would come with me. Mrs Broughton agreed to remain in her own room for five minutes if the blinds were drawn up and all the doors left open.

"So Broughton and I, leaning stiffly one against the other, went down to my room. By the morning light that filtered past the blinds we could see our way, and I released the blinds. There was nothing wrong in the room from end to end, except smears of my own blood on the end of the bed, on the sofa, and on the carpet where I had torn the thing to pieces."

Colvin had finished his story. There was nothing to say. Seven bells stuttered out from the fo'c'sle, and the answering cry wailed through the darkness. I took him downstairs.

"Of course I am much better now, but it is a kindness of you to let me sleep in your cabin."

The Yellow Sign

[ROBERT W. CHAMBERS]

So far we have dealt with horrors more or less based upon authentic folklore. But as the 19th century neared its end, horrors invented purely from the imagination of the writer began to emerge. In a partial response to the ever increasing modernity around them, the "Decadents," themselves late Romantics, burrowed ever more deeply into the worlds within their own heads.

This story is set within a mythology invented wholly by the author (borrowing the name "Carcosa" from an Ambrose Bierce tale). Basically, the whole cycle revolves around a mysterious play, called The King in Yellow *(which also gave its title to the 1895 collection in which this piece first appeared). Although we are never given much information about the play (save its setting in "Lost Carcosa" and a few of its characters), what little we do know is upsetting in the extreme; those who read it, cover to cover, are doomed to madness or worse, as happens here. Not only are the tales frightening in their own right: they have inspired a host of other horror and fantasy writers, from H. P. Lovecraft down to*

Paul Zimmer, who have used various Carcosan motifs in their own work.

Along the shore the cloud waves break,
The twin suns sink behind the lake,
The shadows lengthen
   In Carcosa

Strange is the night where black stars rise,
And strange moons circle through the skies,
But stranger still is
   Lost Carcosa

Songs that the Hyades shall sing,
Where flap the tatters of the King,
Must die unheard in
   Dim Carcosa

Song of my soul, my voice is dead,
Die though, unsung, as tears unshed
Shall dry and die in
   Lost Carcosa.

   Cassilda's Song in *The King in Yellow*
   act 1, scene 2.

I

"Let the red dawn surmise
What we shall do,
When this blue starlight dies
And all is through."

There are so many things which are impossible to explain! Why should certain chords in music make me think of the brown and golden tints of autumn foliage? Why should the Mass of Sainte Cécile send my thoughts wandering among caverns whose walls blaze with ragged masses of virgin silver? What was it in the roar and turmoil of Broadway at six o'clock that flashed before my eyes the picture of a still Breton forest where sunlight filtered through spring foliage and Sylvia bent, half curiously, half tenderly, over a small green lizard, murmuring: "To think that this is also a little ward of God!"

When I first saw the watchman his back was toward me. I looked at him indifferently until he went into the church. I paid no more attention to him than I had to any other man who lounged through Washington Square that morning, and when I shut my window and turned back into my studio I had forgotten him. Late in the afternoon, the day being warm, I raised the window again and leaned out to get a sniff of the air. A man was standing in the courtyard of the church, and I noticed him again with as little interest as I had that morning. I looked across the square to where the fountain was playing and then, with my mind filled with vague impressions of trees, asphalt drives, and the moving groups of nursemaids and holidaymakers, I started to walk back to my easel. As I turned, my listless glance included the man below in the churchyard. His face was toward me now, and with a perfectly involuntary movement I bent to see it. At the same moment he raised his head and looked at me. Instantly I thought of a coffin-worm. Whatever it was about the man that repelled me I did not know, but the impression of a plump white grave-worm was so intense and nauseating that I must have shown it in my expression, for he turned his puffy face away with a movement which made me think of a disturbed grub in a chestnut.

I went back to my easel and motioned the model to resume her pose. After working awhile I was satisfied that I was spoiling what I had done as rapidly as possible, and I took up a palette knife and scraped the color out again. The flesh tones were sallow and unhealthy, and I did not understand how I could have painted such sickly color into a study which before that had glowed with healthy tones.

I looked at Tessie. She had not changed, and the

clear flush of health dyed her neck and cheeks as I frowned.

"Is it something I've done?" she said.

"No—I've made a mess of this arm, and for the life of me I can't see how I came to paint such mud as that into the canvas," I replied.

"Don't I pose well?" she insisted.

"Of course, perfectly."

"Then it's not my fault?"

"No. It's my own."

"I'm very sorry," she said.

I told her she could rest while I applied rag and turpentine to the plague spot on my canvas, and she went off to smoke a cigarette and look over the illustrations in the *Courier Français*.

I did not know whether it was something in the turpentine or a defect in the canvas, but the more I scrubbed the more that gangrene seemed to spread. I worked like a beaver to get it out, and yet the disease appeared to creep from limb to limb of the study before me. Alarmed I strove to arrest it, but now the color on the breast changed and the whole figure seemed to absorb the infection as a sponge soaks up water. Vigorously I plied palette knife, turpentine, and scraper, thinking all the time what a seance I should hold with Duval who had sold me the canvas; but soon I noticed that it was not the canvas which was defective nor yet the colors of Edward.

"It must be the turpentine," I thought angrily, "or else my eyes have become so blurred and confused by the afternoon light that I can't see straight." I called Tessie, the model. She came and leaned over my chair blowing rings of smoke into the air.

"What *have* you been doing to it?" she exclaimed.

"Nothing," I growled, "it must be this turpentine!"

"What a horrible color it is now," she continued. "Do you think my flesh resembles green cheese?"

"No, I don't," I said angrily, "did you ever know me to paint like that before?"

"No, indeed!"

"Well, then!"

"It must be the turpentine, or something," she admitted.

She slipped on a Japanese robe and walked to the window. I scraped and rubbed until I was tired and finally picked up my brushes and hurled them through the canvas with a forcible expression, the tone alone of which reached Tessie's ears.

Nevertheless she promptly began: "That's it! Swear and act silly and ruin your brushes! You have been three weeks on that study, and now look! What's the good of ripping the canvas? What creatures artists are!

I felt about as much ashamed as I usually did after such an outbreak, and I turned the ruined canvas to the wall. Tessie helped me clean my brushes, and then danced away to dress. From the screen she regaled me with bits of advice concerning whole or partial loss of temper, until, thinking, perhaps, I had been tormented sufficiently, she came out to implore me to button her waist where she could not reach it on the shoulder.

"Everything went wrong from the time you came back from the window and talked about that horrid-looking man you saw in the churchyard," she announced.

"Yes, he probably bewitched the picture," I said, yawning. I looked at my watch.

"It's after six, I know," said Tessie, adjusting her hat before the mirror.

"Yes," I replied, "I didn't mean to keep you so long." I leaned out the window but recoiled with disgust, for the young man with the pasty face stood below in the churchyard. Tessie saw my gesture of disapproval and leaned from the window.

"Is that the man you don't like?" she whispered.

I nodded.

"I can't see his face, but he does look fat and soft. Someway or other," she continued, looking at me, "he reminds me of a dream—an awful dream I once had. Or," she mused looking down at her shapely shoes, "was it a dream after all?"

"How should I know?" I smiled.

Tessie smiled in reply.

"You were in it," she said, "so perhaps you might know something about it."

"Tessie! Tessie!" I protested, "don't you dare flatter by saying you dream about me!"

"But I did," she insisted; "shall I tell you about it?"

"Go ahead," I replied, lighting a cigarette.

Tessie leaned back on the open window-sill and began very seriously.

"One night last winter I was lying in bed thinking about nothing at all in particular. I had been posing for you and I was tired out, yet it seemed impossible for me to sleep. I heard the bells in the city ring ten, eleven, and midnight. I must have fallen asleep about midnight because I don't remember hearing the bells after that. It seemed to me that I had scarcely closed my eyes when I dreamed that something impelled me to go to the window. I rose, and raising the sash, leaned out. Twenty-fifth Street was deserted as far as I could see. I began to be afraid; everything outside seemed so—so black and uncomfortable. Then the sound of wheels in the distance came to my ears, and it seemed to me as though that was what I must wait for. Very slowly the wheels approached, and, finally, I could make out a vehicle moving along the street. It came nearer and nearer, and when it passed beneath my window I saw it was a hearse. Then, as I trembled with fear, the driver turned and looked straight at me. When I awoke I was standing by the open window shivering with cold, but the black-plumed hearse and the driver were gone. I dreamed this dream again in March last, and again awoke beside the open window. Last night the dream came again. You remember how it was raining; when I awoke, standing at the open window, my nightdress was soaked."

"But where did I come into the dream?" I asked.

"You—you were in the coffin; but you were not dead."

"In the coffin?"

"Yes."

"How did you know? Could you see me?"

"No; I only knew you were there."

"Had you been eating Welsh rarebits, or lobster salad?" I began laughing, but the girl interrupted me with a frightened cry.

"Hello! What's up?" I said, as she shrank into the embrasure by the window.

"The—the man below in the churchyard;—he drove the hearse."

"Nonsense," I said, but Tessie's eyes were wide with terror. I went to the window and looked out. The man was gone. "Come, Tessie," I urged, "don't be foolish. You have posed too long; you are nervous."

"Do you think I could forget that face?" she murmured. "Three times I saw that hearse pass below my window, and every time the driver turned and looked up at me. Oh, his face was so white and—and soft? It looked dead—it looked as if it had been dead a long time."

I induced the girl to sit down and swallow a glass of Marsala. Then I sat down beside her and tried to give her some advice.

"Look here, Tessie," I said, "you go to the country for a week or two, and you'll have no more dreams about hearses. You pose all day, and when night comes your nerves are upset. You can't keep this up. Then again, instead of going to bed when your day's work is done, you run off to picnics at Sulzer's Park, or go to the Eldorado or Coney Island, and when you come down here in the morning you are fagged out. There was no real hearse. That was a soft-shell crab dream."

She smiled faintly.

"What about the man in the churchyard?"

"Oh, he's an ordinary unhealthy, everyday creature."

"As true as my name is Tessie Reardon, I swear to you, Mr. Scott, that the face of the man below in the churchyard is the face of the man who drove the hearse!"

"What of it?" I said. "It's an honest trade."

"Then you think I *did* see a hearse?"

"Oh," I said diplomatically, "if you really did, it might not be unlikely that the man below drove it. There is nothing in that."

Tessie rose, unrolled her scented handkerchief, and taking a bit of gum from a knot in the hem, placed it in her mouth. Then drawing on her gloves she offered me her hand, with a frank, "Goodnight, Mr. Scott," and walked out.

II

The next morning, Thomas, the bellboy, brought me the *Herald* and a bit of news. The church next door had been sold. I thanked Heaven for it, not that being a Catholic I had any repugnance for the congregation next door, but because my nerves were shattered by a blatant exhorter, whose every word echoed through the aisle of the church as if it had been my own rooms, and who insisted on his r's with a nasal persistence which revolted my every instinct. Then, too, there as a fiend in human shape, an organist, who reeled off some of the grand old hymns with an interpretation of his own, and I longed for the blood of a creature who could play the doxology with an amendment of minor chords which one hears only in a quartet of very young undergraduates. I believe the minister was a good man, but when he bellowed: "And the Lorrrrd said unto Moses, the

Lorrrrd is a man of war; the Lorrrrd is his name. My wrath shall wax hot and I will kill you with the sworrrrd!" I wondered how many centuries of purgatory it would take to atone for such a sin.

"Who bought the property?" I asked Thomas.

"Nobody that I knows, sir. They do say the gent wot owns this 'ere 'Amilton flats was lookin' at it. 'E might be a bildin' more studios."

I walked to the window. The young man with the unhealthy face stood by the churchyard gate, and at the mere sight of him the same overwhelming repugnance took possession of me.

"By the way, Thomas," I said, "who is that fellow down there?"

Thomas sniffed. "That there worm, sir? 'E's night-watchman of the church, sir. 'E maikes me tired a-sittin' out all night on them steps and lookin' at you insultin' like. I'd a punched 'is 'ed, sir—beg pardon sir—"

"Go on, Thomas."

"One night a comin' 'ome with 'Arry, the other English boy, I sees 'im a sittin' there on them steps. We 'ad Molly and Jen with us, sir, the two girls on the tray service, an' 'e looks so insultin' at us that I up and sez: 'Wat you looking hat, you fat slug?'—beg pardon, sir, but that's 'ow I sez, sir. Then 'e don't say nothin' and I sez; 'Come out and I'll punch that puddin' 'ed.' Then I hopens the gate an' goes in, but

'e don't say nothin', only looks insultin' like. Then I
'its 'im one, but ugh! 'is 'ed was that cold and mushy
it ud sicken you to touch 'im."

"What did he do then?" I asked, curiously.

"'Im? Nawthin'."

"And you, Thomas?"

The young fellow flushed in embarrassment and
smiled uneasily.

"Mr. Scott, sir, I ain't no coward an' I can't make it
out at all why I run. I was with the 5th Lawncers, sir,
bugler at Tel-el-Kebir, an' was shot by the wells."

"You don't mean to say you ran away?"

"Yes, sir; I run."

"Why?"

"That's just what I want to know, sir. I grabbed
Molly an' run, an' the rest of us just as frightened as I."

"But what were they frightened at?"

Thomas refused to answer for a while, but now
my curiosity was aroused about the repulsive young
man below and I pressed him. Three years' sojourn
in America had not only modified Thomas's cock-
ney dialect but had given him the American's fear of
ridicule.

"You won't believe me, Mr. Scott, sir?"

"Yes, I will."

"You will lawf at me, sir?"

"Nonsense!"

He hesitated. "Well, sir, it's God's truth that when

I 'it 'im 'e grabbed me wrists, sir, and when I twisted 'is soft, mushy fist one of 'is fingers come off in me 'and."

The utter loathing and horror of Thomas's face must have been reflected in my own for he added:

"It's orful, an' now when I see 'im I just go away. 'E maikes me hill."

When Thomas had gone I went to the window. The man stood beside the church-railing with both hands on the gate, but I hastily retreated to my easel again, sickened and horrified, for I saw that the middle finger of his right hand was missing.

At nine o'clock Tessie appeared and vanished behind the screen with a merry "Good-morning, Mr. Scott." While she had reappeared and taken her pose upon the model-stand I started a new canvas much to her delight. She remained silent as long as I was on the drawing, but as soon as the scrape of the charcoal ceased and I took up my fixative she began to chatter.

"Oh, I had such a lovely time last night. We went to Tony Pastor's."

"Who are 'we'?" I demanded.

"Oh, Maggie, you know, Mr. Whyte's model, and Pinkie McCormick—we call her Pinkie because she's got that beautiful red hair you artists like so much—and Lizzie Burke."

I sent a shower of fixative over the canvas and said: "Well, go on."

"We saw Kelly and Baby Barnes the skirt-dancer and—and all the rest. I made a mash."

"Then you have gone back on me, Tessie?"

She laughed and shook her head.

"He's Lizzie Burke's brother, Ed. He's a perfect gen'l'man."

I felt constrained to give her some parental advice concerning mashing, which she took with a bright smile.

"Oh, I can take care of a strange mash," she said, examining her chewing gum, "but Ed is different. Lizzie is my best friend."

Then she related how Ed had come back from the stocking mill in Lowell, Massachusetts, to find her and Lizzie grown up, and what an accomplished young man he was, and how he thought nothing of squandering half a dollar for ice-cream and oysters to celebrate his entry as clerk into the woolen department of Macy's. Before she finished I began to paint, and she resumed the pose, smiling and chattering like a sparrow. By noon I had the study fairly well rubbed in and Tessie came to look at it.

"That's better," she said.

I thought so too, and ate my lunch with a satisfied feeling that all was going well. Tessie spread her lunch on a drawing table opposite me and we drank our claret from the same bottle and lighted our cigarettes from the same match. I was very much attached to Tessie. I had watched her shoot up into a slender but exquisitely formed woman from a frail, awkward child. She had posed for me during the last three years, and among all my models she was my favorite. It would have troubled me very much indeed had she become "tough" or "fly," as the phrase goes, but I had never noticed any deterioration of her manner, and felt at heart that she was all right. She and I never discussed morals at all, and I had no intention of doing so, partly because I had none myself, and partly because I knew she would do what she liked in spite of me. Still I did hope she would steer clear of complications, because I wished her well, and then also I had a selfish desire to retain the best model I had. I knew that mashing, as she termed it, had no significance with girls like Tessie, and that such things in America did not resemble in the least the same things in Paris. Yet, having lived with my eyes open, I also knew that somebody would take Tessie away some day in one manner or another, and though I professed to myself that marriage was nonsense, I sincerely hoped that, in this case, there would be a priest at the end of the vista. I am a Catholic. When I listen to high mass, when I sign myself, I feel that everything, including myself, is more cheerful, and when I confess, it does me good. A man who lives as much alone as I do, must confess to somebody. Then, again, Sylvia was Catholic, and it was reason enough for me. But I was speaking of Tessie, which is very different. Tessie also was Catholic and much more devout than I, so, taking it all in all, I had little fear for my pretty model until she should fall in love. But *then* I knew that fate alone would decide her future for her, and I prayed inwardly that fate would keep her away from men like me and throw into her path nothing but Ed Burkes and Jimmy McCormicks, bless her sweet face!

Tessie sat blowing smoke up to the ceiling and tinkling the ice in her tumbler.

"Do you know, Kid, that I also had a dream last night?" I observed. I sometimes called her "the Kid."

"Not about that man," she laughed.

"Exactly. A dream similar to yours, only much worse."

It was foolish and thoughtless of me to say this, but you know how little tact the average painter has.

"I must have fallen asleep about 10 o'clock," I continued, "and after a while I dreamt that I awoke. So plainly did I hear the midnight bells, the wind in the tree-branches, and the whistle of steamers from the bay, that even now I can scarcely believe that I was not awake. I seemed to be lying in a box which had a glass cover. Dimly I saw the street lamps as I passed, for I must tell you, Tessie, the box in which I reclined appeared to lie in a cushioned wagon which jolted me over a stony pavement. After a while I became impatient and tried to move but the box was too narrow. My hands were crossed on my breast so I could not raise them to help myself. I listened and then tried to call. My voice was gone. I could hear the trample of the horses attached to the wagon and even the breathing of the driver. Then another sound broke upon my ears like the raising of a window sash. I managed to turn my head a little, and found I could look, not only through the glass cover of my box, but also through the glass panes in the side of the covered vehicle. I saw houses, empty and silent, with neither light nor life about any of them excepting one. In that house a window was open on the first floor and a figure all in white stood looking down into the street. It was you."

Tessie had turned her face away from me and leaned on the table with her elbow.

"I could see your face," I resumed, "and it seemed to me to be very sorrowful. Then we passed on and turned into a narrow black lane. Presently the horses stopped. I waited and waited, closing my eyes with fear and impatience, but all was silent as the grave. After what seemed to me hours, I began to feel uncomfortable. A sense that somebody was close to me made me unclose my eyes. Then I saw the white face of the hearse-driver looking at me through the coffin-lid—"

A sob from Tessie interrupted me. She was trembling like a leaf. I saw I had made an ass of myself and attempted to repair the damage.

"Why, Tess," I said, "I only told you this to show you what influence your story might have on another person's dreams. You don't suppose I really lay in a coffin, do you? What are you trembling for? Don't you see that your dream and my unreasonable dislike for that inoffensive watchman of the church simply set my brain working as soon as I fell asleep?"

She laid her head between her arms and sobbed as if her heart would break. What a precious triple donkey I had made of myself! But I was about to break my record. I went over and put my arm about her

"Tessie, dear, forgive me," I said; "I had no business to frighten you with such nonsense. You are too sensible a girl, too good a Catholic to believe in dreams."

Her hand tightened on mine and her head fell back upon my shoulder, but she still trembled and I petted her and comforted her.

"Come, Tess, open your eyes and smile."

Her eyes opened with a slow languid movement

and met mine, but their expression was so queer that I hastened to reassure her again.

"It's all humbug, Tessie, you surely are not afraid that any harm will come to you because of that."

"No," she said, but her scarlet lips quivered.

"Then what's the matter? Are you afraid?"

"Yes. Not for myself."

"For me, then?" I demanded gaily.

"For you," she murmured in a voice almost inaudible, "I—I care—for you."

At first I started to laugh, but when I understood her, a shock passed through me and I sat like one turned to stone. This was the crowning bit of idiocy I had committed. During the moment which elapsed between her reply and my answer I thought of a thousand responses to that innocent confession. I could pass it by with a laugh, I could misunderstand her and reassure her as to my health, I could simply point out that it was impossible she could love me. But my reply was quicker than my thoughts and I might think and think now when it was too late, for I had kissed her on the mouth.

That evening I took my usual walk in Washington Park, pondering over the occurrences of the day. I was thoroughly committed. There was no back out now, and I stared the future straight in the face. I was not good, not even scrupulous, but I had no idea of deceiving either myself or Tessie. The one passion of my life lay buried in the sunlit forests of Brittany. Was it buried forever? Hope cried "No!" For three years I had been listening to the voice of Hope, and for three years I had waited for a footstep on my threshold. Had Sylvia forgotten? "No!" cried Hope.

I said that I was not good. That is true, but still I was not exactly a comic opera villain. I had led an easy-going reckless life, taking what invited me of pleasure, deploring and sometimes bitterly regretting consequences. In one thing alone, except my paint- ing, I was serious, and that was something which lay hidden if not lost in the Breton forests.

It was too late now for me to regret what had occurred during the day. Whatever it had been, pity, a sudden tenderness for sorrow, of the more brutal instinct of gratified vanity, it was all the same now, and unless I wished to bruise an innocent heart my path lay marked before me. The fire and strength, the depth of passion of a love which I had never even suspected, with all my imagined experience in the world, left me no alternative but to respond or send her away. Whether because I am so cowardly about giving pain to others, or whether it was that I have little of the gloomy Puritan in me, I do not know, but I shrank from disclaiming responsibility for that thoughtless kiss, and in fact had no time to do so before the gates of her heart opened and the flood poured forth. Others who habitually do their duty and find a sullen satisfaction in making themselves and everybody else unhappy, might have withstood it. I did not. I dared not. After the storm had abated I did tell her that she might better have loved Ed Burke and worn a plain gold ring, but she would not hear of it, and I thought perhaps that as long as she had decided to love somebody she could not marry, it had better be me. I, at least, could treat her with an intelligent affection, and whenever she became tired of her infatuation she could go none the worse for it. For I was decided on that point although I knew how hard it would be. I remembered the usual termination of Platonic liaisons and thought how disgusted I had been whenever I heard of one. I knew I was undertaking a great deal for so unscrupulous a man as I was, and I dreaded the future, but never for one moment did I doubt that she was safe with me. Had it been anybody but Tessie I should not have bothered my head about scruples. For it did not occur to me to sacrifice Tessie as I would have sacrificed a woman of the world. I looked the future squarely in the face and saw the several probable endings to the affair. She would either tire of the whole thing, or become so unhappy that I should have either to marry her or go away. If I married her we would be unhappy. I with a wife unsuited to me, and she with a husband unsuitable for any woman. For my past life could scarcely entitle me to marry.

If I went away she might either fall ill, recover, and marry some Eddie Burke, or she might recklessly or deliberately go and do something foolish. On the other hand if she tired of me, then her whole life would be before her with beautiful vistas of Eddie Burkes and marriage rings and twins and Harlem flats and Heaven knows what. As I strolled along through the trees by Washington Arch, I decided that she should find a substantial friend in me anyway and the future could take care of itself. Then I went into the house and put on my evening dress for the little faintly perfumed note on my dresser said, "Have a cab at the stage door at eleven," and the note was signed "Edith Carmichael, Metropolitan Theater, June 19th, 189-."

I took supper that night, or rather we took supper, Miss Carmichael and I, at Solari's and the dawn was just beginning to gild the cross on the Memorial Church as I entered Washington Square after leaving Edith at the Brunswick. There was not a soul in the park as I passed among the trees and took the walk which leads from the Garibaldi statue to the Hamilton Apartment House, but as I passed the churchyard I saw a figure sitting on the stone steps. In spite of myself a chill crept over me at the sight of the white puffy face, and I hastened to pass. Then he said something which might have been addressed to me or might merely have been a mutter to himself, but a sudden furious anger flamed up within me that such a creature should address me. For an instant I felt like wheeling about and smashing my stick over his head, but I walked on, and entering the Hamilton went to my apartment. For some time I tossed about the bed trying to get the sound of his voice out of my ears, but could not. It filled my head, that muttering sound, like thick oily smoke from a fat-rendering vat or an odor of noisome decay. And as I lay and tossed about, the voice in my ears seemed more distinct, and I began to understand the words he had muttered. They came to me slowly as if I had forgotten them, and at last I could make some sense out of the sounds. It was this:

"Have you found the Yellow Sign?"
"Have you found the Yellow Sign?"
"Have you found the Yellow Sign?"

I was furious. What did he mean by that? Then with a curse upon him and his I rolled over and went to sleep, but when I awoke later I looked pale and haggard, for I had dreamed the dream of the night before and it troubled me more than I cared to think.

I dressed and went down into my studio. Tessie sat by the window, but as I came in she rose and put both arms around my neck for an innocent kiss. She

looked so sweet and dainty that I kissed her again
and then sat down before the easel.

"Hello! Where's the study I began yesterday?" I
asked.

Tessie looked conscious, but did not answer. I
began to hunt among the piles of canvases, saying,
"Hurry up, Tess, and get ready; we must take advantage of the morning light."

When at last I gave up the search among the other
canvases and turned to look around the room for the
missing study I noticed Tessie standing by the screen
with her clothing still on.

"What's the matter," I asked, "don't you feel
well?"

"Yes."

"Then hurry."

"Do you want me to pose as—as I have always
posed?"

Then I understood. Here was a new complication.
I had lost, of course, the best nude model I had ever
seen. I looked at Tessie. Her face was scarlet. Alas!
Alas! We had eaten of the tree of knowledge, and
Eden and native innocence were dreams of the
past—I mean—for her.

I suppose she noticed the disappointment on my
face, for she said: "I will pose if you wish. The study
is behind the screen here where I put it."

"No," I said, "we will begin something new"; and I went to my wardrobe and picked out a Moorish costume which fairly blazed with tinsel. It was a genuine costume, and Tessie retired to the screen with it enchanted. When she came forth again I was astonished. Her long black hair was bound above her forehead with a circlet of turquoises, and the ends curled about her glittering girdle. Her feet were encased in the embroidered pointed slippers and the skirt of her costume, curiously wrought with arabesques in silver, fell to her ankles. The deep metallic blue vest embroidered with silver and the short Mauresque jacket spangled and sewn with turquoises became her wonderfully. She came up to me and held up her face smiling. I slipped my hand into my pocket and drawing out a gold chain with a cross attached, dropped it over her head.

"It's yours, Tessie."

"Mine?" she faltered.

"Yours. Now go and pose." Then with a radiant smile she ran behind the screen and presently reappeared with a little box on which was written my name.

"I had intended to give it to you when I went home tonight," she said, "but I can't wait now."

I opened the box. On the pink cotton inside lay a clasp of black onyx, on which was inlaid a curious symbol or letter in gold. It was neither Arabic nor

Chinese, nor as I found afterwards did it belong to any human script.

"It's all I had to give you for a keepsake," she said, timidly.

I was annoyed, but I told her how much I should prize it, and promised to wear it always. She fastened it on my coat beneath the lapel.

"How foolish, Tess, to go and buy me such a beautiful thing as this," I said.

"I did not buy it," she laughed.

"Where did you get it?"

Then she told me how she had found it one day while coming from the Aquarium in the Battery, how she had advertised it and watched the papers, but at last gave up all hopes of finding the owner.

"That was last winter," she said, "the very day I had the first horrid dream about the hearse."

I remembered my dream of the previous night but said nothing, and presently my charcoal was flying over a new canvas, and Tessie stood motionless on the model-stand.

III

The day following was a disastrous one for me. While moving a framed canvas from one easel to another my foot slipped on the polished floor and I fell heavily on both wrists. They were so badly sprained that it was useless to attempt to hold a brush, and I was obliged to wander about the studio, glaring at unfinished drawings and sketches until despair seized me and I sat down to smoke and twiddle my thumbs with rage. The rain blew against the windows and rattled on the roof of the church, driving me into a nervous fit with its interminable patter. Tessie sat sewing by the window, and every now and then raised her head and looked at me with such innocent compassion that I began to feel ashamed of my irritation and looked about for something to occupy me. I had read all the papers and all the books in the library, but for the sake of something to do I went to the bookcases and shoved them open with my elbow. I knew every volume by its color and examined them all, passing slowly around the library and whistling to keep up my spirits. I was turning to go into the dining-room when my eye fell upon a book bound in yellow, standing in a corner of the top shelf of the last bookcase. I did not remember it and from the floor could not decipher the pale lettering on the back, so I went to the smoking-room and called Tessie. She came in from the studio and climbed to reach the book.

"What is it?" I asked.

"*The King in Yellow.*"

I was dumbfounded. Who had placed it there? How came it to my rooms? I had long ago decided

that I should never open that book, and nothing on
earth could have persuaded me to buy it. Fearful lest
curiosity might tempt me to open it, I had never
even looked at it in book-stores. If I ever had had
any curiosity to read it, the awful tragedy of young
Castaigne, whom I knew, prevented me from
exploring its wicked pages. I had always refused to
listen to any description of it, and indeed, nobody
ever ventured to discuss the second part aloud, so I
had absolutely no knowledge of what those leaves
might reveal. I stared at the poisonous yellow binding as I would at a snake.

"Don't touch it, Tessie," I said, "come down."

Of course my admonition was enough to arouse
her curiosity, and before I could prevent it she took
the book and, laughing, danced away into the studio
with it. I called to her but she slipped away with a
tormenting smile at my helpless hands, and I followed her with some impatience.

"Tessie!" I cried, entering the library, "listen, I am
serious. Put that book away. I do not wish you to
open it!" The library was empty. I went into both
drawing-rooms, then into the bedrooms, laundry,
kitchen, and finally returned to the library and began
a systematic search. She had hidden herself so well
that it was half an hour later when I discovered her
crouching white and silent by the latticed window in
the store-room above. At the first glance I saw she

had been punished for her foolishness. *The King in Yellow* lay at her feet, but the book was open to the second part. I looked at Tessie and saw it was too late. She had opened *The King in Yellow*. Then I took her by the hand and led her into the studio. She seemed dazed, and when I told her to lie down on the sofa she obeyed me without a word. After a while she closed her eyes and her breathing became regular and deep, but I could not determine whether or not she slept. For a long while I sat silently beside her, but she neither stirred nor spoke, and at last I rose and entering the unused store-room took the yellow book in my least injured hand. It seemed heavy as lead, but I carried it into the studio again, and sitting down on the rug beside the sofa, opened it and read it through from beginning to end.

When, faint with the excess of my emotions, I dropped the volume and leaned wearily back against the sofa, Tessie opened her eyes and looked at me.

We had been speaking for some time in a dull and monotonous strain before I realized that we were discussing *The King in Yellow*. Oh the sin of writing such words—words which are clear as crystal, limpid and musical as bubbling springs, words which sparkle and glow like the poisoned diamonds of the Medicis! Oh the wickedness, the hopeless damnation of a soul who could fascinate and paralyze human creatures with such words,—words understood by the ignorant and wise alike, words which are more precious than jewels, more soothing than Heavenly music, more awful than death itself.

We talked on, unmindful of the gathering shadows, and she was begging me to throw away the clasp of black onyx quaintly inlaid with what we now knew to be the Yellow Sign. I never shall know why I refused, though even at this hour, here in my bedroom as I write this confession, I should be glad to know *what* it was that prevented me from tearing the Yellow Sign from my breast and casting it into the fire. I am sure I wished to do so, but Tessie pleaded with me in vain. Night fell and the hours dragged on, but still we murmured to each other of the King and the Pallid Mask, and midnight sounded from the misty spires in the fog-wrapped city. We spoke of Hastur and of Cassilda, while outside the fog rolled against the blank window-panes as the cloud waves roll and break on the shores of Hali.

The house was very silent now and not a sound from the misty streets broke the silence. Tessie lay among the cushions, her face a gray blot in the gloom, but her hands were clasped in mine and I knew that she knew and read my thoughts as I read hers, for we had understood the mystery of the Hyades and the Phantom of Truth was laid. Then as we answered each other, swiftly, silently, thought on thought, the shadows stirred in the gloom about us, and far in the distant streets we heard a sound. Nearer and nearer it came, the dull crunching of wheels, nearer, nearer and yet nearer, and now, outside the door it ceased, and I dragged myself to the window and saw a black-plumed hearse. The gate below opened and shut, and I crept shaking to my door and bolted it, but I knew no bolts, no locks, could keep that creature out who was coming for the Yellow Sign. And now I heard him moving very softly along the hall. Now he was at the door, and the bolts rotted at his touch. Now he had entered. With eyes starting from my head I peered into the darkness, but when he came into the room I did not see him. It was only when I felt him envelop me in his cold soft grasp that I cried out and struggled with deadly fury, but my hands were useless and he tore the onyx clasp from my coat and struck me full in the face. Then, as I fell, I heard Tessie's soft cry and her spirit fled to God, and even while falling I longed to follow her, for I knew that the King in Yellow had opened his tattered mantle and there was only Christ to cry to now.

I could tell more, but I cannot see what help it will be to the world. As for me I am past human help or hope. As I lie here, writing, careless even whether or not I die before I finish, I can see the doctor gathering up his powders and phials with a vague gesture to the good priest beside me, which I understand.

They will be very curious to know the tragedy—they of the outside world who write books and print millions of newspapers, but I will write no more, and the father confessor will seal my last words with the seal of sanctity when his holy office is done. They of the outside world may send their creatures into wrecked homes and death-smitten firesides, and their newspapers will batten on blood and tears, but with me their spies must halt before the confessional. They know that Tessie is dead and that I am dying. They know how the people in the house, aroused by an infernal scream, rushed into my room and found one living and two dead, but they do not know that the doctor said as he pointed to a horrible decomposed heap on the floor—the livid corpse of the watchman from the church: "I have no theory, no explanation. That man must have been dead for months!"

I think I am dying. I wish the priest would—

The Watcher

[ROBERT HUGH BENSON]

*Another theme which began to arise in horror writing, as the hold
of the old folklore lessened, was of "nameless dreads," which simply did not fit the traditional categories. So it is with this scary little short piece, written by the son of a former Archbishop of
Canterbury, whose writing of such pieces was carried on alongside
his historical and controversial output (he was, before World War
I, the best known Catholic priest in England, having converted
from Anglicanism).*

One morning, the priest and I went out
soon after breakfast and walked up and
down a grass patch between two yew
hedges; the dew was not yet off the grass that lay in
shadow; and thin patches of gossamer still hung like
torn cambric on the yew shoots on either side. As
we passed for the second time up the path, the old

man suddenly stooped and, pushing aside a dock-leaf at the foot of the hedge, lifted a dead mouse, and looked at it as it lay stiffly on the palm of his hand. I saw that his eyes filled slowly with the ready tears of old age.

"He had chosen his own resting-place," he said. "Let him lie there. Why did I disturb him?"—And he laid him gently down again; and then gathering a fragment of wet earth he sprinkled it over the mouse. "Earth to earth, ashes to ashes," he said, "in sure and certain hope"—and then he stopped; and straightening himself with difficulty walked on, and I followed him.

"You once expressed an interest," he said, "in my tales of the visions of Nature I have seen. Shall I tell you how once I saw a very different sight?

"I was eighteen years old at the time, that terrible age when the soul seems to have dwindled to a spark overlaid by a mountain of ashes—when blood and fire and death and loud noises seem the only things of interest, and all tender things shrink back and hide from the dreadful noonday of manhood. Someone gave me one of those shot-pistols that you may have seen, and I loved the sense of power that it gave me, for I had never had a gun. For a week or two in the summer holidays I was content with shooting at a mark, or at the level surface of water, and delighted to see the cardboard shattered, or the

quiet pool torn to shreds along its mirror where the
sky and green lay sleeping. Then that ceased to
interest me, and I longed to see a living thing suddenly stop living at my will. Now," and he held up a
deprecating hand, "I think sport is necessary for
some natures. After all, the killing of creatures is
necessary for man's food, and sport as you will tell
me is a survival of man's delight in obtaining food,
and it requires certain noble qualities of endurance
and skill. I know all that, and I know further that for
some natures it is a relief—an escape for humours
that will otherwise find an evil outlet. But I do
know this—that for me it was not necessary.

"However, there was every excuse, and I went out
in good faith one summer evening, intending to
shoot some rabbits as they ran to cover from the
open field. I walked along the inside of a fence with
a wood above me and on my left, and the green
meadow on my right. Well, owing probably to my
own lack of skill, though I could hear the patter and
rush of the rabbits all round me, and could see them
in the distance sitting up listening with cocked ears,
as I stole along the fence, I could not get close
enough to fire at them with any hope of what I fancied was success; and by the time that I had arrived at
the end of the wood I was in an impatient mood.

"I stood for a moment or two leaning on the fence
looking out of that pleasant coolness into the open

meadow beyond; the sun had at that moment dipped behind the hill before me and all was in shadow except where there hung a glory about the topmost leaves of a beech that still caught the sun. The birds were beginning to come in from the fields, and were settling one by one in the wood behind me, staying here and there to sing one last line of melody. I could hear the quiet rush and then the sudden clap of a pigeon's wings as he came home, and as I listened I heard pealing out above all other sounds the long liquid song of a thrush somewhere above me. I looked up idly and tried to see the bird, and after a moment or two caught sight of him as the leaves of the beech parted in the breeze, his head lifted and his whole body vibrating with the joy of life and music. As someone has said, his body was one beating heart. The last radiance of the sun over the hill reached him and bathed him in golden warmth. Then the leaves closed again as the breeze dropped, but still his song rang out.

"Then there came on me a blinding desire to kill him. All the other creatures had mocked me and run home. Here at least was a victim, and I would pour out the sullen anger that had been gathering during my walk, and at least demand this one life as a substitute. Side by side with this I remembered clearly that I had come out to kill for food: that was my one justification. Side by side I saw both these things, and I had no excuse—no excuse.

"I turned my head every way and moved a step or two back to catch sight of him again, and, although this may sound fantastic and over-wrought, in my whole being was a struggle between light and darkness. Every fibre of my life told me that the thrush had a right to live. Ah! he had earned it, if labour were wanting, by this very song that was guiding death towards him, but black sullen anger had thrown my conscience, and was now struggling to hold it down till the shot had been fired. Still I waited for the breeze, and then it came, cool and sweet-smelling like the breath of a garden, and the leaves parted. There he sang in the sunshine and in a moment I lifted the pistol and drew the trigger.

"With the crack of the cap came silence overhead, and after what seemed an interminable moment came the soft rush of something falling and the faint thud among last year's leaves. Then I stood half terrified, and stared among the dead leaves. All seemed dim and misty. My eyes were still a little dazzled by the bright background of sunlit air and rosy clouds on which I had looked with such intensity, and the space beneath the branches was a world of shadows. Still I looked a few yards away, trying to make out the body of the thrush, and fearing to hear a struggle of beating wings, among the dry leaves.

"And then I lifted my eyes a little, vaguely. A yard

or two beyond where the thrush lay was a rhodo-
dendron bush. The blossoms had fallen and the outline of dark, heavy leaves was unrelieved by the
slightest touch of colour. As I looked at it, I saw a
face looking down from the higher branches.

"It was a perfectly hairless head and face, the thin
lips were parted in a wide smile of laughter, there
were innumerable lines about the corners of the
mouth, and the eyes were surrounded by creases of
merriment. What was perhaps most terrible about it
all was that the eyes were not looking at me, but
down among the leaves; the heavy eyelids lay droop-
ing, and the long, narrow, shining slits showed how
the eyes laughed beneath them. The forehead sloped
quickly back, like a cat's head. The face was the
colour of earth, and the outlines of the head faded
below the ears and chin into the gloom of the dark
bush. There was no throat, or body or limbs so far as
I could see. The face just hung there like a down-
turned Eastern mask in an old curiosity shop. And it
smiled with sheer delight, not at me, but at the
thrush's body. There was no change of expression so
long as I watched it, just a silent smile of pleasure
petrified on the face. I could not move my eyes
from it.

"After what I suppose was a minute or so, the face
had gone. I did not see it go, but I became aware that
I was looking only at leaves.

"No; there was no outline of leaf, or play of shadows that could possibly have been taken for form of a face. You can guess how I tried to force myself to believe that that was all; how I turned my head this way and that to catch it again; but there was no hint of a face.

"Now, I cannot tell you how I did it; but although I was half beside myself with fright, I went forward towards the bush and searched furiously among the leaves for the body of the thrush; and at last I found it, and lifted it. It was still limp and warm to the touch. Its breast was a little ruffled, and one tiny drop of blood lay at the root of the beak below the eyes, like a tear of dismay and sorrow at such an unmerited, unexpected death.

"I carried it to the fence and climbed over, and then began to run in great steps, looking now and then awfully at the gathering gloom of the wood behind, where the laughing face had mocked the dead. I think, looking back as I do now, that my chief instinct was that I could not leave the thrush there to be laughed at, and that I must get it out into the clean, airy meadow. When I reached the middle of the meadow I came to a pond which never ran quite dry even in the hottest summer. On the bank I laid the thrush down, and then deliberately but with all my force dashed the pistol into the water; then emptied my pockets of the cartridges and threw them in too.

"Then I turned again to the piteous little body, feeling that at least I had tried to make amends. There was an old rabbit hole near, the grass growing down in its mouth, and a tangle of web and dead leaves behind. I scooped a little space out among the leaves, and then laid the thrush there; gathered a little of the sandy soil and poured it over the body, saying, I remember, half unconsciously, 'Earth to earth, ashes to ashes, in sure and certain hope'—and then I stopped, feeling I had been a little profane, though I do not think so now. And then I went home.

"As I dressed for dinner, looking out over the darkening meadow where the thrush lay, I remember feeling happy that no evil thing could mock the defenceless dead out there in the clean meadow where the wind blew and the stars shone down."

The Dead Valley

[RALPH ADAMS CRAM]

*Although Cram was an architect of unsparing Gothic Tradition-
alism (he was responsible for very many churches, schools, and college buildings throughout the United States), when it came to
horror fiction, he was quite advanced. In this selection he uses to
the full the new technique of fright without explanation and
without reason. Despite the lack of traditional folkloric accompa-
niment, or indeed, any mythos at all, his presentation of pure terror is very effective.*

I have a friend, Olof Ehrensvärd, a Swede by
birth, who yet, by reason of a strange and
melancholy mischance of his early boyhood, has
thrown his lot with that of the New World. It is a
curious story of a headstrong boy and a proud and
relentless family: the details do not matter here, but
they are sufficient to weave a web of romance

around the tall yellow-bearded man with the sad eyes and the voice that gives itself perfectly to plaintive little Swedish songs remembered out of childhood. In the winter evenings we play chess together, he and I, and after some close, fierce battle has been fought to a finish—usually with my own defeat—we fill our pipes again, and Ehrensvärd tells me stories of the far, half-remembered days in the fatherland, before he went to sea: stories that grow very strange and incredible as the night deepens and the fire falls together, but stories that, nevertheless, I fully believe.

One of them made a stronge impression on me, so I set it down here, only regretting that I cannot reproduce the curiously perfect English and the delicate accent which to me increased the fascination of the tale. Yet, as best I can remember it, here it is.

"I never told you how Nils and I went over the hills to Hallsberg, and how we found the Dead Valley, did I? Well, this is the way it happened. I must have been about twelve years old, and Nils Sjöberg, whose father's estate joined ours, was a few months younger. We were inseparable just at that time, and whatever we did, we did together.

"Once a week it was market day in Engelholm, and Nils and I went always there to see the strange sights that the market gathered from all the surrounding country. One day we quite lost our hearts, for an old man from across the Elfborg had brought

a little dog to sell, that seemed to us the most beautiful dog in all the world. He was a round, woolly
puppy, so funny that Nils and I sat down on the
ground and laughed at him, until he came and
played with us in so jolly a way that we felt that
there was only one really desirable thing in life, and
that was the little dog of the old man from across the
hills. But alas! we had not half money enough
wherewith to buy him, so we were forced to beg the
old man not to sell him before the next market day,
promising that we would bring the money for him
then. He gave us his word, and we ran home very
fast and implored our mothers to give us money for
the little dog.

"We got the money, but we could not wait for the
next market day. Suppose the puppy should be sold!
The thought frightened us so that we begged and
implored that we might be allowed to go over the
hills to Hallsberg where the old man lived, and get
the little dog ourselves, and at last they told us we
might go. By starting early in the morning we
should reach Hallsberg by three o'clock, and it was
arranged that we should stay there that night with
Nils's aunt, and, leaving by noon the next day, be
home again by sunset.

"Soon after sunrise we were on our way, after having received minute instructions as to just what we
should do in all possible and impossible circum-

stances, and finally a repeated injunction that we should start for home at the same hour the next day, so that we might get safely back before nightfall.

"For us, it was magnificent sport, and we started off with our rifles, full of the sense of our very great importance: yet the journey was simple enough, along a good road, across the big hills we knew so well, for Nils and I had shot over half the territory this side of the dividing ridge of the Elfborg. Back of Engelholm lay a long valley, from which rose the low mountains, and we had to cross this, and then follow the road along the side of the hills for three or four miles, before a narrow path branched off to the left, leading up through the pass.

"Nothing occurred of interest on the way over, and we reached Hallsberg in due season, found to our inexpressible joy that the little dog was not sold, secured him, and so went to the house of Nils's aunt to spend the night.

"Why we did not leave early on the following day, I can't quite remember; at all events, I know we stopped at a shooting range just outside of the town, where most attractive pasteboard pigs were sliding slowly through painted foliage, serving so as beautiful marks. The result was that we did not get fairly started for home until afternoon, and as we found ourselves at last pushing up the side of the mountains with the sun dangerously near their summits, I think we were a little scared at the prospect of the examination and possible punishment that awaited us when we got home at midnight.

"Therefore we hurried as fast as possible up the mountainside, while the blue dusk closed in about us, and the light died in the purple sky. At first we had talked hilariously, and the little dog had leaped ahead of us with the utmost joy. Latterly, however, a curious oppression came on us; we did not speak or even whistle, while the dog fell behind, following us with hesitation in every muscle.

"We had passed through the foothills and the low spurs of the mountains, and were almost at the top of the main range, when life seemed to go out of everything, leaving the world dead, so suddenly silent the forest became, so stagnant the air. Instinctively we halted to listen.

"Perfect silence—the crushing silence of deep forests at night; and more, for always, even in the most impenetrable fastnesses of the wooded mountains, is the multitudinous murmur of little lives, awakened by the darkness, exaggerated and intensified by the stillness of the air and the great dark: but here and now the silence seemed unbroken even by the turn of a leaf, the movement of a twig, the note of night bird or insect. I could hear the blood beat through my veins; and the crushing of the grass under our feet as we advanced with hesitating steps sounded like the falling of trees.

"And the air was stagnant—dead. The atmosphere seemed to lie upon the body like the weight of sea on a diver who has ventured too far into its awful depths. What we usually call silence seems so only in relation to the din of ordinary experience. This was silence in the absolute, and it crushed the mind while it intensified the senses, bringing down the awful weight of inextinguishable fear.

"I know that Nils and I stared towards each other in abject terror, listening to our quick, heavy breathing, that sounded to our acute senses like the fitful rush of waters. And the poor little dog we were leading justified our terror. The black oppression seemed to crush him even as it did us. He lay close on the ground, moaning feebly, and dragging himself painfully and slowly closer to Nils's feet. I think this exhibition of utter animal fear was the last touch, and must inevitably have blasted our reason—mine anyway; but just then, as we stood quaking on the bounds of madness, came a sound, so awful, so ghastly, so horrible, that it seemed to rouse us from the dead spell that was on us.

"In the depth of the silence came a cry, beginning as a low, sorrowful moan, rising to a tremulous shriek, culminating in a yell that seemed to tear the

night in sunder and rend the world as by a cataclysm.
So fearful was it that I could not believe it had actual
existence: it passed previous experience, the powers
of belief, and for a moment I thought it the result of
my own animal terror, an hallucination born of tot-
tering reason.

"A glance at Nils dispelled this thought in a flash.
In the pale light of the high stars he was the embod-
iment of all possible human fear, quaking with an
ague, his jaw fallen, his tongue out, his eyes protruding like those of a hanged man. Without a word we
fled, the panic of fear giving us strength, and
together, the little dog caught close in Nils's arms,
we sped down the side of the cursed mountains—
anywhere, goal was of no account: we had but one
impulse—to get away from that place.

"So under the black trees and the far white stars
that flashed through the still leaves overhead, we
leaped down the mountainside, regardless of path or
landmark, straight through the tangled underbrush,
across mountain streams, through fens and copses,
anywhere, so only that our course was downward.

"How long we ran thus, I have no idea, but by and
by the forest fell behind, and we found ourselves
among the foothills, and fell exhausted on the dry
short grass, panting like tired dogs.

"It was lighter here in the open, and presently we
looked around to see where we were, and how we

were to strike out in order to find the path that would lead us home. We looked in vain for a familiar sign. Behind us rose the great wall of black forest on the flank of the mountain: before us lay the undulating mounds of low foothills, unbroken by trees or rocks, and beyond, only the fall of black sky bright with multitudinous stars that turned its velvet depth to a luminous gray.

"As I remember, we did not speak to each other once: the terror was too heavy on us for that, but by and by we rose simultaneously and started out across the hills.

"Still the same silence, the same dead, motionless air—air that was at once sultry and chilling: a heavy heat struck through with an icy chill that felt almost like the burning of frozen steel. Still carrying the helpless dog, Nils pressed on through the hills, and I followed close behind. At last, in front of us, rose a slope of moor touching the white stars. We climbed it wearily, reached the top, and found ourselves gazing down into a great, smooth valley, filled half way to the brim with—what?

"As far as the eye could see stretched a level plain of ashy white, faintly phosphorescent, a sea of velvet fog that lay like motionless water, or rather like a floor of alabaster, so dense did it appear, so seemingly capable of sustaining weight. If it were possible, I think that sea of dead white mist struck even greater terror into my soul than the heavy silence or the deadly cry—so ominous was it, so utterly unreal, so phantasmal, so impossible, as it lay there like a dead ocean under the steady stars. Yet through that mist *we must go!* There seemed no other way home, and, shattered with abject fear, mad with the one desire to get back, we started down the slope to where the sea of milky mist ceased, sharp and distinct around the stems of the rough grass.

"I put one foot into the ghostly fog. A chill as of death struck through me, stopping my heart, and I threw myself backward on the slope. At that instant came again the shriek, close, close, right in our ears, in ourselves, and far out across that damnable sea I saw the cold fog lift like a water-spout and toss itself high in writhing convolutions towards the sky. The stars began to grow dim as thick vapor swept across them, and in the growing dark I saw a great, watery moon lift itself slowly above the palpitating sea, vast and vague in the gathering mist.

"This was enough: we turned and fled along the margin of the white sea that throbbed now with fitful motion below us, rising, rising, slowly and steadily, driving us higher and higher up the side of the foothills.

"It was a race for life; that we knew. How we kept it up I cannot understand, but we did, and at last we saw the white sea fall behind us as we staggered up the end of the valley, and then down into a region that we knew, and so into the old path. The last thing I remember was hearing a strange voice, that of Nils, but horribly changed, stammer brokenly, 'The dog is dead!' and then the whole world turned around twice, slowly and resistlessly, and consciousness went out with a crash.

"It was some three weeks later, as I remember, that I awoke in my own room, and found my mother sitting beside the bed. I could not think very well at first, but as I slowly grew strong again, vague flashes of recollection began to come to me, and little by little the whole sequence of events of that awful night in the Dead Valley came back. All that I could gain from what was told me was that three weeks before I had been found in my own bed, raging sick, and that my illness grew fast into brain fever. I tried to speak of the dread things that had happened to me, but I saw at once that no one looked on them save as the hauntings of a dying frenzy, and so I closed my mouth and kept my own counsel.

"I must see Nils, however, and so I asked for him. My mother told me that he also had been ill with a strange fever, but that he was now quite well again. Presently they brought him in, and when we were alone I began to speak to him of the night on the mountain. I shall never forget the shock that struck me down on my pillow when the boy denied everything: denied having gone with me, ever having heard the cry, having seen the valley, or feeling the deadly chill of the ghostly fog. Nothing would shake his determined ignorance, and in spite of myself I was forced to admit that his denials came from no policy of concealment, but from blank oblivion.

"My weakened brain was in a turmoil. Was it all but the floating phantasm of delirium? Or had the horror of the real thing blotted Nils's mind into blankness so far as the events of the night in the Dead Valley were concerned? The latter explanation seemed the only one, else how explain the sudden illness which in a night had struck us both down? I said nothing more, either to Nils or to my own people, but waited, with a growing determination that, once well again, I would find that valley if it really existed

"It was some weeks before I was really well enough to go, but finally, late in September, I chose a bright, warm, still day, the last smile of the dying summer, and started early in the morning along the path that led to Hallsberg. I was sure I knew where the trail struck off to the right, down which we had come from the valley of dead water, for a great tree grew by the Hallsberg path at the point where, with a sense of salvation, we had found the home road. Presently I saw it to the right, a little distance ahead.

"I think the bright sunlight and the clear air had

worked as a tonic to me, for by the time I came to the foot of the great pine, I had quite lost faith in the verity of the vision that haunted me, believing at last that it was indeed but the nightmare of madness. Nevertheless, I turned sharply to the right, at the base of the tree, into a narrow path that led through a dense thicket. As I did so I tripped over something. A swarm of flies sung into the air around me, and looking down I saw the matted fleece, with the poor little bones thrusting through, of the dog we had bought in Hallsberg.

"Then my courage went out with a puff, and I knew that it all was true, and that now I was frightened. Pride and the desire for adventure urged me on, however, and I pressed into the close thicket that barred my way. The path was hardly visible: merely the worn road of some small beasts, for, though it showed in the crisp grass, the bushes above grew thick and hardly penetrable. The land rose slowly, and rising grew clearer, until at last I came out on a great slope of hill, unbroken by trees or shrubs, very like my memory of that rise of land we had topped in order that we might find the dead valley and the icy fog. I looked at the sun; it was bright and clear, and all around insects were humming in the autumn air, and birds were darting to and fro. Surely there was no danger, not until nightfall at least; so I began to whistle, and with a rush mounted the last crest of brown hill.

"There lay the Dead Valley! A great oval basin, almost as smooth and regular as though made by man. On all sides the grass crept over the brink of the encircling hills, dusty green on the crests, then fading into ashy brown, and so to a deadly white, this last color forming a thin ring, running in a long line around the slope. And then? Nothing. Bare, brown, hard earth, glittering with grains of alkali, but otherwise dead and barren. Not a tuft of grass, not a stick of brushwood, not even a stone, but only the vast expanse of beaten clay.

"In the midst of the basin, perhaps a mile and a half away, the level expanse was broken by a great dead tree, rising leafless and gaunt into the air. Without a moment's hesitation I started down into the valley and made for this goal. Every particle of fear seemed to have left me, and even the valley itself did not look so very terrifying. At all events, I was driven by an overwhelming curiosity, and there seemed to be but one thing in the world to do—to get to that Tree! As I trudged along over the hard earth, I noticed that the multitudinous voices of birds and insects had died away. No bee or butterfly hovered through the air, no insects leaped or crept over the dull earth. The very air itself was stagnant.

"As I drew near the skeleton tree, I noticed the glint of sunlight on a kind of white mound around its roots, and I wondered curiously. It was not until I had come close that I saw its nature.

"All around the roots and barkless trunk was heaped a wilderness of little bones. Tiny skulls of rodents and of birds, thousands of them, rising about the dead tree and streaming off for several yards in all directions, until the dreadful pile ended in isolated skulls and scattered skeletons. Here and there a larger bone appeared—the thigh of a sheep, the hoofs of a horse, and to one side, grinning slowly, a human skull.

"I stood quite still, staring with all my eyes, when suddenly the dense silence was broken by a faint, forlorn cry high over my head. I looked up and saw a great falcon turning and sailing downward just over the tree. In a moment more she fell motionless on the bleaching bones.

"Horror struck me, and I rushed for home, my brain whirling, a strange numbness growing in me. I ran steadily, on and on. At last I glanced up. Where was the rise of hill? I looked around wildly. Closely before me was the dead tree with its pile of bones. I had circled it round and round, and the valley wall was still a mile and a half away.

"I stood dazed and frozen. The sun was sinking,

red and dull, towards the line of hills. In the east the
dark was growing fast. Was there still time? *Time!* It
was not *that* I wanted, it was *will!* My feet seemed
clogged as in a nightmare. I could hardly drag them
over the barren earth. And then I felt the slow chill
creeping through me. I looked down. Out of the
earth a thin mist was rising, collecting in little pools
that grew ever larger until they joined here and
there, their currents swirling slowly like thin blue
smoke. The western hills halved the copper sun.
When it was dark I should hear that shriek again,
and then I should die. I knew that, and with every
remaining atom of will I staggered towards the red
west through the writhing mist that crept clammily
around my ankles, retarding my steps.

"And as I fought my way off from the Tree, the
horror grew, until at last I thought I was going to
die. The silence pursued me like dumb ghosts, the
still air held my breath, the hellish fog caught at my
feet like cold hands.

"But I won! though not a moment too soon. As I
crawled on my hands and knees up the brown slope,
I heard, far away and high in the air, the cry that
already had almost bereft me of reason. It was faint
and vague, but unmistakable in its horrible intensity.
I glanced behind. The fog was dense and pallid,
heaving undulously up the brown slope. The sky was

gold under the setting sun, but below was the ashy gray of death. I stood for a moment on the brink of this sea of hell, and then leaped down the slope. The sunset opened before me, the night closed behind, and as I crawled home weak and tired, darkness shut down on the Dead Valley."

The Middle Toe of the Right Foot

[AMBROSE BIERCE]

"Bitter Bierce" was far in advance of his contemporaries in many ways, not least in the use of psychology and illusion in fiction, most notably perhaps in his "Occurrence at Owl Creek Bridge." In this piece, the setting of the stage is everything, and the climax—swift.

I

It is well known that the old Manton house is haunted. In all the rural district near about, and even in the town of Marshall, a mile away, not one person of unbiased mind entertains a doubt of it; incredulity is confined to those opinionated persons who will be called "cranks" as soon as the useful word shall have penetrated the intellectual demesne of the Marshall *Advance*. The evidence that the house is haunted is of two kinds: the testimony of disinterested witnesses who have had ocular proof, and that of the house itself. The former may be disregarded and ruled out on any of the various grounds of objection which may be urged against it by the ingenious; but facts within the observation of all are material and controlling.

In the first place, the Manton house has been unoccupied by mortals for more than ten years, and with its outbuildings is slowly falling into decay—a circumstance which in itself the judicious will hardly venture to ignore. It stands a little way off the loneliest reach of the Marshall and Harriston road, in an opening which was once a farm and is still disfigured with strips of rotting fence and half covered with brambles over-running a stony and sterile soil long unacquainted with the plow. The house itself is in tolerably good condition, though badly weatherstained and in dire need of attention from the glazier, the smaller male population of the region having attested in the manner of its kind its disapproval of dwelling without dwellers. It is two stories in height, nearly square, its front pierced by a single doorway flanked on each side by a window boarded up to the very top. Corresponding windows above, not protected, serve to admit light and rain to the rooms of the upper floor. Grass and weeds grow

pretty rankly all about, and a few shade trees, somewhat the worse for wind, and leaning all in one
direction, seem to be making a concerted effort to
run away. In short, as the Marshall town humorist
explained in the columns of the *Advance*, "the
proposition that the Manton house is badly haunted
is the only logical conclusion from the premises."
The fact that in this dwelling Mr. Manton thought
it expedient one night some ten years ago to rise
and cut the throats of his wife and two small children, removing at once to another part of the country, has no doubt done its share in directing public
attention to the fitness of the place for supernatural
phenomena.

To this house, one summer evening, came four
men in a wagon. Three of them promptly alighted,
and the one who had been driving hitched the team
to the only remaining post of what had been a fence.
The fourth remained seated in the wagon "Come,"
said one of his companions, approaching him, while
the others moved away in the direction of the
dwelling—"this is the place."

The man addressed did not move. "By God!" he
said harshly, "this is a trick, and it looks to me as if
you were in it."

"Perhaps I am," the other said, looking him
straight in the face and speaking in a tone which had
something of contempt in it. "You will remember,

however, that the choice of place was with your own assent left to the other side. Of course if you are afraid of spooks——"

"I am afraid of nothing," the man interrupted with another oath, and sprang to the ground. The two then joined the others at the door, which one of them had already opened with some difficulty, caused by rust of lock and hinge. All entered. Inside it was dark, but the man who had unlocked the door produced a candle and matches and made a light. He then unlocked a door on their right as they stood in the passage. This gave them entrance to a large, square room that the candle but dimly lighted. The floor had a thick carpeting of dust, which partly muffled their footfalls. Cobwebs were in the angles of the walls and depended from the ceiling like strips of rotting lace, making undulatory movements in the disturbed air. The room had two windows in adjoining sides, but from neither could anything be seen except the rough inner surfaces of boards a few inches from the glass. There was no fireplace, no furniture; there was nothing: besides the cobwebs and the dust, the four men were the only objects there which were not a part of the structure.

Strange enough they looked in the yellow light of the candle. The one who had so reluctantly alighted was especially spectacular—he might have been called sensational. He was of middle age, heavily built, deep chested and broad shouldered. Looking at his figure, one would have said that he had a giant's strength; at his features, that he would use it like a giant. He was clean shaven, his hair rather closely cropped and gray. His low forehead was seamed with wrinkles above the eyes, and over the nose these became vertical. The heavy black brows followed the same law, saved from meeting only by an upward turn at what would otherwise have been the point of contact. Deeply sunken beneath these, glowed in the obscure light a pair of eyes of uncertain color, but obviously enough too small. There was something forbidding in their expression, which was not bettered by the cruel mouth and wide jaw. The nose was well enough, as noses go; one does not expect much of noses. All that was sinister in the man's face seemed accentuated by an unnatural pallor—he appeared altogether bloodless.

The appearance of the other men was sufficiently commonplace: they were such persons as one meets and forgets that he met. All were younger than the man described, between whom and the eldest of the others, who stood apart, there was apparently no kindly feeling. They avoided looking at each other.

"Gentlemen," said the man holding the candle and keys, "I believe everything is right. Are you ready, Mr. Rosser?"

The man standing apart from the group bowed and smiled. "And you, Mr. Grossmith?"

The heavy man bowed and scowled.

"You will be pleased to remove your outer clothing."

Their hats, coats, waistcoats and neckwear were soon removed and thrown outside the door, in the passage. The man with the candle now nodded, and the fourth man—he who had urged Grossmith to leave the wagon—produced from the pocket of his overcoat two long, murderous-looking bowie-knives, which he drew now from their leather scabbards.

"They are exactly alike," he said, presenting one to each of the two principals—for by this time the dullest observer would have understood the nature of this meeting. It was to be a duel to the death.

Each combatant took a knife, examined it critically near the candle and tested the strength of blade and handle across his lifted knee. Their persons were then searched in turn, each by the second of the other.

"If it is agreeable to you, Mr. Grossmith," said the man holding the light, "you will place yourself in that corner."

He indicated the angle of the room farthest from the door, whither Grossmith retired, his second parting from him with a grasp of the hand which had nothing of cordiality in it. In the angle nearest the door Mr. Rosser stationed himself, and after a whispered consultation his second left him, joining the other near the door. At that moment the candle was suddenly extinguished, leaving all in profound darkness. This may have been done by a draught from the opened door; whatever the cause, the effect was startling.

"Gentlemen," said a voice which sounded strangely unfamiliar in the altered condition affecting the relations of the senses—"gentlemen, you will not move until you hear the closing of the outer door."

A sound of trampling ensued, then the closing of the inner door; and finally the outer one closed with a concussion which shook the entire building.

A few minutes afterward a belated farmer's boy met a light wagon which was being driven furiously toward the town of Marshall. He declared that behind the two figures on the front seat stood a third, with its hands upon the bowed shoulders of the others, who appeared to struggle vainly to free themselves from its grasp. This figure, unlike the others, was clad in white, and had undoubtedly boarded the wagon as it passed the haunted house. As the lad could boast a considerable former experience with the supernatural thereabouts his word had the weight justly due to the testimony of an expert.

The story (in connection with the next day's events) eventually appeared in the *Advance*, with some slight literary embellishments and a concluding intimation that the gentlemen referred to would be allowed the use of the paper's columns for their version of the night's adventure. But the privilege remained without a claimant.

II

The events that led up to this "duel in the dark" were simple enough. One evening three young men of the town of Marshall were sitting in a quiet corner of the porch of the village hotel, smoking and discussing such matters as three educated young men of a Southern village would naturally find interesting. Their names were King, Sancher, and Rosser. At a little distance, within easy hearing, but taking no part in the conversation, sat a fourth. He was a stranger to the others. They merely knew that on his arrival by the stage-coach that afternoon he had written in the hotel register the name Robert Grossmith. He had not been observed to speak to any one except the hotel clerk. He seemed, indeed, singularly fond of his own company—or, as the *personnel* of the *Advance* expressed it, "grossly addicted to evil associations." But then it should be said in justice to the stranger that the *personnel* was himself of a too convivial disposition fairly to judge one differently gifted, and had, moreover, experienced a slight rebuff in an effort at an "interview."

"I hate any kind of deformity in a woman," said King, "whether natural or—acquired. I have a theory that any physical defect has its correlative mental and mortal defect."

"I infer, then," said Rosser, gravely, "that a lady lacking the moral advantage of a nose would find the struggle to become Mrs. King an arduous enterprise."

"Of course you may put it that way," was the reply; "but, seriously, I once threw over a most charming girl on learning quite accidentally that she had suffered amputation of a toe. My conduct was brutal if you like, but if I had married that girl I should have been miserable for life and should have made her so."

"Whereas," said Sancher, with a light laugh, "by marrying a gentleman of more liberal views she escaped with a parted throat."

"Ah, you know to whom I refer. Yes, she married Manton, but I don't know about his liberality; I'm not sure but he cut her throat because he discovered that she lacked that excellent thing in woman, the middle toe of the right foot."

"Look at that chap!" said Rosser in a low voice, his eyes fixed upon the stranger.

That chap was obviously listening intently to the conversation.

"Damn his impudence!" muttered King—"what ought we to do?"

"That's an easy one," Rosser replied, rising. "Sir," he continued, addressing the stranger, "I think it would be better if you would remove your chair to the other end of the veranda. The presence of gentlemen is evidently an unfamiliar situation to you."

The man sprang to his feet and strode forward with clenched hands, his face white with rage. All were now standing. Sancher stepped between the belligerents.

"You are hasty and unjust," he said to Rosser; "this gentleman has done nothing to deserve such language."

But Rosser would not withdraw a word. By the custom of the country and the time there could be but one outcome to the quarrel.

"I demand the satisfaction due to a gentleman," said the stranger, who had become more calm. "I have not an acquaintance in this region. Perhaps you, sir," bowing to Sancher, "will be kind enough to represent me in this matter."

Sancher accepted the trust—somewhat reluctantly it must be confessed, for the man's appearance and manner were not at all to his liking. King, who dur-

ing the colloquy had hardly removed his eyes from
the stranger's face and had not spoken a word, consented with a nod to act for Rosser, and the upshot
of it was that, the principals having retired, a meeting
was arranged for the next evening. The nature of the
arrangements has been already disclosed. The duel
with knives in a dark room was once a commoner
feature of Southwestern life than it is likely to be
again. How thin a veneering of "chivalry" covered
the essential brutality of the code under which such
encounters were possible we shall see.

III

In the blaze of a midsummer noonday the old Manton house was hardly true to its traditions. It was of
the earth, earthy. The sunshine caressed it warmly
and affectionately, with evident disregard of its bad
reputation. The grass greening all the expanse in its
front seemed to grow, not rankly, but with a natural
and joyous exuberance, and the weeds blossomed
quite like plants. Full of charming lights and shadows and populous with pleasant-voiced birds, the
neglected shade trees no longer struggled to run
away, but bent reverently beneath their burdens of
sun and song. Even in the glassless upper windows
was an expression of peace and contentment, due to

the light within. Over the stony fields the visible heat danced with a lively tremor incompatible with the gravity which is an attribute of the supernatural.

Such was the aspect under which the place presented itself to Sheriff Adams and two other men who had come out from Marshall to look at it. One of these men was Mr. King, the sheriff's deputy; the other, whose name was Brewer, was a brother of the late Mrs. Manton. Under a beneficent law of the State relating to property which has been for a certain period abandoned by an owner whose residence cannot be ascertained, the sheriff was legal custodian of the Manton farm and appurtenances thereunto belonging. His present visit was in mere perfunctory compliance with some order of a court in which Mr. Brewer had an action to get possession of the property as heir to his deceased sister. By a mere coincidence, the visit was made on the day after the night that Deputy King had unlocked the house for another and very different purpose. His presence now was not of his own choosing: he had been ordered to accompany his superior and at the moment could think of nothing more prudent than simulated alacrity in obedience to the command.

Carelessly opening the front door, which to his surprise was not locked, the sheriff was amazed to see, lying on the floor of the passage into which it opened, a confused heap of men's apparel. Examination showed it to consist of two hats, and the same number of coats, waistcoats, and scarves, all in a remarkably good state of preservation, albeit somewhat defiled by the dust in which they lay. Mr. Brewer was equally astonished, but Mr. King's emotion is not of record. With a new and lively interest in his own actions the sheriff now unlatched and pushed open a door on the right, and the three entered. The room was apparently vacant—no; as their eyes became accustomed to the dimmer light something was visible in the farthest angle of the wall. It was a human figure—that of a man crouching close in the corner. Something in the attitude made the intruders halt when they had barely passed the threshold. The figure more and more clearly defined itself. The man was upon one knee, his back in the angle of the wall, his shoulders elevated to the level of his ears, his hands before his face, palms outward, the fingers spread and crooked like claws; the white face turned upward on the retracted neck had an expression of unutterable fright, the mouth half open, the eyes incredibly expanded. He was stone dead. Yet, with the exception of a bowie-knife, which had evidently fallen from his own hand, not another object was in the room.

In thick dust that covered the floor were some confused footprints near the door and along the wall through which it opened. Along one of the adjoining walls, too, past the boarded-up windows, was the trail made by the man himself in reaching his corner. Instinctively in approaching the body the three men followed that trail. The sheriff grasped one of the outthrown arms; it was as rigid as iron, and the application of a gentle force rocked the entire body without altering the relation of its parts. Brewer, pale with excitement, gazed intently into the distorted face. "God of mercy!" he suddenly cried, "it is Manton!"

"You are right," said King, with an evident attempt at calmness: "I knew Manton. He then wore a full beard and his hair long, but this is he."

He might have added: "I recognized him when he challenged Rosser. I told Rosser and Sancher who he was before we played him this horrible trick. When Rosser left this dark room at our heels, forgetting his outer clothing in the excitement, and driving away with us in his shirt sleeves—all through the discreditable proceedings we knew whom we were dealing with, murderer and coward that he was!"

But nothing of this did Mr. King say. With his better light he was trying to penetrate the mystery of the man's death. That he had not once moved from the corner where he had been stationed; that his posture was that of neither attack nor defense; that he had dropped his weapon; that he had obviously perished of sheer horror of something that he *saw*—these were circumstances which Mr. King's disturbed intelligence could not rightly comprehend.

Groping in intellectual darkness for a clew to his maze of doubt, his gaze, directed mechanically downward in the way of one who ponders momentous matters, fell upon something which, there, in the light of day and in the presence of living companions, affected him with terror. In the dust of years that lay thick upon the floor—leading from the door by which they had entered, straight across the room to within a yard of Manton's crouching corpse—were three parallel lines of footprints—light but definite impressions of bare feet, the outer ones those of small children, the inner a woman's. From the point at which they ended they did not return; they pointed all one way. Brewer, who had observed them at the same moment, was leaning forward in an attitude of rapt attention, horribly pale.

"Look at that!" he cried, pointing with both hands at the nearest print of the woman's right foot, where she had apparently stopped and stood. "The middle toe is missing—it was Gertrude!"

Gertrude was the late Mrs. Manton, sister to Mr. Brewer.

The Vampire of Croglin Grange

[AUGUSTUS HARE]

This last of our stories is most puzzling; it may well be true. Certainly, Hare told it to friends before he wrote it down (the celebrated Lord Halifax, who almost edged Churchill out of the Prime Ministry in 1941, had been told it by him and duly frightened as a child). In 1924, one Charles G. Harper went to Croglin, and discovered there was no such house as Croglin Grange. Instead, there were two houses, Croglin Low Hall and Croglin High Hall, neither of which was near the church. The story seemed exploded.

In the 1930s, however, an F. Clive-Ross visited the village, and determined that in fact a church had once stood near Croglin Low Hall. Moreover, local legend placed the occurrence in the 1680s rather than the 1870s, the approximate period of the story which you are about to read. Moreover, the Thorncombe Estate in Surrey to which the story has the Fishers moving, was in fact inhabited by them; Conway Fisher-Rowe of that place was

Hare's godson. That Estate was eventually inherited by the come-
dienne Beatrice Lillie in 1937, and subdivided and sold by her.

So we end as we began, with the possibility that the horrors we
have been describing may not be purely literary at all. Something
to reflect on, late at night, when you are all alone.

"Fisher," said the Captain, "may sound a very plebeian name, but this family is of very ancient lineage, and for many hundreds of years they have possessed a very curious old place in Cumberland, which bears the weird name of Croglin Grange. The great characteristic of the house is that never at any period of its very long existence has it been more than one story high, but it has a terrace from which large grounds sweep away towards the church in the hollow, and a fine distant view.

"When, in lapse of years, the Fishers outgrew Croglin Grange in family and fortune, they were wise enough not to destroy the long-standing characteristic of the place by adding another story to the house, but they went away to the south, to reside at Thorncombe near Guildford, and they let Croglin Grange.

"They were extremely fortunate in their tenants, two brothers and a sister. They heard their praises from all quarters. To their poorer neighbours they were all that is most kind and beneficent, and their

neighbours of a higher class spoke of them as a welcome addition to the little society of the neighbourhood. On their part the tenants were greatly
delighted with their new residence. The arrangement of the house, which would have been a trial to
many, was not so to them. In every respect Croglin
Grange was exactly suited to them.

"The winter was spent most happily by the new
inmates of Croglin Grange, who shared in all the little social pleasures of the district, and made themselves very popular. In the following summer there
was one day which was dreadfully, annihilatingly
hot. The brothers lay under the trees with their
books, for it was too hot for any active occupation.
The sister sat in the verandah and worked, or tried to
work, for in the intense sultriness of that summer
day work was next to impossible. They dined early,
and after dinner they still sat out in the verandah,
enjoying the cool air which came with evening, and
they watched the sun set, and the moon rise over the
belt of trees which separated the grounds from the
churchyard, seeing it mount the heavens till the whole
lawn was bathed in silver light, across which the long
shadows from the shrubbery fell as if embossed, so
vivid and distinct were they.

"When they separated for the night, all retiring to
their rooms on the ground-floor (for, as I said, there
was no upstairs in that house), the sister felt that the

heat was still so great that she could not sleep, and having fastened her window, she did not close the shutters—in that very quiet place it was not necessary—and, propped against the pillows, she still watched the wonderful, the marvellous beauty of that summer night. Gradually she became aware of two lights, two lights which flickered in and out in the belt of trees which separated the lawn from the churchyard; and, as her gaze became fixed upon them, she saw them emerge, fixed in a dark substance, a definite ghastly something, which seemed every moment to become nearer, increasing in size and substance as it approached. Every now and then it was lost for a moment in the long shadows which stretched across the lawn from the trees, and then it emerged larger than ever, and still coming on. As she watched it, the most uncontrollable horror seized her. She longed to get away, but the door was close to the window and the door was locked on the inside, and while she was unlocking it, she must be for an instant nearer to it. She longed to scream, but her voice seemed paralysed, her tongue glued to the roof of her mouth.

"Suddenly, she never could explain why afterwards, the terrible object seemed to turn to one side, seemed to be going round the house, not to be coming to her at all, and immediately she jumped out of bed and rushed to the door; but as she was unlocking it, she heard scratch, scratch, scratch upon the window, and saw a hideous brown face with flaming eyes glaring in at her. She rushed back to the bed, but the creature continued to scratch, scratch, scratch upon the window. She felt a sort of mental comfort in the knowledge that the window was securely fastened on the inside. Suddenly the scratching sound ceased, and a kind of pecking sound took its place. Then, in her agony, she became aware that the creature was unpicking the lead! The noise continued, and a diamond pane of glass fell into the room. Then a long bony finger of the creature came in and turned the handle of the window, and the window opened, and the creature came in; and it came across the room, and her terror was so great that she could not scream, and it came up to the bed, and it twisted its long, bony fingers into her hair, and it dragged her head over the side of the bed, and it bit her violently in the throat.

"As it bit her, her voice was released, and she screamed with all her might and main. Her brothers rushed out of their rooms, but the door was locked on the inside. A moment was lost while they got a poker and broke it open. Then the creature had already escaped through the window, and the sister, bleeding violently from a wound in the throat, was lying unconscious over the side of the bed. One brother pursued the creature, which fled before him through the moonlight with gigantic strides, and eventually seemed to disappear over the wall into the churchyard. Then he rejoined his brother by the sister's bedside. She was dreadfully hurt, and her wound was a very definite one; but she was of strong disposition, not either given to romance or superstition, and when she came to herself she said, 'What has happened is most extraordinary, and I am very much hurt. It seems inexplicable, but of course there is an explanation, and we must wait for it. It will turn out that a lunatic has escaped from some asylum and found his way here.' The wound healed, and she appeared to get well, but the doctor who was sent for would not believe that she could bear so terrible a shock so easily, and insisted that she must have change, mental and physical; so her brothers took her to Switzerland.

"Being a sensible girl, when she went abroad she threw herself at once into the interests of the country she was in. She dried plants, she made sketches, she went up mountains, and, as autumn came on, she was the person who urged that they should return to Croglin Grange. 'We have taken it,' she said, 'for seven years, and we have only been there one; and we shall always find it difficult to let a house which is only one story high, so we had better return there; lunatics do not escape every day.' As she urged it, her brothers wished nothing better, and the family returned to Cumberland. From there being no upstairs to the house it was impossible to make any great change in their arrangements. The sister occupied the same room, but it is unnecessary to say she always closed her shutters, which, however, as in many old houses, always left one top pane of the window uncovered. The brothers moved, and occupied a room together, exactly opposite that of their sister, and they always kept loaded pistols in their room.

'The winter passed most peacefully and happily. In the following March the sister was suddenly awakened by a sound she remembered only too well— scratch, scratch, scratch upon the window, and, looking up, she saw quite clearly in the topmost pane of the window the same hideous brown shrivelled face, with glaring eyes, looking in at her. This time she screamed as loud as she could. Her brothers rushed out of their room with pistols, and out of the front door. The creature was already scudding away across the lawn. One of the brothers fired and hit it in the leg, but still with the other leg it continued to make way, scrambled over the wall into the churchyard, and seemed to disappear into a vault which belonged to a family long extinct.

"The next day the brothers summoned all the tenants of Croglin Grange, and in their presence the vault was opened. A horrible scene revealed itself.

The vault was full of coffins; they had been broken open, and their contents, horribly mangled and distorted, were scattered over the floor. One coffin alone remained intact. Of that the lid had been lifted, but still lay loose upon the coffin. They raised it, and there, brown, withered, shrivelled, mummified, but quite entire, was the same hideous figure which had looked in at the windows of Croglin Grange, with the marks of a recent pistol-shot in the leg; and they did the only thing that can lay a vampire—they burnt it."

AUTHOR BIOGRAPHIES

PHILOSTRATUS (c. A.D. 170–249)
Born on the Greek island of Lemnos, he became one of the leading sophists or orators of his day, spent some years at the Roman imperial court, and wrote several books, among which are a very entertaining "Lives of the Sophists" and the biography of Apollonius of Tyana.

SIR WALTER SCOTT (1771–1832)
Born in Edinburgh, Scott simply *was* Scotland to his contemporaries, as Robert Burns had been to the previous generation. His voluminous output allowed him to maintain himself financially, and his influence reached all over Europe and into America.

WASHINGTON IRVING (1783–1859)
The first American writer known overseas, Irving will be forever connected with Rip Van Winkle and the Headless Horseman. Irving had many interests including writing, architecture and landscape design, traveling, and diplomacy.

NATHANIEL HAWTHORNE (1804–1864)
Known to every American school child, Hawthorne produced quite a body of strange tales. He saw a

ghost himself at the Salem Athenaeum, but pronounced himself too timid to speak to it.

H.B. MARRYAT (1792–1848)
After a naval career very much like that of the fictional Horatio Hornblower, Captain Marryat turned to a literary career. Turning out novels and stories in the Romanticist manner, he acquired great fame during his lifetime (and enough money to survive both his own extravagance and several financial reverses).

NIKOLAY GOGOL (1809–1852)
Best known for his 1842 *Dead Souls*, Gogol is considered one of the best Russian (and Ukrainian) writers. He often used supernatural themes even in his "mainstream" works.

CHARLES DICKENS (1812–1870)
As the foremost English writer of the 19th century, Dickens requires little introduction.

RUDYARD KIPLING (1865–1936)
Born in Bombay, Kipling was sent to school in England at age five, returning to Lahore 11 years later. A varied life took him to Vermont (where he lived for a time with his American wife), South Africa, and many other places; eventually he settled in Sussex. He

wrote an incredible amount of novels, short stories, and poetry, and is once again coming back into favor.

SAKI (H. H. MUNRO) (1870–1916)

Born in Burma, Munro was raised by aunts in England. Having been both an historian and a journalist, his cynical, witty style soon won (and has maintained) a large following. He was killed in France during World War I.

R. S. HAWKER (1803–1875)

Hawker was parson of the parish of Morwenstow on the desolate north Cornish coast for forty-one years. He first became known for his work in rescuing and burying the remains of shipwreck victims washed up on the jagged rocks below his church. He was one of the finest poets of his period, and his Arthurian masterpiece, *The Quest of the Sangraal*, drew from Tennyson the acclamation: "Hawker has beaten me on my own ground." His eccentricity was a by-word. He dressed in claret-coloured coat, blue fisherman's jersey, long sea-boots and pink brimless hat. He talked to birds, invited his nine cats into church, and excommunicated one of them when it caught a mouse on a Sunday. His *Footprints Of Former Men In Cornwall* contains many weird tales. Hawker's deathbed conversion to Catholicism was the cause of a great controversy at the time.

PERCEVAL LANDON (1869–1927)

Landon was present for the *Times* at the Battle of Magersfontein and at the surrender of General Piet Cronje to Lord Roberts at Paaderburg at the end of February 1900. He was one of three journalists to enter into Bloemfontein before Roberts' army a fortnight later. Landon was also the correspondent for the *Times* during the Younghusband mission to Lhasa in 1903–4. He also wrote extensively about Nepal and Tibet.

ROBERT W. CHAMBERS (1865–1933)

An artist who studied in Paris, as mentioned in the note for *The Yellow Sign*, Chambers also had a literary influence, which has lasted to the present. But most of his later work involved commonplace romantic stories, for which many horror aficionados have considered him something of a Benedict Arnold.

ROBERT HUGH BENSON (1871–1914)

The son of E. W. Benson, Archbishop of Canterbury, Msgr. Benson converted to Catholicism in 1903. In his time one of the best known authors in Great Britain, and his brothers—A. C. Benson and E. F. Benson—were highly acclaimed writers on their own. Benson wrote 15 novels, mostly historical. A few, such as *The Necromancers*, dealt with the occult, as did a number of his short stories. C. C.

Martindale, S.J, treated Benson's interests in these matters at length in his biography.

RALPH ADAMS CRAM (1863–1942)
As noted, Crams was a famous architect who wrote some chilling horror tales. He was also very much involved in the Anglo-Catholic wing of Anglicanism. His political and social views were rather anti-Modern, having much in common with the Arts and Crafts Movement.

AMBROSE BIERCE (June 24, 1842–??)
Bierce was an Ohio-born writer and journalist who mysteriously disappeared in 1913 while attempting to join Pancho Villa in Mexico. He was famous for his Civil War and supernatural stories, as well as for his legendary wit—best appreciated by reading his *Devil's Dictionary*. His strange vanishing in Mexico forms a part of the 1989 film, *The Old Gringo*, wherein he is portrayed by Gregory Peck.

AUGUSTUS HARE (1834–1903)
Born into an aristocratic English family, Hare wrote a great deal, primarily travel books about Italy and elsewhere. His six-volume autobiography, *Story of My Life*, is filled with ghost tales picked up in various places.